"Your Life is Only As Big As The Dream You Dare To Live"

~ *Garrett W. Hillerman*

Other Books by
Elayne Gineve James

THE LIGHTBRIDGE LEGACY
Series

A young, reclusive teen born with a
unique *soul signature* is chosen by a
race of ancients to inherit the most
powerful magical object in the world.

*"A soul-searching YA Adventure
Fantasy that will have you turning
pages late into the night."*

—— BOOK ONE ——
The Secret Half

—— BOOK TWO ——
The Hidden Gates

—— BOOK THREE ——
The Lost Path

—— BOOK FOUR ——
The Dark Below

FOR MORE EGJ BOOKS & RELEASE UPDATES, VISIT ELAYNEJAMES.COM

The Saint
of
Carrington

A Spirited Christmas Story
of Hope, Healing, and the
Power of Believing

Elayne Gineve
James

A MISCHIEVOUS MUSE BOOK

MISCHIEVOUS MUSE
Press

The Saint of Carrington
A Spirited Christmas Story of Hope,
Healing, and the Power of Believing
A Mischievous Muse book, December 2020

Published by
Mischievous Muse Press
Los Angeles County, CA USA

Library of Congress Cataloging-in-Publication Data
James, Elayne Gineve
The Saint of Carrington/
Fiction / Christmas / Holiday Novel

Paperback Edition ISBN: 978-1-9382081-6-4

10 9 8 7 6 5 4 3 2 1
BVG

Printed in the USA

DEDICATION

For anyone who has ever lost someone dear to
them, lost hope, lost faith, lost their way, or
simply lost the wonder of Christmas,
this book is for you.

*May it guide your
heart back to
believing.*

The Saint
of
Carrington

In The Beginning...

There once was a town called Carrington, nestled high upon a snowy mountaintop where none but the lucky dwelled. In fact, it may still be there, just hidden from view, known only to a privileged few.

There was a time the people of this sleepy little town knew how special it was. Like a precious gem hidden away for safekeeping, they kept their secret well, telling only their children, and their children's children, what made their little town so remarkable.

Although the townsfolk thought that it would always be true, their story changed one stormy night, as stories often do. And I will soon tell you what sad and tragic thing occurred on that fateful night, but for now, it is enough to say that after this storm of storms struck on Christmas Eve, the town was never the same.

What once made Carrington a magical place, soon existed merely as memory. And it wasn't long before the kindhearted people of this fine town began to forget, and in their forgetting, they stopped believing.

Now, as some may know, and others may guess, when people cease to believe in magic, the wonder in their hearts dims, and it is as if the winter inside them never ends.

That tragic night is where this story truly begins, but if you will permit me, I'll venture to start elsewhere, for my part in this story commences nearly forty years later. And in truth, as strange as it may seem, this bright new beginning for me, served also as a harbinger of my fate.

It is December 1899. A new century soon will turn, and a grand new era shall begin. Being who and what I am, I know only this for certain... that everything in Carrington is about to change again.

Garrett W. Hillerman
1849 – 1898

CHAPTER ONE
THE SECRET IN THE ATTIC

S he handed him the tarnished silver key.

William Thomas stared at it in astonishment. So many times he'd admired it from afar, in all its ornate splendor, hanging just out of reach, like the star atop the Christmas tree he wished upon every year.

It wasn't just the intricacies of the key that interested him, but what it represented—entry to a forever-locked door at the top of cleverly hidden stairs—the same door that, for as long as he could remember, had barred his access to untold treasures and secrets.

He'd never been allowed anywhere near the attic. Not in all his years on earth, which measured exactly twelve on his last birthday.

"William," said his mother, snapping him back to attention, "I need you to go up to the attic and retrieve Grammy's old sewing kit, the one that looks like a picnic basket. Then I want you to take it over to Miss Tully across the street. Can you do that for me?"

He peered up at his mother in confusion. "You want *me* to go into the attic?"

"You are the man of the house now, are you not?"

William nodded somberly.

"Well, then, you're old enough to go into the attic. Just be careful."

"Yes ma'am."

"And William, take care not to lose the key. There is no replacement."

"I won't. I promise!"

She smiled one of her knowing smiles and said, "Go on then."

William dashed up to the second floor, and down a long hallway, passing his bedroom and then his sisters', before skidding to a stop. Peering up into the dark stairwell that led to the attic, he caught his breath. Despite his bursting excitement, he climbed the steep narrow steps with deliberate caution. His mother would certainly never grant him access again if he hurt himself . . . *or* for that matter, damaged any of the precious heirlooms awaiting discovery inside.

At the top of the attic stairs he stood before the mysterious door, clutching the skeleton key, savoring the significance of the moment. After taking in a long deep breath, he placed the key in the lock . . . and turned.

The door opened with a groan at the hinges. Before stepping inside, he pulled a handkerchief from his pocket, wrapped the key up tight, and returned it to his pocket for safekeeping.

A century of buried stories and secrets invited him in. Pools of darkness loomed to either side of a small window that split the room with a shaft of dusty light. The attic air, thin in his lungs, smelled of damp rags and old newspaper. As his eyes adjusted, he began to see the relics of bygone days that beckoned and begged for immediate excavation.

A tingle of discovery pulsed through him. His love of all things past and ancient took over now. He could spend days, weeks, even months up here sifting and organizing, and never tire of the task.

That one idea made him happier than he had been in a very long time. He secretly hoped to find something of Father's here. Something that might somehow bring him closer, for the distance between Heaven and Earth seemed far too vast an expanse to separate a father and son.

He took a small step, careful not to displace anything. Floorboards creaked under unaccustomed weight.

A second step disturbed an industrious spider. Will slapped away sticky strands of web, hoping its architect wasn't caught in his uncombed hair.

Another step roused a tiny brown mouse that skittered over his foot, across the floor, and into a hole. An involuntary jump left him scrambling to steady a teetering porcelain vase.

William let out a quick breath. Nothing would dissuade him from this adventure, not even spiders and mice.

Good thing Becca isn't here, he thought, with a little half-grin. Places like this always scared his little sister, but he didn't share Bec's dread of the unknown. For William, places like this were full of intrigue and possibility; like buried treasure without the threat of pirates.

First order of business, find Grammy's sewing kit.

He squinted, scanning the pockets of darkness.

There. Picnic basket on a stand next to the window.

Easy enough. Now a quick jaunt across the street to deliver the basket to Miss Tully, and then back up the stairs to—

William halted midstride. A small wooden box lit by the half-light of the winter sun had caught his attention. Fastened to the top with twine was a handwritten note.

"That's father's handwriting," he said aloud, though none but the attic ghosts could hear.

He rested on his knees, took the box into his lap, and read the attached note. "Save for Christmas."

His heart constricted with a familiar ache. It had been almost a year now, but still he missed his father each morning when he woke to realize all over again that he was gone.

"Father," he whispered, looking up to the heavens, "would it be all right if I opened this box? I know it's not Christmas yet, but it *is* right around the corner since today is December first."

As he waited for an answer, he filled the time with a thorough inspection of the box's construction. It was the size of a small shoebox, finished wood, with a simple carving of a rose on the lid. It had a petite circular latch but no lock. That meant he needn't search for a key. He could just open—

"No." William set the box on the floor where he'd found it, feeling suddenly disrespectful, as if Father were watching.

He stared at it a moment, and then, with an outstretched index finger, inched it back into place to match its rectangular dust mark on the floor.

"But . . . what if I'm the only one who knows it's here? Mother hasn't been to the attic since before last Christmas," he muttered to himself. "Maybe she doesn't even know about it. Whatever's in here could be important. If I don't open it, who will?"

In that moment, without knowing how or why, William knew he had to open the box, as if Father had whispered in his ear, *'Go ahead, my boy. It is your discovery and yours alone. No longer is it my secret.'*

William freed the twine that held the note in place, swung the latch from its catch, and opened the lid. The musty, sweet smell of dried rose petals tickled his nose.

Inside, he found four items: a carved wooden Christmas tree ornament in the shape of a star, a pocket-size tintype photograph of a couple with a newborn, and two numbered envelopes with the words *Merry Christmas from Papa* written on the front.

He opened envelope number one, and as he read the letter inside, the words began to blur.

William read to its end, blinked to clear his vision, and then opened the second envelope.

Eyes wide, he gasped, stuffed the contents back into the box, and slammed the lid shut. He wedged the whole thing under his arm and dashed out the attic door.

Down the stairs he flew, forgetting all about his promise to be careful. "Mother! Mother!" he called, running through the house and into the kitchen.

His mother looked up from her mixing bowl and dried her hands on her apron. "William Thomas! You know better than to run in the house!"

"Mother, I found something!"

"The sewing basket, I hope?"

"No. Something important! Look! It's from Father! And this tag was on top."

Nora read the note. "Save for Christmas?"

"Did you know about this box?"

"That's your father's rosewood keepsake box. I haven't seen it in a very long time," she said with a faraway look in her eyes. "It was a gift from your Grammy Beatrice on the day you were born. I'd forgotten all about it."

"Open it!" he said, holding the box at arm's length.

She drew up the lid and peered inside.

"Look in the envelope!" said Will. "The one on top."

"Train tickets?" she said, confused. "To New York City?"

"And boat tickets too!" said William.

"To Europe!" she said, reading the destination on the second set of tickets.

"They're from Father. Look at the date! We're supposed to leave in one week!"

"Oh William, you mustn't get your hopes up. It's not—"

"There's a letter too! He wrote us a Christmas letter! You should read it before you decide." Will fished the other envelope out of the box, handed it to her and said in a near-whisper, "Read it, Mother."

Eyes misting, breath shallow, she read the words written in her husband's skillful hand...

My Sweet Family,

The tickets you will find within may seem a rather odd and impulsive Christmas gift, considering we've not discussed the possibility of travel for the holidays, but I wanted it to be a genuine surprise, and truth be told, I have been thinking on this for some time now, and only just felt the moment ripe to set the plan in motion.

I've arranged for everything. The White Star Oceanliner out of New York City will carry us across the Atlantic to France, and from there, we'll be boarding a train through the Swiss Alps, and finally, a carriage ride to our destination, a place not on any map, nor in anyone's address book.

Now I admit, embarking on a lengthy and arduous passage such as this, to seek out a place no one has ever heard of, sounds a bit extravagant, but it is meant to be a grand adventure and, in a way, a homecoming as well.

I realize this makes little sense to you at the moment, but when we are there, I shall introduce you to a very significant

5

individual, and we will all begin to understand just how important this journey is for our family.

The town we are traveling so far to reach is called Carrington. It is a special place. And I believe, with all my heart and soul, that this is truly the best Christmas gift I could ever give you. I promise you'll understand once we've arrived.

Merry Christmas, my darlings.
All my love,

Papa

P.S. And for you, Nora, my beautiful wife, because I know how you dislike being away from home during the holidays, I've made an offer on a splendid piece of property there, and the sale has just gone through. We now own The Carrington Grand Hotel, and I've reserved the residential suite for our stay. It can be your home away from home, my love.

Nora's hand moved to cover her heart. "I had no idea."

"He wants us to go, Mother. He says it's important. It's all there in the letter!"

She peered into the envelope, pulled out the last piece of paper and gasped.

Will hadn't noticed it before. "What is it?"

"It's . . . a receipt. Your father bought these tickets just before he—" Her voice failed her.

Will looked at the date on the receipt. "Mother, don't you see? If buying these tickets for us was the last thing he did before he died," Will took the tickets from his mother, "and this is the last Christmas present he'll ever give us, then we have to go!"

"William. It's not a simple thing. And departure in six days! It's just not enough time to prepare for—"

"We have to honor his wish, his *last* wish for us, don't we?"

"I . . . I must think about this, William. There is much to consider."

"No! We have to go! Read it again! He said we'll understand when we get there! He said he'd introduce us to a 'very significant individual.' What if that person is waiting for us?"

Nora's expression betrayed her carefully shunted emotions. Lips pressed together; she peered at her husband's words through pinched eyes. The letter shook in her trembling hands.

"Mother?" William said in a soft voice. "Are you all right?"

Nora caught her breath. "Perhaps . . . " She steadied herself. "Perhaps you're right. We . . . must honor his wishes."

William held out the family portrait he'd found in the Christmas box. "Is this Father?" he asked, pointing to the baby in the woman's arms.

She studied the photograph. "Where did you get this?"

"It was in the box with the tickets. It's father as a baby, isn't it? And those are my grandparents."

She narrowed her eyes to read the date. "You could be right, William. By the date, he would have been six months."

"And the child in the picture—?"

"—could very well be six months, yes." She stared at the faces in fascination. "There *is* a family resemblance, but I've never seen this photograph before. When we married, he confessed he possessed no evidence of his birth or his parents, and we did not speak of it again." She paused and smiled. "Part of the surprise," she said more to herself than to her son. She offered the photo back to Will. "Would you like to keep this?"

"Yes, please!" He took the photo, tucked into a shirt pocket and turned on his heels.

"Where are you off to, young man? We have much to do!"

"I'm going to get Grammy's sewing kit, for Miss Tully."

"Oh," said Nora. "Thank you for remembering, William."

"And then I'm going next door to fetch Becca and tell her Father is taking us on a great adventure!"

"I want you both back here in ten minutes."

Will nodded and dashed out.

Nora took another look at the letter, and then pressed it to her heart. "Oh Garrett, how you loved surprises. And you have managed to surprise me yet again."

"Merry Christmas, my love," Garrett whispered in her ear, but all she heard was the sound of distant music.

7

CHAPTER TWO
THE CARRINGTON GRAND HOTEL

"There she is!" called André the coachman, as he brought the sleigh over a rise. He slowed the horses to offer his passengers their first glimpse of The Carrington Grand in the distance.

Breathless, Nora and the children turned their attention from the grandeur of the jagged, white-capped mountains, to the stately hotel rising up like a castle in the sky as they crested the knoll.

The crown jewel of Carrington stood tall on a snow-covered slope overlooking the cobblestone streets of the town.

"This is my favorite view," said André. "It never fails to ignite my soul."

Nora gasped in spite of herself. "That's The Carrington Grand?"

"She's quite something, isn't she?" said André. "She's our inspiration, and she can be seen from nearly any point in town by anyone who cares to look up."

"You make it sound as if the hotel has a beating heart," said Nora.

"Indeed she does, Mrs. Hillerman," said André. "She watches over us. She's a symbol of hope to all who live here."

"Why is our hotel a symbol of hope?" asked little Becca, ever curious about the why and how of things.

8

"Well, you see, Miss Rebecca" said André, "The Grand not only represents what once was—faithfully preserving Carrington's enchanting history—but also represents what might someday be again. As long as she stands, there is still hope."

Becca wrinkled her nose in confusion.

The coachman grinned. "You will understand once you get to know her."

"When was she built?" asked William, intrigued.

"They began construction in 1598."

Will calculated. "It's . . . three hundred years old?"

"Every colossal alabaster brick of her," said André.

"It looks like a castle built by giants!" said Becca.

André laughed. "Near enough!"

William knew well his father's affinity for monumental hotels, but this one was unlike any Father had built or acquired in America. And though Will had never beheld its equal, it possessed an odd dream-like familiarity that captured his imagination.

"Wait until you see inside," said the coachman, grinning.

André pulled the sleigh up to the front entrance and hopped out. "Fortunate the weather held," he said, opening the door for his passengers. He offered a hand.

Nora stepped out first, took in her surroundings with a quick sweep of the eye, and nodded to her children. William jumped down and helped his little sister out of the sleigh.

"Come here, sweetheart," said Nora, pulling her daughter close. She whisked Becca's cornsilk hair away from her face and twisted it into a graceful swirl, securing it with a single hairpin pilfered from her own dark tresses.

"Welcome to The Grand," said André, with an outswept arm. "Ben will see to your luggage, while I take Mrs. Prescott into town for a bit of shopping."

"André," Nora said, pressing a generous tip into the coachman's palm. "Just a little something to show our appreciation. You are an excellent driver. The sleigh ride up the hill was quite breathtaking."

"I am pleased you enjoyed it as much as I did, Mrs. Hillerman."

Nora shook André's hand. "You're American, yes?"

"Yes ma'am. My parents were originally from France, but I was born and raised in New York City."

"It's nice to meet a fellow countryman so far from home," she said.

André touched the brim of his cap. "My carriage and sleigh are at your service, ma'am, day or night."

"Thank you, André."

"It's been a true pleasure, Mrs. Hillerman. Miss Rebecca. Master William." He bowed to each of them separately and then turned to tend the horses as a younger man came to collect their luggage.

Nora and the children climbed the marble steps to the colossal, frosted-glass and iron-flourished double doors that parted when they drew near. The doorman wore the same gold-buttoned, double-breasted, red velvet waistcoat that the coachman wore beneath his warm, shoulder-caped overcoat.

As they entered the lobby of The Carrington Grand Hotel, they all three stopped, stunned by its majesty.

A warm, bright ambiance charged the atmosphere, as flickering firelight caught the bends and folds of twisted gold ribbon. The sparkle of the room made it seem almost mystical, as if light and magic conspired to paint the scene with more color and beauty than the eye could behold.

A dozen or so hotel guests milled about, greeting one another with holiday cheer. Nora and the children entered the lobby, richly decorated in burgundy and gold, glowing in the warmth of oil lamps. Pine-scented garlands and a freshly cropped candlelit Christmas tree, standing proud in the spacious front window, perfumed the air. A sizable holly wreath trimmed in red velvet, accented the front desk.

Becca's gaze wandered from the elaborate scenes painted on the vaulted ceiling high above to the gold inlay of the white marble floors at their feet. "It's a palace, Mama," uttered Becca. "A princess should live here."

"Have you ever seen a Christmas tree so tall?" said William, pointing. "It must be thirty feet high."

Dazzled by the shimmer and glimmer of the most beautiful chandelier she'd seen in all her days, Nora leaned in to whisper to her children, "I had no idea. It's more beautiful than I could have imagined. I see now why your father chose it."

"I wish he were here," said Becca with a sniffle.

"Me too," added Will.

Nora felt it too—that pang of pain in her heart that came every time she had the thought, *Garrett should be here to see this.* She pushed back tears and exhaled slowly, not noticing until just then that she'd been holding her breath.

Needing to steer her children toward happier thoughts, she knelt to put an arm around each of them and said, "If your father were here, do you know what he would say?"

Her children peered at her, their sweet faces sad but expectant, looking so much like their father it frayed her heart.

"He would tell us not to be melancholy," she continued, softly. "He would tell us to find the worth of the moment, for in every circumstance something worthy can be found."

"I found something," said William.

Becca covered her mouth to hide a giggle as Will pointed to a cluster of local children adding their own finishing touches to the front desk wreath. Angry paper cutout eyes and a frowning mouth transformed the entire thing into a scowling face. And next to it, they placed a chalkboard sign that read 'Mean old Mr. Staub' with an arrow pointing to the wreath.

William stepped up to one of the boys who watched the others from afar, tapped him on the shoulder, and asked, "Who is Mr. Staub?"

The boy pointed to a stuffy man in a black suit and a burgundy tie. "The hotel manager. He doesn't like anyone under the age of thirty, so don't expect him to be nice to you."

Though the children snickered and laughed throughout their antics, the hotel manager, stern in demeanor and stiff in posture, appeared quite oblivious to their mischief.

William returned to his mother and sister, but continued to observe the man who was busily greeting the arriving guests, seemingly pleased and surprised at their numbers. He looked to be a man who was proud of his profession—the sort of man who might know all there was to know about the administration and operation of such a prominent hotel, but perhaps, Will thought, not as proficient in the handling of children. And the town kids seemed to know well his discomfort, taking pleasure in tormenting him in front of his new arrivals.

As the hotel manager began to make his way back to his place at the front desk, the town kids scattered, leaving their artistic additions to the wreath in plain view of the distinguished visitors.

Nora felt a light touch on her arm.

"Mama," whispered Becca, "may we go look around?"

"No, darling, we must check in first."

"Then can we go explore?" asked Will.

"After we settle into our suite, and rest up a bit, it'll be time for supper."

William expressed his disappointment with a grunt.

"There will be plenty of chances to explore the hotel and grounds tomorrow," Nora assured them.

Becca giggled again as Will gestured to the defaced wreath and the finely pressed man now busily attempting to right the unfortunate situation, muttering grievances under his breath.

"William, it is impolite to point," said Nora, stifling a smile.

When finally Mr. Staub turned and noticed the family awaiting his assistance, he stashed the offending artwork among a pile of papers on the front desk and mumbled an apology before offering his standard salutation.

"Season's greetings and warm tidings! Welcome to The Carrington Grand Hotel!"

"Good afternoon, sir," said Nora with a slight nod of her head. "I'm Mrs. Garrett Hillerman. I believe you are expecting us?" She removed her travel hat and offered a gloved hand.

"Yes, of course," said Mr. Staub, clearing his throat again before extending his hand to shake hers. "We've eagerly awaited your arrival, Mrs. Hillerman. It is a privilege to meet the new owners of The Carrington Grand! I am Mr. Friedrich Aschwin Staub, hotel manager and concierge, at your service."

"You certainly have a lovely hotel here, Mr. Staub," said Nora, "and I must say, I am surprised and pleased that you and your staff speak such excellent English."

"Oh, not just English, ma'am. All who live in Carrington have a remarkable gift for languages. We've to hear a word or phrase but once to comprehend its meaning and speak it from there on."

"Truly?" said Nora, intrigued. "That is a peculiarity I might like to discuss in more depth at a later time."

"Just one of the many special qualities about our little hamlet. May we take your coats?" he asked, snapping his fingers to summon a young woman in a staff uniform to assist.

"And will Mr. Hillerman be joining us soon?"

"Oh, ah, I . . ." Nora stumbled over her words. "I didn't realize you . . . no of course, you would not have received word. Our holiday in Carrington was so hushed, it would not have occurred to anyone to inform you."

"I'm afraid I don't understand," said the manager.

"My husband won't be joining us, Mr. Staub. There was an accident you see." Nora glanced at her children who were too fascinated with their surroundings to overhear her conversation with the hotel manager, and for that she was grateful.

Mr. Staub read the sorrow in her eyes. "Oh no. I—"

"Good Afternoon, ma'am," interrupted a sweet-faced young woman with a cheerful exuberance. She curtsied and then smoothed her crisp, white and goldenrod uniform before helping Nora off with her coat.

"This is Ada," said Mr. Staub, a bit upturned. "She presides over the cloakroom in the foyer, and assists Fiona in the main kitchen on notable occasions."

Mr. Staub forced a smile as the children stepped up to shed their winter wear. "Ah, and these must be your lovely children."

"Yes, Rebecca Rose is almost ten, and William Thomas recently turned twelve," Nora said proudly.

"We've never been to Switzerland before," offered Becca, in an almost-shy voice. "We crossed the sea on a big ocean liner. That was a little scary. Then we rode over an entire mountain range on a steam locomotive. That was more fun. Then we had to take a carriage from two towns over and a sleigh ride up the hill. That was my favorite part. But it sure took a long time to get here." Becca glanced at Will before returning her gaze to Mr. Staub. "This is the farthest we've ever been from home."

"My, what a talkative child you are," said Mr. Staub. "Well, you must be weary after all your adventures. You'll no doubt want to rest before your evening meal."

"Why doesn't the train come to Carrington?" asked Becca.

"Carrington has no train station, Miss."

"Why not?"

"Rebecca darling," Nora said, "let the gentleman do his job." She turned to the manager. "Thank you, Mr. Staub."

Staub gave a quick nod and called to a waiting bellhop.

"Ben, Mrs. Hillerman and her children will be occupying one of our residential suites. Two-twelve. Please see to their luggage."

Nora watched as the bellhop stacked their bags on a valet cart, crowning the load with a midnight blue satin drawstring pouch, which appeared to be in imminent danger of toppling.

"Wait!" called Nora, running to catch it as it teetered. She caught it just in time. "I'll carry this myself, thank you, Ben."

"Ma'am?"

"It is very precious to me," she said, clutching it to her breast.

Mr. Staub shot Ben a disapproving look and then waved him on with a quick flick of the wrist. "I shall personally escort the Hillermans to their suite."

As the family followed Mr. Staub through a white stone archway and up the grand marble staircase leading to the hotel's second-floor rooms, Nora's gaze settled momentarily on an old man snoozing against the polished granite hearth of the lobby's oversized fireplace.

By the look of him, she assumed the man to be a vagabond—his clothes, old and worn, his coat mended in so many places it could have passed for a patchwork quilt had it not been so frightfully thin. Certainly much too thin for winter, Nora thought.

The disheveled man looked as though he had no place to go. And although Nora couldn't imagine him as a paying guest at The Grand, neither could she imagine the hotel manager allowing a vagrant to take up residence in the lobby.

The man sat, eyes closed, propped up on the sleek stone frame of the impressive fireplace, which by its sheer size drew a fair amount of attention. It was unquestionably the centerpiece of the entire lobby, which made the unkempt man next to it an uncomfortably prominent fixture.

Something about him made Nora uneasy, and more than a little curious. She resolved to ask Mr. Staub about him after she and the children had settled in and rested.

14

CHAPTER THREE
THE UNINVITED

The steam locomotive approached the station, hailed by a rumbling quake, the score of metal on metal, and finally the squeal of brakes. The engine slowed, belching a thick puff of dark smoke, and as it came to a full stop, the great iron horse hissed its relief with the release of pressure, announcing its arrival. This gave way to the sound of doors parting, the patter of disembarking passengers and the chatter of people on the platform waiting to greet them.

When all had found their loved ones and made their way to wherever it was they were going; when those few travelers standing by to board the train had found their seats and were eagerly awaiting the start of their journey; when the bustling rail station had once again fallen into expectant silence, then and only then did the last arriving passenger step from his private cabin at the back of the train.

The stately gentleman placed one foot on the railway platform, looking left, then right, before stepping free of the locomotive. His dark brimmed top hat had been tipped forward just enough to obscure his face. He clutched an ebony staff in his right hand, but did not use it to aid him. In his left, he carried a small patent leather suitcase secured by a single-tumbler lock; his black-gloved fingers wrapped so tight around its handle that one could see the boney contours of his knuckles and joints.

The man walked toward the station exit but stopped at the gate, halted by an obstruction. A young boy wrapped in rags, shivering from the cold, sat on the icy ground tending to a wounded dog, effectively blocking the man's passage.

"Remove yourself from my path," commanded the man.

The boy peered up at the tall stranger through red-ringed eyes. "He's hurt. I have to help him."

"The condition of this mangy beast is of no interest to me. However, you, or more precisely, your position on this walkway, and the fact that you are blocking my exit, is of immediate concern. Leave now or I will have you extricated."

"If I move him I might hurt him more," said the boy.

"If you do not, I assure you, his condition will worsen."

"I can't," cried the boy. "He might die!"

"Then I shall move him myself," said the man.

"No!" the boy screamed.

The tall man opened the gate and with one swift kick, sent the dog tumbling onto the snow-flanked railroad tracks.

The pup's piercing yelp punctuated the boy's cries as he ran to the whimpering dog.

The man nodded his satisfaction. "For every problem, there is a determinant and expedient solution," he said as if it were the credo he lived by. He stepped through the gate and exited the station to a waiting carriage.

The coachman, spotting his fare, hopped down from the driver's seat to open the carriage door for the approaching gentleman. "May I take your luggage, sir?" he said, tipping his hat.

"No," said the man, stepping into the carriage. He pulled a handkerchief from his pocket and wiped his boot.

Once his passenger had been comfortably installed, the coachman waited for his instructions.

The dark stranger uttered a single word, "Carrington."

The coachman hesitated. "Carrington, sir?"

"Is there a problem?" he said with obvious displeasure.

"It shall require an arduous full day's ride from here, sir. Perhaps longer, if we meet with foul weather."

"Then I suggest you cease to further delay our departure with inconsequential details," said the man. "Go!"

CHAPTER FOUR
THE MAN BY THE FIRE

Late that afternoon, as snow began to fall outside The Carrington Grand's picturesque bay windows, Nora and the children returned to the lobby dressed for dinner.

Nora chose her dark green gown of rough spun silk with black velvet trim for the evening's attire, and had swept her hair into a graceful bun. She wore a small ruby-crested rosebud brooch over her heart, the only embellishment she allowed herself since her husband's death.

Little Becca sported a navy blue satin frock, her stockinged knees poking out beneath a white lace hem, and William Thomas, in his dark blue suit and tie, looked the proper little gentleman.

Many a head turned as the Hillermans made their way downstairs. Word had spread that they now owned The Grand. There was not a single guest in the hotel who wasn't curious to know them. They watched Nora and the children as they made their way over to the front desk.

"They're all staring at us," Becca whispered to her brother.

"That's because you're so funny looking," Will whispered back.

Becca looked down at her dress and frowned.

"William Thomas," chided Nora, "don't tease your sister." She squeezed her daughter's hand. "You look lovely, sweetheart."

The hotel manager gave a slight bow of his head to acknowledge their approach. "Dinner shall be served shortly,

Mrs. Hillerman. You have time enough, to go for a short stroll around the grounds. Shall I call for your coats?"

"Tomorrow perhaps" said Nora. For now, we are content to stay warm and dry here in the lobby until our meal."

"As you wish," he said, studying her expression.

To Mr. Staub's keen eye, some of Mrs. Hillerman's earlier sparkle had diminished. It was almost imperceptible. She held herself well. But Mr. Staub had made a career of knowing his guests' needs even before requests were made and the new owner of his hotel, he determined, would be no different.

After a brief deliberation, Mr. Staub said, "Although I hadn't the chance to express my condolences earlier ..." He hesitated. "I wanted to convey how sorry I am to hear of Mr. Hillerman's passing. He was a good man and will be missed."

"That is . . . kind of you, Mr. Staub," said Nora fingering the rose brooch on her lapel. "Did you know my husband well?"

"Oh, not well. That is to say, I—" Staub hesitated again, noting Mrs. Hillerman's subtle shift in demeanor, not wanting to add to her unease. He cleared his throat and softened his voice. "I never had the pleasure of meeting Mr. Hillerman in person, but I did enjoy our correspondences."

"Correspondences, Mr. Staub?"

"Why yes, your husband penned a very fine letter." Mr. Staub closed the guest book and returned the feather pen to its holder. "Of course, at first it was simply to inquire about the hotel, but after his questions had been answered, we continued to keep in touch. Although it was only a few times a year, usually around the holidays, I grew very fond of our exchanges."

"A few times a year? How long were you and my husband corresponding?"

"It would have been twelve years this Christmas."

"Twelve years? But my husband only purchased The Grand last year."

"Yes, just after he learned of the plans to tear it down."

"It was to be torn down?"

"Yes ma'am. Mr. Hillerman became adamant in his efforts to save The Carrington Grand. He said it had been standing for more than three hundred years and if he had any say in it, it would stand for three hundred more!" The hotel manager checked his enthusiasm, cleared his throat, and added, "Those were the last words of his final letter to me."

"His . . . final letter," muttered Nora.

Mr. Staub straightened his back. "Your husband single-handedly saved our lovely hotel, Mrs. Hillerman, and we are all exceedingly grateful."

"I had no idea he'd known about it for so long," said Nora, as much to herself as to Mr. Staub. "All those years and he never mentioned it." Nora's brows drew together.

William approached unnoticed and tugged on Nora's arm to get her attention. "Mother, may I have a coin please?"

"A coin? And what might this coin be for?"

"He looks hungry." William nodded toward the old man at the fireplace who appeared to have moved not an inch since Nora observed him the previous night. He still snoozed on the hearth, propped against its frame, his knobby fingers entwined around a stained porcelain cup displaying the hotel insignia.

Nora dug into her evening bag and handed William a coin. "Here you go, but don't bother the man if he's dozing."

William nodded and made his way over to the fireplace.

"Mr. Staub," said Nora with a look of concern, "who is that man sitting by the fire? Do you know him? Is he a guest here?"

"Guest? Ah, well, no. I wouldn't call him a guest. Not strictly speaking. His given name is Nicholas. I don't know his surname. No one does." Mr. Staub lowered his voice. "I really must apologize, Mrs. Hillerman."

"What for, Mr. Staub?"

"For Nicholas, ma'am."

"Why, is there a problem?"

"Well no, not in the strictest sense . . . he's just a bit, dare I say, peculiar."

"Peculiar, Mr. Staub?" Nora frowned. Her eyes shifted to her son. "Is it safe?"

"Oh, don't misunderstand, Nicholas is quite harmless. All the children love him. He tells them stories and such. 'Quite the friendly old chap,' as one of our regular guests, Mr. Dodsworth, is fond of saying."

"Well," said Nora, "I believe he's been here since our arrival this morning."

"Oh, he's been here quite a bit longer than that."

"Has he no place to go? Does he not have a home?"

"In a sense."

Nora's brows drew together. "You're being rather elusive, Mr. Staub."

"I don't mean to be, Mrs. Hillerman. It's just a bit difficult to explain."

"Perhaps you should make a better effort, Mr. Staub."

"Yes, of course." He straightened again and said with all the authority allotted his position, "Nicholas has a home, ma'am. He lives here."

"Here, in the hotel?"

"No. Here." Staub pointed to the floor. "In the lobby."

Nora looked around at the guests in their evening finery, the rich velvet upholstery, the crystal chandeliers—not at all the proper place for a homeless man to take up shelter. "I'm not sure I understand, Mr. Staub."

"He's been here for years, ma'am. He came long before I arrived."

"And how long ago was that?"

"I've managed The Carrington Grand Hotel for the past nineteen years," he said proudly.

"And in all that time you've given no thought to rectifying the situation?"

"Oh, many times, ma'am. His presence here represents the only blemish on the otherwise perfect standard of excellence we uphold here at The Grand. But I'm afraid he came with the property, Mrs. Hillerman, along with a full pardon. The previous owners insisted on it."

"The same owners who planned to tear down the hotel?"

"No. No. When the previous owners, Harold and Gertrude Mills, were unable to maintain the installments on the restoration monies they'd borrowed, a development company purchased the bank note and assumed ownership of the property. The Mills' had owned The Grand for nearly sixty years. It broke their hearts to have it taken from them in such a manner. It was they who insisted Nicholas not be displaced for any reason."

The line of Nora's mouth tightened. "Well, as the new owner of The Carrington Grand, I suppose I shall have to take it upon myself to remedy this man's unfortunate circumstance.

We can't very well have vagabonds living in our lobby now can we, Mr. Staub?"

"Oh, I assure you, I agree. Wholeheartedly. However, Mr. Hillerman himself gave explicit instructions that nothing be changed—no furniture removed, no fixtures replaced—and well, Nicholas was listed as one of those things, ma'am."

"My husband knew of this man?"

"Yes ma'am."

"And said that he was not to be removed?"

"Under no circumstance. Those were his exact words. I have a file full of letters in my office, written in your husband's own hand, if you'd like to verify these statements for yourself." He motioned to a door behind the front desk with a tarnished brass nameplate that read 'Concierge.'

Nora gave an almost imperceptible nod. "I . . . would like to see my husband's letters, yes, thank you," she said with a catch in her throat.

Mr. Staub stiffened, bowed slightly, and turned to open the office door. "After you, Mrs. Hillerman."

Nora glanced back at her children.

"Not to worry. They're perfectly safe. And you'll be able to keep an eye on them through the observation window."

Five swollen wood steps led up to the manager's office, elevated, no doubt, to keep a keen eye on the staff and guests via a lengthy observation window, which offered a view of the entire lobby.

Once inside, Nora glanced around the office to discern the measure of the man who worked within its walls.

Everything seemed to have a place, and everything was in its place with one notable exception. A highly wrought metal birdcage hung on an ironwork stand, somewhat at odds with its purpose, for no bird perched within. Nora, though curious, chose not to inquire about the oddity, feeling it might constitute a breach of privacy. She could ill afford to alienate the manager of her husband's hotel, from whom she had much to learn.

"You appear to be very organized, Mr. Staub."

"Efficiency is the mark of an uncluttered mind," he said, as if for the hundredth time. He moved to one of the many

21

teak filing cabinets on the far wall, withdrew a thick file marked 'Hillerman' and offered it to Nora. "This is every letter I received from Mr. Hillerman, in order of receipt."

She took the folder and held it closed for a moment, sandwiched between her hands.

"The last exchange, there on top, is the document to which I refer."

Nora opened the file and placed a hand on her husband's letter, her fingertips tracing the delicate raised surface of the dried ink.

"Mrs. Hillerman?"

Steeling herself against a tidal wave of emotion, she closed the file with a bit more force than she'd intended and said, "May I . . . keep these for a few days? I would like to review them in private."

"Of course," said Mr. Staub. "You will find everything precisely as I have said. Mr. Hillerman did indeed make provisions for Nicholas."

Mr. Staub's apparent distress drew Nora back to the situation at hand. "I'm sure," she muttered, breathless.

"And if you review the previous correspondences in the file," he continued, "you will see that Mr. Hillerman's persistent inquiries about Nicholas more than prove his interest in the man's well-being and concern for his future."

Nora looked up. "Oh, it's not that I doubt your word, Mr. Staub. Not in the least. It's all just so very odd," she said, trying to fathom her husband's intentions. For reasons unknown to her, Garrett had cared a great deal about this man of misfortune. Her gaze shifted to the office window. "Very odd indeed," she mumbled, peering across the lobby at the curious scene taking shape in front of the fireplace.

William stopped shy, waiting and watching to see if the old man was indeed asleep or just resting his eyes, as old folk tended to do.

He inched closer to the rumpled man. "Are you asleep?" he whispered. "Because if you are, my mother says I'm not to disturb you."

The man made no response.

"But if you're just pretending to be asleep so people will leave you be, I understand. I do that sometimes too."

The man still did not stir.

"All right," he said, continuing to whisper, "I just wanted to give you this." He plopped the coin into the man's cup.

The man opened one eye, then the other, and peered at Will. Then, scratching his tangled salt and pepper beard, he said, "Hello there."

William opened his mouth, ready to apologize for disturbing the old man's nap.

The old man peeked into his cup. "And what's this?" He fished the coin out and bit it lightly between his front teeth. "Nope, not edible. And I certainly can't drink it."

"It's a coin, sir," William said.

"Ah, so it is. But there's just one problem."

"Problem?" asked Will.

"This cup here," said the tattered man, "it's for water, or hot cocoa if I'm lucky. You like hot cocoa, don't you, Will?"

"Of course," answered William, not noticing the old man somehow magically knew his name. "It's my favorite!"

"Mine too," said the man. "Now you wouldn't want to go ruining a perfectly good cup of cocoa with a tarnished old coin, would you?"

"No sir."

"Tell you what, my friend," he said as he returned the coin to William's palm. "Take this back to your mother and ask her to tip the bellhop with it instead. You can do that, can't you Will?"

"Sure, I can do that."

Nicholas grinned at the boy and reached up to ruffle his hair. "I'm Nicholas."

"Nice to meet you Nicholas, I'm—" Will stopped, finally realizing that the old man already knew his name.

"Go on then," said Nicholas, indicating William's mother, who appeared to be keeping a watchful eye on her boy.

William zipped back to where his mother stood speaking with the hotel manager after emerging from the concierge office.

Nora's eyebrows shot up. "What's this?" she said as Will held up the coin.

"He said the cup is for hot cocoa."

Mr. Staub nodded. "That sounds like our Nicholas all right."

"He won't take money?" asked Nora.

"Not a franc."

"How extraordinary."

William offered the coin back to his mother. "He told me to tell you to tip the bellhop with it."

"That's a splendid idea," said Nora. "Why don't you do it for me. Tell him it's a little extra for a job well done."

Nora watched as her son caught up to Ben, gave him the coin and then pointed to Nicholas, crediting the old man for the gift, but before Ben could walk over to properly thank him, Mr. Staub intervened.

"Ben! There are guests waiting for their bags. Room 104."

"Yes sir," said Ben, turning toward the stairs.

While William acquainted himself with the more peculiar residents of the hotel, Becca took an interest in the place itself. She walked the length of the lobby, slowly running her fingers over the backs of chairs and sofas to feel the softness of the velvet.

She breathed in the sweet aroma of fresh cut lilacs and evening primrose displayed in the many stone vases throughout the lobby and stood to stare for a time at the lavishly decorated Christmas tree, inspecting the intricate wooden ornaments depicting tiny scenes of the town. One she found particularly beautiful—a miniature model of The Carrington Grand itself, carved from a single block of wood by someone who obviously shared her love of detail.

Spotting a curious pair of statues flanking one of the large picture windows, Becca crossed the length of the lobby to get a closer look. She stopped before a life-sized bronze of a woman in a windblown cloak cradling a dove. "What's your name?" she asked the statue. "You don't have a name? Well, that won't do. I'll call you Arabella. It's the prettiest name I can imagine." As she gazed up at the serene figure, a face appeared in the window to her right, drawing her attention away from the sculpture. The face belonged to a young boy whose focus seemed intent upon Nicholas and William.

Becca waved to the boy.

Realizing he'd been caught, the boy ducked out of sight. Becca raced to the window but saw only the white of snow banking the court and the misty spot the boy's breath left on the glass.

CHAPTER FIVE
THE INVITATION

The next morning, light streamed through the vividly colored stained-glass windows that sprinkled the east-facing wall of the cafe hall, saturating the room with vibrant greens, blues, and reds.

The guests were all abuzz during breakfast, for each had risen that morning to discover a gold and white engraved invitation slipped under their hotel room door sometime in the night.

After finishing their meal of baked eggs with ham, porridge and cream, and toasted sweet bread in the dining hall, Nora and the children took a stroll around the hotel grounds.

Upon their return, Nora approached Mr. Staub at the front desk to ask about the mysterious invitations.

"Are you speaking of the Christmas party? I assumed the invitations were from you."

"Why, no, Mr. Staub, they aren't from me," said Nora. "In fact, I received one as well." She held up the white and gold envelope.

"Quite puzzling," said Mr. Staub, taking their coats. "The ballroom was reserved months ago, and payment arrived by courier along with instructions, but there was no name or signature. It appears our host prefers to remain anonymous.

But it is to be a grand affair. That much was clear. Will you be attending, Mrs. Hillerman?"

Nora shook her head. "Oh no, I couldn't leave the children alone."

"I assumed you would bring the children," said Mr. Staub.

"Will there be other children there?"

"I presume so. The Dreschers have three children. Boris and Isadora Anosov have a little girl about the same age as yours. And Mrs. Stow has six," he said with evident distaste, "though she insists they are all well behaved. Her husband hasn't yet made an appearance, but I believe he may disagree with that assessment when, or rather, if he arrives."

"Well," said Nora, with some amusement, "if the children are invited, then I suppose you'd better add three more to your confirmation list."

"Excellent," said Staub.

A small scuffle transpired as a gangly boy led a group of ragamuffin children through the lobby, heading for Nicholas, who waved them in.

"Would you excuse me a moment, Mrs. Hillerman," said Staub as he huffed off toward them.

Several unpleasant words were exchanged as Mr. Staub demanded their prompt exit.

Soon the children ran pell-mell through the lobby toward the front entrance. The obvious leader of the group snatched a holiday invitation off the front desk on the way out.

A flustered Staub reappeared, loosening his collar. He cleared his throat. "Again, my apologies, Mrs. Hillerman. The children of this town have no respect for the dignity of this fine establishment."

"Well," said Nora, "they are, after all, only children."

A stout woman entered through the marble archway outfitted with a chef's hat and apron over The Carrington Grand starched staff uniform.

"Ah, Fiona!" called Staub. "This is Mrs. Hillerman, our new owner. She and her children are staying through to January."

"Aye, 'tis a pleasure to be makin' your acquaintance, ma'am," said Fiona in a thick Scottish brogue. She extended a hand after a quick pat of her apron. "Fiona McFarland, head chef . . . *and* head of housekeeping, I might well add."

"Pleased to meet you, Fiona."

"Should ye be needin' anything, anything a'tall, I'll be the one ye be callin'." Fiona drew close. "When Mr. Staub told us ye were comin', I took great care to ready yer suite myself."

"Ah," said Nora. "I wondered who did such a fine job with the flowers."

"I thought ye could do with a wee bit of bright in yer room. Flowers are a grand reminder that life abounds."

"A very thoughtful gesture." Nora glanced around the lobby at the many other floral arrangements. "How ever did you find such glorious blooms in the dead of winter?"

"'Tis a might bit of magic, no? Carrington is rich with it. We grow them ourselves in the conservatory behind the kitchen, alongside the herbs, spices, and vegetables we use for meals. A triumph to be certain, and one we're all quite proud of."

Nora smiled. "It would appear our hotel is in good hands."

"We do our best, ma'am." Then, lowering her voice in a conspiratorial manner she added, "Ye may have noticed, we're miserably shorthanded, with only Mr. Staub, the four senior heads of staff including myself, and a handful of underlings left to run the hotel."

"Oh, I didn't realize," said Nora, stalling to collect her thoughts. She hadn't adequately prepared herself for the responsibility of the title she now held and silently chided herself for the oversight. Nodding slowly to appear supervisory, she said, "I've not been apprised of your situation."

Fiona gave a little huff. "I can tell ye full well, 'tis a might poor situation at that. We've closed off the east wing entirely. Most of the west tower as well, but that still leaves us with nearly a hundred rooms to manage, not counting the great hall, the parlor room, and the like. Our staff has plummeted from four hundred to forty in the last few years, and that includes the night staff. 'Tis a right disgrace, it is."

Nora's eyes scanned the room, seeing what she'd not seen upon arrival, dazzled as she was by the splendor of it all. The details did indeed tell a tale of neglect: dust in the folds of the drapery and tapestries, the accumulation of ash in the hearth, chipped marble at the foot of the stairs, threadbare rugs worn so thin in places you could glimpse the marblestone below.

"A staff of forty for a hotel of this size? It would never pass in America. How ever do you manage, Fiona?"

"Oh, well, there are only a handful of suites occupied at the moment. And we all of us hold numerous stations here, to offset the deficiency. Your coachman, André, is also groom and stable hand. Ben, your bellhop, works as valet, page, and footman. My housekeeping staff, they are all chamber and parlormaids as well as scullery maids and cooks." Her eyes flashed to her superior. "Why, even our good man Mr. Staub works in the wee hours of the morn as a secret gardener of the grounds durin' spring and summer, though he claims to take great pleasure in it."

Nora raised an eyebrow. "Truly?"

Fiona lowered her voice another notch and added, "Oh, best be keepin' that bit'a knowin' between us. It wouldn't do ta' have folks privy to our troubles. But seein' as how you're in a position to do somethin' 'bout it now, well, you catch my meanin' aye?"

"Yes, yes of course. I shall look into it immediately."

"That will be all, Fiona," snapped Mr. Staub, no doubt overhearing his name amid the women's hushed exchange as he approached.

"You'll nae forget?" said Fiona quickly.

"You have my word," answered Nora.

"Fiona! Haven't you important duties to attend to?"

"Why yes, Mr. Staub, how good of you to acknowledge that what I do is important," sassed Fiona, mimicking the hotel manager's stately mannerisms. She curtsied mockingly, and then said loud enough for all to hear, "Mrs. Hillerman, how would ye like a lovely cup of rose petal tea to coax the mornin' chill from yer bones?"

"That would be lovely," said Nora.

"Right then," Fiona said, turning on her heels. "I'll fetch ye when it's ready."

"Mama?" Becca interrupted. "May we go play outside?"

Nora peered out the front window at a thin shaft of sunlight glistening on the melting snow. "You may," she said to her daughter, "fetch your coats from the cloakroom."

The children disappeared into the foyer and returned a moment later with their arms full.

Mr. Staub tugged the bottom of his vest and straightened his already perfectly straight bowtie. "You must forgive Fiona and her manner of speaking her mind, Mrs. Hillerman. She is indispensable here, but I fear her Scottish frankness lacks the proper sense of etiquette for a noble establishment such as The Carrington Grand."

"Not to worry, Mr. Staub," said Nora, kneeling to help Becca on with her coat and mittens. "I like Fiona. And I wish to be informed where improvements are needed, which includes staffing concerns."

"Of course, Mrs. Hillerman."

By the time Nora had topped Becca off with scarf and hat, her daughter could barely be seen amid all the wool and fur. She then turned to her son. "You too, Will."

"Must I, Mother?" He pointed to the window. "The sun is shining."

"That doesn't mean it's not cold." She reached for his coat. "I don't want you catching a chill."

"You don't have to help me," grumbled Will. "I can do it myself."

"Of course you can. I forget sometimes how independent you have both become . . . but that doesn't mean you can wander off. I want you to stay together, and you're not to leave the hotel grounds. Understood?"

"Yes ma'am," the children chorused.

"And look after your sister, William!"

"I will," said Will.

"All right then," she said, waving them out the door. "Have fun. Stay warm. Be careful."

Nora buttoned her own coat and followed her children to the courtyard at the back of the hotel. As she stood on a stone terrace to watch them play, her heart constricted with a familiar fear. It happened every time they ventured out on their own. She knew she'd been overprotective of her children since Garrett's death, but she couldn't help herself. Something might happen to them—something horrible. What if she wasn't there when they needed her?

She hadn't been there for Garrett. His men said it was an accident, that no one could have prevented it.

He and his chief architect were visiting the construction site of his newest Charleston hotel. A cable snapped. A beam fell. It happened in an instant. Garrett saved the architect's life, but not his own. Nora was a quarter mile away, having tea with an old friend.

Just one-quarter mile, she thought over and over. One thousand, three hundred and twenty feet. Just a handful of steps and she could have been there with him. She might not have been able to prevent the tragedy, but she could have been by his side at the end. She could have looked into his eyes and whispered I love you. She could have—

Fiona approached, drawing Nora out of her sullen introspection. "What're ye doin' out here in the frigid air? Come inside, Mrs. Hillerman. I've set a place for ye in the parlor. I've put ye at our best table. It has a lovely view of the town, it does, and mountains beyond."

Nora would have preferred to watch her children play, but propriety demanded a more genteel response. She followed Fiona into the sunny parlor and sat at a table positioned near a sweeping picture window.

"Thank you, Fiona. The view is stunning, as promised."

"With yer leave, I'll go look in on my kitchen staff to see how supper preparations are comin'. There'll be a choice of roast wild duck or fillet of pheasant, with soupe à la Reine. And for dessert: apricot tart, raspberry cream, or maple custard."

Nora took a sip of tea, still feeling quite full from Fiona's scrumptious breakfast. "I look forward to it."

Outside, William and Rebecca breathed in the chill winter air. Becca reached down with a fuzzy-mittened hand, picked up a fistful of freshly fallen snow and tossed it in the air. It fell like soft white confetti all around them.

"Let's go on a treasure hunt!" said Becca.

"I have a better idea," said Will. "Let's look for clues!"

Becca gave a little tilt of the head. "Clues to what?"

"Clues to what makes this place so special."

"Can we do both?"

"Of course!" said Will. "Which way first?"

Becca spun around twice with eyes closed, then made an abrupt stop and pointed. "That way!"

"Perfect." William grabbed his sister's hand. "Let's go!"

They ran down a meandering slushy footpath that led to a sleeping garden with roseless rose bushes, bare-branched archways, imposing stone angels blanketed in white, and a large frozen fountain at its center.

Stopping before one of the winged statues, Becca gazed up at the figure's angelic face. For a moment she was transfixed by its beauty. The kneeling angel wore a smile of joy, of grace, eyes closed, head bowed, with her arms crossed over her heart. In her right hand was a single rose.

"This statue is different from the others," said Becca, but William didn't hear her. His attention was fixed on something in the distance.

Becca removed the mitten warming her right hand and touched the stone statue expecting it to be cold, but it wasn't.

"I know you're different from the others," she whispered, "and I know why. You're an angel made by angels, and if you're from heaven that means you can get a message to Papa for me."

CHAPTER SIX
THE FROZEN CLUE

Standing before the stone angel, Becca bent on one knee, crossed her arms over her heart and bowed her head, mirroring the angel's stance. "I know you can hear me," she whispered. "Please tell Papa I love him very much and I miss him every day. Tell him I wish he could be here with us for Christmas, and ask him to help Mama not be so sad."

Becca opened her eyes and again the magnificent angel filled her field of vision. She blinked as the sunlight glistened like diamonds on her snow-coated wings, and in that instant Becca saw the angel tilt her head in acknowledgement.

"Thank you for delivering my message," Becca whispered, knowing with utter certainty that Papa had heard her wish.

"Bec, what are you doing? You should be looking for clues!"

"Have you ever seen anything so beautiful?" said Becca.

"Sure," said Will, with a brotherly impatience, "it's a pretty angel, but I think I found a real clue!" He led her to the frozen fountain at the courtyard's center. "Look!" He brushed a bit of snow from its base to reveal words carved in the white stone.

Magic is Real for He Who Hath the Key
Seeing is Not Believing
One Must Believe to See

Becca read it aloud, emphasizing every word. "What does it mean?"

"It means what it says," snapped her brother.

"I know, but what is it telling us about Carrington?"

"That's what we have to figure out. It's a clue."

Becca's gaze returned to the winged statue. "Then I think the angel is also a clue. Willy, I think Papa is—"

"Bec look!" William pointed across the court.

Becca watched in wonder as the bare branched rose bushes began to sprout tiny pink and yellow buds, which grew and unfurled to full bloom, first one by one, then nearly all at once, until there were thousands of beautiful roses filling the entire garden with a warm-sweet sent. It was as though the protracted course of spring raced toward summer all in a single moment.

"It's father!" cried Becca with a wave of chills rippling through her the same way the roses had blossomed through the courtyard. "He heard my message! He's answering me!"

"What are you on about?"

"The roses!"

"What roses?"

"Because Rose is my middle name! He's using them to send a message!"

"Bec, it's the middle of winter. These rose bushes won't bloom until spring comes."

Becca visibly deflated. "You can't see them." She peered at the lovely garden that had bloomed only for her and let out a sigh, her breath forming a tiny white cloud in the frigid air before evaporating. Then, quick as one beat of a heart, the roses wilted back to bare branches, returning to their winter dormancy.

"They're gone," she said, excitement wilting with the flowers. She looked up at her brother. "You couldn't see them. I guess that means you don't believe anymore."

"You're making even less sense than usual, Bec."

"The fountain says you won't see the magic until you believe in it. Oh Willy, you have to start believing again or you'll miss so much of what's worth seeing!"

"I have to help Mother now, Becca. I can't be a starry-eyed child anymore. Father's gone and I have to be the man of the house. You understand, don't you?"

Becca slowly nodded. "I'm sorry, Willy. I wish you could have seen it." Her gaze fell to the frozen ground.

"Me too, Bec." William had grieved the loss of his father, but in that moment he felt the loss of something else, something he never knew he had until it was gone.

"Wait," said Becca, suddenly remembering how their conversation started. "If you couldn't see the garden, then what were you pointing at?"

Will motioned to the far end of the court. "Aren't those the kids who got kicked out of the hotel earlier?"

Becca squinted. "Where?"

"There. By the stables. Let's go see what they're up to."

"Mother wouldn't like us hanging around them, Willy. I overheard Mr. Staub saying bad things about them."

"What bad things?"

"Words like . . . imp—impudent, and . . . au—dacious, and brazen."

"You don't even know what those words mean."

"Neither do you," argued Becca.

"I know what brazen means," said Will, puffing himself up. "It means bold. That's not such a bad thing, is it?"

"I don't think I want to be friends with them."

"Oh Becca, you're always so afraid of everything. Be bold for once. Come on. I just want to know what they're talking about."

Becca glared at her brother. "You want to eavesdrop on them?"

"Sure, why not? Maybe we'll learn something."

"Because it's not very nice."

"It's all just part of our investigation," said Will. "Don't forget, we're still looking for clues." William motioned for his sister to follow as he snuck out of the garden, along the back fence and across to the stables.

By the time they found the children, the group had dispersed and there were only two left; Trev, a gangly thirteen-year-old in a worn out coat and grubby newsy cap, and Finn, a short, skinny boy with bucked front teeth.

34

William and Becca edged close enough to hear what they were saying and ducked into an empty horse stall nearby to listen.

"All right, Finn," said the taller and older of the two. "The others are gone. What's so important? And make it quick. I got things to do."

"You saw the new kids, right?"

"Yeah, I seen 'em," said Trev. "What of it?"

"The boy was talking to Nicholas."

Trev stiffened. "What was he saying?"

"Don't know," said Finn. "Watched 'em through the window. But it looked like he was trying to give Nick some money."

"Stupid kids. They don't know nothin'. They think Nick is just some homeless loafer that hangs around the hotel lobby looking for handouts."

"I think their father owns The Grand now. I heard Mr. Staub talking to Ben."

"Nick should own that hotel," spat Trev, "not some rich snobs showin' up here outta nowhere who don't know nothin' about anythin'!"

"I also heard Ben say they moved into the residential suite. Maybe they're going to stay."

"They're just here for the holidays. They're not gonna stay."

"How do you know?" asked Finn. "Maybe they're going to change things. What if they don't let Nicholas live in the lobby anymore?"

"They're *not* staying."

"What should we do?"

"Just leave it to me." Trev produced the Christmas party invitation from a hidden coat pocket, threw it to the ground, and kicked dirty snow over it.

"Trev, they're kids. They're going to find out about Nick. You know they will. *All* the kids know. The adults may be too thick to see what's right in front of them but kids can see how it is. They're going to find out."

"No one's gonna find out nothin', now go bother someone else. I got business."

"What are you going to do?"

"I said go!"

Finn dashed off.

Will and Becca held their breath, peering through the wooden slats of the horse stall.

Trev waited just inside the barn doors, pacing and mumbling about plans and schemes.

Then William understood why.

A tall slender man shrouded in a sleek black cloak stepped out of the shadows and advanced toward Trev.

The broad brim of the man's top hat obscured his face, but William didn't need to see his expression to know what kind of man he was. His knotted stomach and thumping heart was warning enough.

"I know who you are," said Trev.

"Oh? And just how is it you think you know me?"

"Mrs. Brimby, the baker's wife, keeps an old photograph of you in her storage room. When I asked her about it, she got sad and said that once, long ago, before she married Mr. Brimby, she was in love with a boy and they dreamed of running away together."

The man's commanding posture weakened a bit. "She kept the photograph all these years?"

Trev nodded. "She says she keeps it there to remind her of what can happen when you allow evil to poison your heart. She says she wants to remember what it looks like in case she meets the devil on the road to Heaven so she'll be able to see through his disguise and never be fooled by him again."

William shuddered as the man scanned his surroundings as if sensing he was being watched. Will and Becca drew back into the darkness of the barn.

"That's a charming story," said the man, stiffening, "but it has nothing to do with me."

"Old wounds heal slow," said Trev with a smirk. "Denying them will only make it harder for you."

"Imp!" The man swung open-palmed at the lanky teen, but Trev ducked the slap and whirled around to face him. "I'm not afraid of you, old man."

"You're awfully sure of yourself for a scrawny street urchin."

"And you're awfully bony for an evil ogre."

36

The man laughed out loud, but then stopped abruptly, took a step closer to Trev, dropped his voice to a low snarl and said, "Now that we've established a rapport, perhaps you will tell me what we are doing here in this filthy, reeking stable?"

Trev didn't flinch. "I think we might be useful to each other."

The man raised a single eyebrow. "Useful?"

"I see and hear more than anyone around," said Trev. "I know what's happening in this town before they do."

The man held up Trev's note. "That is precisely why I took the trouble to meet with you despite your odious choice of locale. I have been observing you."

"Oh, that's not creepy at all."

"I intend to employ you."

"You want to give me a job?" said Trev, arms crossed. "And what makes you think I'll be interested?"

"You're not interested in the job," said the man, "you're interested in the money."

"How much?"

"More than you'll see in a year of begging and stealing, I'll wager."

"I don't beg."

"Then I suspect you'll take this job regardless of your obvious disdain for me."

"And what do I have to do for this pay?"

"The same thing you do every day. Keep your eyes and ears sharp."

"And?"

"And report back to me here at exactly five o'clock each night."

William peered at the dark stranger, squinting in an attempt to see his face but it was no use. Between the severe angle of his hat and the shadowy barn, details were impossible to make out. But in that instant, the man halted the conversation and turned. A hand went up to silence Trev's next question.

The man glared in Will's and Becca's direction as if he knew they were there. William closed his eyes as a dizzying sensation blurred his vision. All at once, there came a rush of images, fragments of a distant past that was not his own.

Will's mind capsized—filled to capacity with unbidden memories, misty and nebulous, flooding in to drown him.

William gasped.

"Who's there!" yelled the man. "Show yourself!"

Heart thudding, head pounding, William grabbed Becca's hand and dashed out of the barn.

They didn't stop running until they reached The Grand.

Becca halted on the front marble steps and would go no further. "What happened to you, Willy?"

"Nothing."

"You're lying. Something happened." Becca's labored breath punctuated her words.

"I was just surprised, that's all. It seemed like he knew we were there."

"I don't like that man," said Becca. "He scares me. I think we need to stay away from him."

"Far away," Will agreed.

"Tell me what happened," said Becca, still attempting to catch her breath.

Will shook his head.

"You stopped breathing for a second," she said, "and then you had this far off look in your eyes, like you have when you're sleepwalking."

William, still trying to make sense of it all, whispered, "I don't know, Bec. For a second it felt like I was somewhere else."

"What do you mean, somewhere else?"

"I can't explain it, but I saw . . . I saw . . . I don't know what I saw. It's like a dream you can't remember after you wake up."

William looked into his little sister's worried eyes. "Don't fret about it, Bec. Everything will be fine."

"Are you sure?"

"As sure as I'll ever be." William frowned at his scrunch-faced sister. "What's the matter now?"

"Did you hear what those kids said about the old man in the lobby?"

"His name is Nicholas."

"What did they mean when they said we'd find out? Find out what?"

"I don't know. It's another clue. They're keeping a secret for him, that much is certain. And whatever it is, I'm going to figure it out."

"If it's a secret, maybe it's none of our business," said Becca.

"This is Father's hotel. That makes it ours too. What goes on here *is* our business, Bec, and it's not just Nicholas, it's Carrington too."

"What do you mean?"

"The reason Father brought us here."

Becca huffed. "He wanted us to have Christmas here. Isn't that enough of a reason?"

"There's more to it than that, Bec. I can feel it. There's something else happening here and I won't stop searching until I know what it is."

CHAPTER SEVEN
ENCOUNTERS IN THE NIGHT

It happened to be late, very late, when William Thomas tiptoed downstairs in his forest green flannel pajamas and red knit slippers. He'd thrown on his travel coat to top it off, which did little to conceal the awkward ensemble.

The night clerk dozed behind the front desk, neither hearing nor seeing the boy sneak by, headed for the lobby where Nicholas knelt at the fireplace coaxing sleepy embers back into flame with an iron prod.

"Hello, William. I've been expecting you," Nicholas said without looking up. "That's a fine pair of slippers, young man."

"Want them? I have another pair upstairs," Will said, peering at the old man's shabby shoes.

"That is oh-so-generous of you, my boy, but these ole beat-up boots of mine are like treasured friends—worn in just enough to be as comfortable as slippers, but still reliable and true."

Nicholas hung the hot poker on a black hook and then turned from the fire, which burned bright once more.

"Come," said Nicholas. "Sit with me a spell."

They sat in the two overstuffed leather chairs facing to the hearth.

"You never look up to see who's approaching," said Will. "How do you always know it's me?"

"How could it not be? You are you, are you not?" Nicholas' smile glowed as warm as the fire. "Are you ever anyone else?"

William considered the man's strange question, feeling a bit like he was being tested for admittance into some secret club. "No. I suppose not."

"Well then," said Nick, "mystery solved. So, tell me, good Will, why aren't you tucked warm in your bed, sleeping the night away?"

"A dream woke me. An odd dream."

"And what happened in this odd dream that beckoned you out of your slumber?"

"I was . . . standing out in the snow at night. I had no shoes, no coat, but I wasn't cold. I was in the garden, staring at the frozen fountain . . . talking to it. I told the fountain that it was the same as me, frozen inside, suspended in time, remembering what it was like to move, to be free, to be useful. And then the fountain spoke back."

"And what did the fountain say?"

"It said that winter is like a little death each year until spring coaxes everything back to life. Then I said ever since Father died I feel like I've been stuck in an unending winter. After I said that, I looked down and saw that my bare feet had frozen to the ground and my legs were turning to ice."

Nicholas leaned forward in his chair. "And what did the fountain say then?"

"It said no winter is unending, even though it may seem that way. The sun always returns. Ice always melts. Hearts always heal."

"It would seem you and I have something in common."

"What's that?"

"The ability to dream Truth. It is a great gift."

"When I woke I knew I had to come talk to you," said Will, "because you were there. In my dream. You were frozen like the fountain. Like me."

"I suppose we have more in common than one might imagine," said Nicholas.

Will removed his coat and settled in. "There's something I've been wondering."

"About the truth of things?"

Will nodded. "What do the words on the fountain mean? It says, 'Magic is real for he who hath the key. Seeing is not believing. One must believe to see.' I memorized it because it seemed important."

"Indeed, it is," said Nicholas. "It's one of the secrets to life—a key to open any door. Believing comes before perceiving, and not just with magic. It is requisite to any great achievement. You cannot manifest your dreams and aspirations without belief—belief not only in the path you've chosen, but also in yourself."

"That seems too simplistic to be true."

"All great truths are simple. And this one can be applied to a great many things."

"What do you mean?"

"Well, for example, if you do not *believe* that your life is beautiful, you will not see its beauty."

William pondered Nick's words for a moment. Since Father died, nothing about life seemed beautiful. If anything, it seemed cruel, and no words of wisdom, no magic, no dream could make him feel differently. But that didn't change the fact that he was here to get answers.

"Go on," said Nick.

William looked up. "What?"

"I believe you have other questions you'd like to ask me?"

"I do," agreed Will, surprised again. *How does he always—*

"I have a knack for knowing what's in a child's heart," said Nick, cutting off William's thought. "You might say it's another one of my gifts, like truth-dreaming."

"You do seem to know a lot for someone who doesn't get out much," said William.

Nick laughed at that—a deep-in-the-belly kind of laugh—and then said, "So? What's your question, good Will?"

"Um, Ben says you live here. In the lobby."

"I'm afraid that doesn't qualify as a question. You'll have to try again."

"Okay. Why do you live in the lobby of a hotel? Is it because you're homeless?"

"Homeless." Nick said it as if he'd never considered the notion. He glanced at his surroundings. "I can't imagine living

42

anywhere else. The Carrington Grand *is* my home. But how I came to live here, well, that is a long story."

"Is it a sad story? Is that the reason you don't want to tell it?"

"Hmmm. You are quite perceptive for such a young lad."

"Did you lose hope? My father said the saddest stories are from people who've lost hope."

"Quite so." Nicholas peered at William over his spectacles. "You have a sad story of your own, don't you, Will."

William nodded. "My father. He's gone. He um, died last Christmas."

Nick reached out to touch Will's arm. "Life-shattering. That's what it is to lose a parent. Especially so young."

William bit his bottom lip to keep it from quivering.

"And have you lost your hope, my young friend?"

Will looked away, struggling to keep it all inside. "Sometimes."

"Then you know how it feels."

"Like nothing will ever be the same," said William, in a quiet voice.

Nick nodded. "It's true. Nothing will ever be like it was. The secret is to make it into something different."

"Different?"

"Something new. Something so singular that it helps you to stop comparing the past to the present. That's where healing begins. And then you start to find little flashes of happiness in the between moments, those beautiful fleeting moments of joy that surprise us now and again."

"What happened? What made *you* lose hope?" Will asked. "Did your father die too?"

"My present circumstance has nothing to do with my father."

"What does it have to do with?"

"It's not important," said Nick, with a sigh of resignation. "What happened, happened, and I ended up here. This is where I belong now."

"Where did you belong before?"

"I had a home once," said Nicholas, "people who loved me." He sat a little taller in his high-backed chair. "I was a well-respected citizen of this town, from a prominent family."

"Then how did you become a—" William hesitated, not wanting to offend the man again.

"Tell me, Will, do you believe in Father Christmas?"

William blinked at the old man's abrupt change of subject. "Father Christmas?"

"Pere Noel? Kris Kringle? Santa Claus?"

"Oh."

"Well? Do you?"

"Do I believe in Santa Claus?" Will shook his head. "No, of course not. That's kid's stuff. I'm too old for that."

"Too old? And just how old are you?"

"I'm twelve and two months."

"Well, I'm older than that, and *I* still believe."

"Yeah, but you're—"

"—Just a crazy old man?"

"That wasn't what I was going to s—"

"Before you finish that sentence Will, you should know, I also have a knack for knowing the truth when I hear it, or don't hear it, as the case may be."

"Okay, yes, that's what I was going to say, but I stopped because—"

"—You didn't want to hurt my feelings?"

William nodded.

"I respect that," said Nicholas in a soft, thoughtful tone. "The real reason I live here, in the lobby of The Carrington Grand Hotel, to answer your question Will, is because no one believes in Santa Claus anymore. Not even the children."

"I don't understand. What does that have to do with anything?"

"It has everything to do with everything. You see, long ago—" Nicholas stopped short and glanced toward the grand staircase. "Hmm. Maybe I should tell you my story another time. It's getting rather late."

"You can tell it now. It's not that late."

"Perhaps, but your mother is looking for you."

"No she's not. She fell asleep after reading Becca a bedtime story."

Nora entered the lobby and found her son sitting by the fire next to Nicholas.

"William, there you are," whispered Nora. "What are you doing down here?" She looked him over. "In your nightclothes, no less!"

Will pulled on his coat to cover up his pajamas.

"Get to bed this instant young man, before you wake that poor gentleman!"

"Wake him? We were just talking—" Will looked at Nick, who did indeed appear to be sound asleep, although as Will rose to follow his mother upstairs, he thought he saw the old man wink.

While William did go straight to his room as instructed, he did not go straight to sleep. As he began to ready himself for bed, he heard his sister crying in the adjoining room.

"Becca?" he whispered, stopping in the doorway between their rooms with the candle from his bedside table. "Are you okay?"

She continued to whimper.

Will crossed the moonlit floor and sat on the edge of her bed. "Bec? Becca, wake up."

"What?" Becca started, then rubbed the sleep from her eyes. "Willy? What's wrong?"

"You were having another nightmare. Was it the same one? About father?"

Becca nodded, bleary-eyed. "I can't save him. I watch it over and over. I'm there. I see it happen. I try to move, but I can't. I try to cry out to warn him, but I can't. I have no voice."

"I have the same nightmare," said Will, setting the candle on the bedside table. "So does Mother."

"She does? How do you know?"

"I don't know how I know. I just do."

Becca looked at Will's clothes. "What are you doing up?"

"I was talking to Nicholas. The old man downstairs. I went to ask him about his secret. The one the town kids spoke of."

"You did? What did he say?"

Will shrugged. "Nothing much. We didn't have a chance to finish our conversation. Mother came to fetch me. But he did say something about Santa Claus."

Becca crinkled her nose. "Santa Claus?"

"He said the reason he's homeless is because people don't believe in Santa Claus anymore."

"Do you think he's crazy?"

"Nah," said William. "Well, maybe a little. But I like him."

"You do?" Becca sat up in bed.

"There's something about him that makes me feel like he understands things. And he reminds me of Father a little."

"Papa?"

"Remember how Father always knew things he couldn't have known? Things we didn't tell him, but he knew anyway?"

Becca nodded.

"Well, that's how Nicholas is."

Becca grew quiet.

William reached over to put his arm around her. "I know you don't like talking about Father, but if we don't talk about him, it's like we're making him disappear even more. Not all of it is sad, Bec. There are still lots of happy things to remember about him too."

Becca's countenance brightened a bit. "Like how he used to point out silly faces in the rocks and clouds just to make us giggle?"

William smiled. "Or how he used to laugh at the worst jokes in the world."

"And that made everybody else laugh too," said Becca.

"Or how he loved to give us presents, months before our birthdays, and it was always something we secretly wanted but never told anyone about."

"Right," said Becca. "What did he call them?"

"Pre-presents," William said with a little laugh.

"Oh, and remember how his face would light up whenever he had a surprise for us?" said Becca. "I miss that."

Will's mouth tightened into a straight line. "I miss how he always knew when we were sad even if we were trying to hide it."

"Like now," said Becca.

"And how he could always make things better."

"I wish he were here now so he could tell us everything's going to be all right."

"It will be, Bec. I know it will. And, I know it's not the same, but I'll always be here for you."

Becca rubbed tears from her eyes. "Promise?"

"I promise." William tried to hide the welling of his own eyes. "We have to remember him, Bec, even if it makes our hearts hurt a little."

"Or a lot."

"If we don't remember him, we'll lose him." Will's voice cracked.

"I miss him so much," cried Becca, hugging her brother.

"I miss him too," said Will. He drew away and reached into his front coat pocket. "I want to show you something." He handed his sister the tintype photograph from the box in the attic—of the couple holding their infant son.

Becca squinted at the photograph. "Willy, who are these people?"

"That's Father." Will pointed to the child. "And those are our grandparents."

"How to you know that? Where did this come from?"

"It was in the Christmas box with the tickets and the letter Mother read to you."

"I thought Papa never knew where he came from. Why didn't he show us this?"

"Maybe he found it and realized it was a clue, but wanted to find out more before he told us about it. That's what I would have done." Will took the tintype from his sister. "I just thought you should see it."

"I'm glad you showed it to me." She hugged him again. "I have something to show you too." She held out the charm bracelet Papa had given her on her seventh birthday—the one she wore every day until his death.

"I haven't seen you wear that in a long while," said Will.

"It was in my music box." She pointed to the beautiful ornate box on the bedside table. "I didn't put it there, and I asked Mama. She didn't put it there either. Did you?"

"I haven't seen it for over a year."

"That's because I lost it. I took it off when Papa . . . " She looked down at the bracelet in her hand. "It made me sad so I put it in a drawer." She stopped herself from crying. "I looked for it a few months later but it was . . . gone. I never should have taken it off."

"Well, you found it again, so everything's all right now."

She placed a single charm between her index finger and thumb and let the rest of the chain dangle. "Look at this charm, Willy. It's an angel . . . just like the one in the garden. It wasn't here when Papa gave me the bracelet. I think it means something. I think it's another clue."

"Maybe." Will yawned. "We'll talk about it in the morning, but right now it's time for bed. Lie down and try to get some sleep."

Becca put her head on the pillow and William covered her with soft blankets, stroking her hair for a moment—something Mother always did to help her fall asleep.

"Willy?" she said in a half-whisper, "What if I'm mad at God? Does that make me a bad person?"

"I don't think so. Close your eyes."

"I'm mad at God for taking Papa away from us."

"So am I," said Will.

After a long silence, Becca finally yawned.

"Go to sleep now," said William. "Try to dream of happy things."

She nodded and nestled deeper under the covers.

Will rose and started toward the door that joined their two rooms. "I love you, Bec," he whispered. "Goodnight. Sleep tight. See you with the morning light."

"Night night," mumbled Becca, drifting off to sleep.

William retuned to his room, leaving the door ajar so he could hear his little sister cry out if she had another bad dream.

He sat staring at the old photograph for a long while before placing it back in his coat pocket.

Finally, he took off his coat and slippers, and crawled into bed, but lay awake for some time in the dark, thinking about first Father, then Nicholas, and the mystery that seemed to be unfolding around them both.

CHAPTER EIGHT
THE GREAT GIVER

What William didn't know—couldn't possibly have known—was that a few minutes before he and Nora went back upstairs, Trev had crept into the hotel kitchen using the service entrance, and after plucking a buttermilk roll from a bread basket, continued out through the dining hall, and with the stealth of a jewel thief, slipped easily past the night clerk at the front desk.

Halting to the sound of voices, Trev remained just out of sight to eavesdrop on a conversation in progress and heard enough to know that Nick intended to tell the owner's son everything, and would have, if not for the interruption.

After the boy and his mother went to bed, the lanky teen crossed the lobby to the fireplace, stood over a snoozing Nicholas, and kicked the old man's boot.

"I know you're awake, Nick. You never sleep this time of night. Too many wishes and dreams to listen for."

Nicholas opened one eye. "You're too smart for me, Trev. And you know me too well." He smiled. "Hmm. What's that?" He pointed to an awkward lump in Trev's overcoat pocket.

"This?" Trev produced a well-worn stuffed lion, one of its paws dangling by a thread.

"Ah! A wounded critter that needs my attention!" said Nick. "This is little Jonah's companion, is it not?"

Trev nodded. "He's sick and won't take his medicine until it's mended, so I offered to bring it."

"That was very kind of you, Trev." Nick rummaged through his patchwork pockets and retrieved a needle and thread wrapped in yellowing wax paper. He got straight to work, sewing the lion's torn paw back onto its well-loved, nearly fuzzless torso. "You're a good person, Trev."

"Huh, try telling that to Mr. Staub."

"Oh, Mr. Staub is a bit too preoccupied with the comings and goings of his hotel to see it, but that's okay, because I do."

A moment of silence passed between them and when Trev didn't respond, Nick became concerned.

"What is it, my friend? What's on your mind?"

After a bit of fidgeting, Trev said, "You and me, Nick, we're a team, right? Two of a kind?"

"That's right," said Nick. "Since the day you were born."

"And we'll always be friends, won't we?"

"Of course we will," said Nicholas.

"Even if—" Trev stopped.

Nick's brows knitted. "Even if . . . ?"

"Nothing."

"Has something got you worried, Trev?"

"Nah."

"But there *is* something you'd like to discuss, isn't there?"

"Well," said Trev, "you've heard that The Grand has new owners now, right?"

"The Hillermans, yes. Good folk."

"What if they don't let you stay here anymore?"

"Everything happens for a reason, Trev. Try not to worry so much about how things appear in the moment. It will all unfold the way it's meant to."

"But how can you know for sure? Maybe they—"

"It's not about knowing, it's about believing." Nicholas returned the lion. "See, look. All better." He reached out to tug on Trev's dirty shirtsleeve. "Have faith, my friend."

Trev looked at the once-threadbare stuffed animal, which now appeared somehow miraculously restored. "Thanks, Nick."

Nick smiled. "Thank you for bringing it to me for mending. Now, you carry that little lion back to Jonah, tell him to take his medicine and get a good night's rest. And you get some shut-eye yourself, okay?"

"I will."

"You have a place to lay your head tonight?"

Trev, eyes cast to the floor, mumbled, "Sure. Always find something, don't I?"

"The fire's warm," said Nicholas, nodding to the empty chair beside him. "You're always welcome to share the hearth with me."

"Oh, the night manager will be back from his rounds any minute now, and you know he is Mr. Staub's man. Watches me like he's got a criminal in his midst every time I'm near. Never lets me stay more than a few ticks of the clock."

"Perhaps you have it wrong and he's simply looking after you."

"Nah. Best I make myself scarce before he returns."

"I worry about you, my friend."

"I'll be fine. 'Night, Nick."

"Good night, Trev. Dream well."

The following day, William waited all day for an opportunity to talk to Nicholas, but it never came. Every time he got near the lobby, his mother called him away for one reason or another.

The morning was busy with a lavish breakfast and the meeting of guests, which, much to William and Becca's displeasure, Nora insisted the entire family be present for, asserting that 'cordiality is requisite in a civilized world.'

After breakfast and guest greeting, the three of them snuggled into one of The Grand's horse-drawn sleighs, festively decorated for the holidays, and André, the coachman, took them on a historical tour of Carrington that, despite its enchantments, took far too long for such a small town, in William's opinion.

While they were out, they met polite Mr. Henson, with hat in hand, and Mrs. Ivan Lee, who gave them candy that wasn't at all sweet.

They stopped to feed and rest the horses at O'Malley's Horse and Cart, where Mr. O'Malley told them the story of how his great-great-grandfather came to Carrington so long ago, all the way from Ireland, to take up residence in a place he called 'the gem of the world.'

"I have to say," said Nora, "in our explorations of the town today, I have found Carrington to be surprisingly continental for its limited numbers and remote location."

"Oh, aye," said Mr. O'Malley, with a twinkle in his eye. "People were, once upon a time, drawn to our fair hamlet by, they say, a 'mystical invitation.' Nearly every member of our community is a descendant of the first settlers here nearly four hundred years ago. They came from all over, answerin' the call, and mind you, they had no easy time of it, way back when there was no train a'huffin' and puffin' up the mountain to carry their burdens."

William interrupted. "What exactly is a mystical invitation and how did it call them to Carrington?"

"I ought to warn you," said Nora, watching Mr. O'Malley's expression for any sign of irritation, "we are a curious bunch, given to inquiry, so please pardon our outbursts." She paused as a flush crept into her cheeks, "But I must admit, I too am more than a little intrigued as to the reason behind the allure of the town. I appreciate that Carrington has a charm of its own, but there *is* something different about this place, is there not?"

"Aye. 'Twas *Flaithiúlach. That* is what brought them all here," he said decisively, as if Nora spoke Gaelic.

"Fla-hool-ock," repeated Nora trying out the word for herself. What language is that? I've never heard—then all at once she knew what the word meant. "A grand generosity," she said, with a tiny tingle of enchantment.

"Aye, a grand generosity," echoed Mr. O'Malley. "The gift of giving. You see, the Lord and Master of our once flourishing township was called The Great Giver."

"And who was this man?" asked William. "Where did he come from?"

"If any ever knew the answer to that question," said Mr. O'Malley, "they'd be long dead. All we do know is that he had a kindness about him, a gentleness of spirit, and a powerful pull to draw the right and courageous souls for his—" and here, he

52

slipped back into the same strange language to finish his sentence, and yet, somehow they all understood . . .

"Enterprise of the heart," said Nora, Will, and Becca all at together.

"Aye. Enterprise of the heart," O'Malley repeated, with a knowing smile.

"How—" started William.

"Yer wonderin' how ya can understan' me when I speak Gaelic even though you've never heard it before today?"

"Indeed," said Nora.

"Ah well, 'tis a wondrous gift from The Great Giver. All who find themselves in Carrington have a purpose here. And if they truly belong, they'll understand all that is spoken here, no matter the tongue. 'Tis how he could bring together so many people from so many places the world over and have 'em all workin' together like family."

William, who thus far had been only mildly interested in the events of the day, now found himself fully engaged. A fascinating portrait was taking shape . . . of the town, its people, and its obscure history. Now, more than ever, he was convinced that if he could figure out what makes Carrington so special, he'd understand why Father brought them here. And then, just maybe, he could understand *the why* of all that had happened in the past year. Mr. O'Malley had just offered another clue, and possible confirmation of the magic hinted at by the writing on the fountain.

William wanted to know more, but the instant Will began to ask another question, Mr. O'Malley put a hand up to stop him.

"I'm afraid that is the sum total of my knowledge on the subject, lad. Just what has been passed down through generations of O'Malleys."

"Is there anywhere else I can learn about this town's history?" asked Will.

Mr. O'Malley leaned in. "Legend tells of a great book that holds all the history and secrets of this town and its people. It's called The Book of Christmas." Mr. O'Malley whispered the last few words in Gaelic, but Will understood them perfectly.

"The Book of Christmas?" said William with a wave of goosebumps spreading across his skin.

"Aye," said Mr. O'Malley.

"And where do I find this book?"

"It is hidden, I'm afraid. A secret location. Oh, there are those who've searched, but none have ever found it. Only the Great Giver himself knows where it is for certain."

"But he's gone," said William.

"Died with his secrets still in him, I'm afraid. Most believe the book was buried with him."

William's shoulders drooped.

"Sorry lad."

For a moment, Will had a glimmer of hope that all his questions would be settled, if he could just get his hands on that book. *Doesn't matter*, he thought, *if the answers are here, I will find them.*

After Mr. O'Malley's captivating story, Nora and the children ventured next door for afternoon tea and cakes. The little café had a funny name: Jolly Belly's Best, and the food turned out to be positively scrumptious.

Everyone in town seemed to know who they were, and a steady stream of fancy folk paraded in to meet the new owners of The Carrington Grand Hotel. They even brought welcome gifts—homemade jam and pickled eggs, squares of delicate embroidery, hand-painted stationery, fruit, bread, and cheese baskets decorated with silk ribbon.

All the townsfolk seemed genuinely glad to make their acquaintance—all, that is, except one man who stood outside the cafe, looming at the window; a sinister looking man in a tall black hat and a long black cloak.

"Willy," whispered Becca, squinting at the window, "isn't that the man we saw in the barn yesterday?"

"That's him," said Will. "He's been standing there since we entered the café."

"What's he doing here?"

"I'm not sure, but I don't think it's because he's hungry."

"It's odd, isn't it? Him just staring at us through the window like that?" whispered Becca, clutching at her wrap to pull it tighter around her shoulders. "What does he want?"

William shook his head, feeling instantly protective over his sister and mother. Every muscle in his body tensed.

The man made no attempt to mask his overt stare.

"He scares me," said Becca.

"Oh Bec, you think I'd let anything happen to my little sister?" said William, consciously willing himself to relax. But the rumbling disquiet in the pit of his stomach refused to abate. His instincts told him to investigate this man's intentions, but his upbringing waged a convincing argument in favor of decorum.

"But surely some action is called for," he murmured.

William rose slowly from the table.

"Willy, what are you doing?" whispered Becca. "You're going to get in trouble."

"I'm just going to introduce myself, ask him his name, and find out why he's here."

"No," whispered Becca, "it's too dangerous."

"What are you two on about?" said Nora, turning from her society ladies to her obviously agitated children.

"William Thomas! Where are your manners? Sit down!"

Will sat, balanced on the edge of his chair. He placed his hands on the table, fingers laced. "Mother, may I go speak to that gentleman in the window?"

Nora glanced over her shoulder. "What gentleman?"

William twisted about to have a look.

Gone. Of course, the instant the cloaked man saw that he'd been spotted, he disappeared from sight, leaving Will with no explanation for his behavior.

William shrugged an apology in his mother's direction, sat back in his chair, and they did not speak of it again.

But for the rest of the afternoon, Will secretly fretted over it, rerunning scenarios in his mind of what he might have said to the man had he the chance.

Unable to shake the image of the dark stranger, William vowed to discover as much as he could about the man the next time they were in town.

CHAPTER NINE
REASONS OF THE HEART

"Camilla, have you met the new owner?" said a young girl peeling potatoes in The Grand's main kitchen. "A woman, no less. I am intensely curious about her."

"Not as of yet," said Camilla, searing cutlets at the largest of the stoves, "but Mr. Staub seems quite impressed, and that's as rare as a pig in plaid."

"Oh, I imagine her to be a stately woman, draped in expensive jewels and fur. Dignified and reserved, but secretly passing judgment on all she surveys."

"She's not the queen, Ada, she's a mother of two who has lost her husband. Fiona says she's friendly enough . . . in a modest sort of way."

"Why hasn't she inspected the staff?" said Ada. "Do you think she intends to replace us?"

The other girls in the kitchen stopped working to hear Camilla's answer.

Camilla checked the fire under a heavy iron skillet and then turned to the girls. Lowering her voice, she said, "There's no reason to think our jobs are in jeopardy."

"But that's what new owners do, isn't it?" said Ada. "I've heard the staff chattering on about it."

"I need this job," said one of the other girls, "it's my family's only income."

"We all do," said Camilla, "but—"

"Ladies!" barked Fiona, entering through the pantry, "Less prattle. More preparation. There are hungry guests a'gatherin' just beyond these walls."

"Yes, ma'am," they chorused, even though most of them had finished their work and were already prepping tomorrow's morning meal.

Fiona opened one of several large iceboxes to retrieve a ready-made plate of food leftover from yesterday.

"Hungry?" said Ada, with a sly grin.

"I'll thank ye to mind your own, Miss Ada. What I do with the kitchen discards is no concern of yers."

"And what's *that* for," asked Camilla, pointing to the wool blanket draped over Fiona's arm.

"Return to your tasks, all of ye," barked Fiona, after which, she left through the same door she had just entered.

"Think she's got a secret lover tucked away?" said Camilla.

"Locked away, is more like," said Ada.

The girls all giggled as they continued their work.

Fiona carried the plate of food through the cold, dark storage pantry, and out into the light and relative heat of the conservatory, where the kitchen spices and vegetables grew in glorious abundance.

The conservatory was Fiona's pride and joy. Her mother had instilled in her a passion for gardening—in Scotland, of course, where the rain encouraged everything to grow—but she took added pleasure in growing things at the top of a mountain in the dead of winter. It took dedication, focus, skill, and, most of all, love.

She'd spoken to Mrs. Hillerman of the magic in this garden, and sincerely believed it was so, for nothing she tended to ever died here. And when she harvested the fruits of her labor, they were as flavorful as any she had ever prepared in her sixty-two years on earth. Magic, to be certain.

"Yoo-hoo?" she called. "Are ye here?" She hurried to the far corner of the conservatory where a wooden pallet had been converted into a makeshift bed.

Stooping to set the plate beside the bed, she heard feet shuffling in the dirt directly behind her. Straightening as she turned, she found Trev staring at her.

"Are ye hungry?" asked Fiona. "I brought ye a smatterin' of last night's leftovers."

"I'm always hungry." Trev took the plate, sat on the wooden pallet, and began to devour the food.

"Due ta' the influx of new arrivals," said Fiona, "and the fast approachin' holiday festivities, we're preparing a heap more food this week. I thought ye could do with a wee bit extra. Put some meat on yer' bones."

Fiona watched Trev eat for a moment and then looked down at the blanket draped over her arm. "Oh, and I brought this for ye. The nights are getting colder." She nodded to the shabby coverlet Trev sat upon. "I suspect ye'll soon be needin' more than that to keep ye warm."

"What I have is fine," said Trev. "It's not cold in here."

"Och aye. The conservatory is heated by steam, same as the hotel, but if there be a sudden drop in temperature outside, it can take a bit of time for the system to compensate." Fiona set the blanket down and took a step back. "There's a storm a'brewin', there is. I feel it in m'bones."

Trev looked up. "Why are you always trying to be nice to me? You don't even know me."

"I know ye better than ye might suppose."

Trev's eyes narrowed. "You think so?"

"I know ye steal from the kitchen but not from the guests even though yer a skillful pickpocket. I know ye eat the berries off the vine in the conservatory but ye've also watered and cared for them too. I know ye sing when ye think no one's listening and ye've the voice of an angel, ye do. I know the kids in town look up to ye and ye watch over them, even though they've all got homes of their own."

"So," interrupted Trev. "That don't mean you know me."

"Am I makin' ye uncomfortable, Trev? Are ye scared to have somebody know ye?"

"I'm not scared of nothin'."

"We're all afraid'a somethin' but it's nothin' to be shameful of. 'Tis what makes us human, one'n'all. 'Tis why

58

we need one another. Compassion and companionship keep our demons at bay."

"I'm not scared of nothin' and I don't need nobody."

"Ye do, but yer afraid a'losin' 'em, so ye push 'em away."

Trev laughed.

"Yer mum died when ye were five and the woman who took ye in, she died a few years thereafter, n' since then ye've refused to let anyone look after ye."

"I look after myself," Trev snarled.

"Ye like folks to think yer tough, and in fact, ye are, but yer also sad and soul-weary. Ye make like yer willful and troublesome, but I know deep down yer a good person with a good heart."

Trev's gazed snapped back to Fiona. "You're wrong. I'm not. You don't know what I've done."

"Well, I know Nick believes in ye and that's good enough for me."

Trev looked down at the plate of leftovers, suddenly not hungry. "Maybe he shouldn't."

With a bit of effort, Fiona sat on the pallet beside Trev.

"Don't be so hard on yer'self, ye hear? Things won't always be so bad. Ye'll see."

"I don't want things to change. I want everything to stay just the way it is. The way it's always been."

"The way it is now, Trev, that's not how it's always been. Ye had a home once. A mum who loved ye, and a Da too, though he passed just 'afore ye were born."

"How do you know all this?"

"I never said as much, but I knew yer mum."

"What?"

"Not well, mind ye, but she worked at The Grand for a spell. Came all'a'way over on a boat from America. Couldn't 'a been an easy passage for her, being with child and no husband to dote. Strong-willed, she was, like ye. Hard worker too. And the kindest of souls. I remember she—"

"Do you . . . know how she died? No one ever told me."

"She was ill," said Fiona. "That'd be all any of us knew. But I do know she loved ye more than anythin' on God's great earth. She used to bring ye here on workdays. Nick watched over ye while she'd be cleanin' the rooms. You were just a wee thing

59

then." Fiona smiled at the memory. "All grins and giggles, you were. We all had quite a fondness for ye."

"I don't remember any of that," snapped Trev. "I don't even remember what she looked like."

"Hmmm. I can help ye with that. I believe there be a photograph lyin' about somewheres, an old staff photograph that she appeared in. I'll see if I can find it for ye."

"Don't bother. I don't want to remember. It's me and Nick now, and that's the way it's gonna stay. It's all that matters to me."

"Well, then. I suppose that's that." Fiona labored to her feet, found her balance, and clasped her hands together. "I'll see if I can't spirit away some of tonight's meal for ye before it's picked clean." She bent to prune a few dried leaves off the top of a nearby tomato plant. "I best be gettin' on. Heaps to do 'n'all."

She pointed herself back the way she came and started off.

"Fiona?" called Trev.

She stopped, turned, and raised an eyebrow.

Trev held up the plate, now empty, and shrugged. "Thanks."

"You're quite welcome," said Fiona, whisking the plate away.

Nora, William, and Rebecca sat for their evening meal in The Carrington Grand's main dining hall, a room as splendidly decorated as the lobby and foyer. Gold candlesticks adorned every table, accented by sweet-scented garlands, and tiny glass ornaments. To complete the elaborate centerpieces, hand-woven cornucopias overflowed with exotic fruits and sweets, fresh baked cinnamon cakes and honey bread, none of which, said their mother, were William and Becca allowed to touch.

As dinner neared completion, William eyed the uneaten bread rolls that came with his roast bird and ginger stuffing. When his mother wasn't looking, he stashed one in his pocket, along with a few small pieces of candied fruit from the centerpiece.

"Willy," whispered Becca, "what are you doing?"

"There's no reason all this wonderful food should go to waste as decoration," William whispered back and then turned to his mother. "May I be excused?"

Nora gave him a curious look. "Before dessert?"

"Oh, I . . . uh . . . I'm full," said William, not wanting to lie, but not wanting to tell the truth either.

"Full?" Nora looked at the roll peeking out of her son's pocket. "Ahh. He might appreciate butter to go with that bread."

William bit his bottom lip. "It's not stealing if we own the hotel, right? I just wanted to bring Nicholas something."

Nora grinned, secretly pleased by her son's charitable nature. "You might take a bit of marmalade with you as well," she added, scooting the small bowl of jam over to him. "I believe I heard one of the staff mention it's his favorite."

William smiled.

"All right then," said Nora, "go on. And tell him I'll have the cook put together a plate of whatever is left from the kitchen."

"You're the best mother in the world."

"Well, we can't have him starving in the lobby while we're feasting in the dining room, now can we? It just wouldn't be proper. I'll tell the staff to see that he's fed until we can make other arrangements."

"What do you mean, *other arrangements*?"

"You know he cannot continue to live in the lobby, William."

"But you can't just throw him out in the cold! He'll die!"

"Oh dear, I would never do that," said Nora. "No, no, you misunderstand my intent. I shall make it my personal mission to see him installed some place where he can be warm, safe and happy."

"He's happy here," said Will.

"I'm going to find him a proper home."

"He has a home. He lives at The Grand."

"We shall find him a new home, William," said Nora, resolute. "A better home."

William wanted to talk his mother out of this new plan, but he needed to speak to Nicholas—now more than ever. He retrieved the bowl of marmalade from the table and made his way out of the grand dining room and into the lobby.

Nicholas, as usual, was waiting for him.

"Hello, Will. No dessert tonight?"

William produced the roll, candied fruit, and jam.

"Mmm, marmalade, my favorite," said Nick, taking the food and placing it on the hearth. "It was kind of you to think of me, Will."

"You can tell me your story now."

"Story?"

"Whatever you were going to tell me last night."

"Ahh, but are you willing to listen to my story?"

"That's why I'm here." William worried that the dinner guests would finish eating and interrupt them. He could feel the seconds ticking by.

"I mean, are you ready to *really* listen—to truly hear what I am going to tell you—because this story is very old, much older than most stories will ever be, and it takes time to tell. And my good fellow, you shall be the first soul I've ever told it to . . . that is, if you are willing to listen."

William glanced at the entrance to the dining room. No one emerged. For a brief moment, he wondered what dessert he was missing out on.

"Bread pudding," said Nick, answering his thoughts, "with pumpkin and cinnamon. Very tasty. One of Fiona's specialties. She's a true artist in the kitchen. It will be coming out of the oven in a few minutes, I believe. Served up hot with sweet cream poured over the top. Would you like to join them? We can talk later."

William shook his head and settled into the plush chair next to Nicholas. "I want to hear your story. It's why I came. I'm ready to listen."

"All right then," said Nick, "but before I tell you my story, you must first answer a question."

"What question?"

"You must tell me why you are here."

"I just told you! I'm here to listen to your story."

"No Will, I'm asking why you are in Carrington."

"I'm here because my mother brought me here."

"That is how you got here, not *why* you are here."

"Well, I guess I'm here because my father bought this hotel and purchased passage to Switzerland—because he wanted to show us Carrington, and because he wanted us to spend our Christmas holiday here."

"No William, what I'm asking for is the deeper reason."

Will let out a frustrated breath. "I don't understand."

"What you have offered me are the *outer* reasons you are here. I'm looking for the *inner* reasons. Reasons of the heart."

William grew quiet and still, searching his heart for the answer to Nick's question. Finally he said, "I'm . . . here to solve a mystery—to find out about my Father—the real reason he brought us here. I . . . thought I knew him, but there are secrets here, secrets he was keeping, and I want to know why."

"Better," said Nicholas. "But there's another reason, isn't there? A reason that cuts deeper than all the others."

William nodded, shutting his eyes against unwanted tears. After a long silence, he whispered, "I want to know why God took him. Why he couldn't take somebody else. Somebody nobody likes. Somebody nobody needs. Why take my father. He was a good person. He did good things. He . . . he was my best friend. It's not fair."

Nicholas put an arm around William. "That, my dear boy, is the deeper answer to my question. You have your own questions that need to be answered, questions that need the *deeper* answers. By the time you leave this place, you will know your father in a way that you never could before. A deeper way. And it will heal you a little bit more each day."

Nicholas retrieved the bread roll William had given him, split it in two, and offered half to the boy.

"You and I share a deeper truth now, and because of that bond, I can tell you my story, for *this* is the deeper answer to who *I* am."

CHAPTER TEN
THE TALE OF A THOUSAND YEARS

Nicholas leaned back in his chair. "All right then," he said, "this story begins long, long ago."

"I'm surprised you didn't start with *Once upon a time*," said William, with a little chuckle.

"It's not that kind of story, William. This story holds the truth of a thousand years. I will tell it to you as it was told to me when I was a boy. I was only a year or two younger than you are now, but I memorized every word. Actually, it started out as a song, I'm told, but the tune has been lost to time. I can only offer you the words as I remember them."

Nicholas took in a deep breath, and began:

"It happened, as they say, upon a midnight clear, one starry night so very long ago. Listen carefully, for this is a story you may *think* you know, but there are secrets here, secrets that will tell a different tale . . . that of three brothers traveling afar in Israel, who chose one night to alter their course, and so changed their lives forever.

"Now, as the brothers walked invisible roads, over mountains of sand and desert lands, they met three shepherds who greeted them kindly, who said they followed 'a mystical star that shines in the north.' They journeyed to a place called Bethlehem, with special gifts for a very special child. And these shepherds said unto them, 'Come, walk this path with us, and witness the beginning of which angels have spoken, for an infant king will be born this night, who will lead us from darkness and into the light."

"Wait," said William, paying no mind of the interruption. "I know this story. It's the story of how Jesus was born, right?"

"Young Will, I do believe I heard you say you were ready to *listen*."

"I am. I mean, I will. I just—"

"If you promise not to interrupt again," said Nick, "I shall endeavor to pick up where I left off."

"I'm sorry, Nicholas. I'll be quiet. I promise."

"All right then." Nick cleared his throat before continuing. "So they followed the shepherd's path, and shared their bread, and wrote of all they did and said. The story the shepherds told, though hard to imagine, the brothers' soon believed, for they saw a light in the shepherds' eyes seldom ever seen.

"Now these brothers were expert craftsmen, dedicated artisans all three, and when they glimpsed the holy child, wrapped in a manger asleep, their hearts filled with tenderness and their eyes with grateful tears. So blessed by his light, so moved in his presence, that they too wanted to offer a precious gift to the luminous child. They resolved to create something wholly unique and exceptional just for him.

"The inspired brothers worked on the gift all through the night and into morn . . . and continued on to the next day . . . and the day after that. They each carved one intricate piece of a fine, hand-made toy, hoping it would someday bring the infant king great joy. Each piece fit inside the other, to honor the bond of brother-to-brother. Carved of wood and inlaid with love, 'twas in the shape of the star they'd followed above.

"On the third day, they offered their gift to Mary for her blessed son, knowing that though their journey would be difficult and long, the magic of the star would protect and guide them."

Nicholas stopped.

It took William a second to register the silence. His mind was wandering. "Why did you stop?" asked Will.

"Your mind was wandering," chided Nick.

"I was listening," Will said, in feeble defense.

"Yes, but you were listening only with your ears."

"How else am I to listen?"

"With your heart," said Nicholas.

"How do I do that?"

"Close your eyes." Nick waited for William to close his eyes before continuing. "Now, picture in your mind a vast sand-swept desert at night, brightened by the North Star. Shepherds guide you and your companions to a secret place where a child has been born. A radiant young woman, lit by firelight, cradles her young son in her arms. Can you see her?"

"Yes, I can see her," whispered Will. "She's beautiful."

"Good. Now, by the radiant joy in her eyes, and the palpable reverence in the air, you know you have come to this place to bear witness to a miracle. You feel deep inside that everything is different now. This world, *your* world, has new hope. You find a true sense of belonging that, just yesterday, you couldn't even imagine possible. It's as if you've been lost your entire life and have finally come home." Nick paused. "Can you feel that?"

"Yes," whispered Will, his skin tingling.

"And you know somehow that this new hope will guide your path from this day forward, your life forever changed by what you have witnessed. Can you feel that love, that hope, William?"

Will nodded.

"Now, listen to the rest of my story. Listen with all your heart and soul."

William nodded again, eyes still closed.

Nicholas continued: "When the brothers left that night, they knew they'd never again walk this earth alone, for the child of light was a miracle of God—the greatest gift the world had ever known.

"Seasons passed, and exactly one year later, the brothers gathered to speak of the night that changed all their lives. And it was then they made a sacred vow to one another. The three brothers agreed to honor the birth they had witnessed, by choosing one child each winter upon whom to bestow a gift. And this they did without fail for many years to come.

"But as each year came to pass, they found it harder to choose just one. They felt all children worthy of the honor that they had begun. So they started gifting to all the children in their little village, and then to the surrounding towns. Each winter, they found a way to reach more and more children on the eve of that one special day. And so tradition was made.

"Now, when the time came, they taught their sons the secret, and their sons taught their sons, and eventually, their grandchildrens' grandchildrens' grandchildren, in turn, taught it to me.

"In time, they gave this gift-giving day a name. It came to be known as—

"Christmas!" cheered Will.

"—and today we know it as the same," finished Nick.

William laughed in spite of himself and grinned at the old man. "I like your story, Nicholas. Christmas used to be my favorite time of year. I've read books about it, but I've never heard it told like that. Did you make it up?"

"It's a true story, Will. Every word." Nicholas stood. "Come."

William rose from his chair by the fire. "Where are we going?"

"I would like to show you something."

Nicholas led William to the Christmas tree standing tall in The Grand's front bay window.

"You're looking for clues, William. Clues to what makes Carrington so special. They're all right here. The whole story is hanging on this tree. All our secrets, our entire history, for all to see. But it doesn't matter, because no one believes." He plucked a hand-carved miniature scene from one of the branches. "Each of these Christmas ornaments tell a part of the story, and hold a piece of my family's history."

He offered it to Will.

"The manger scene?" William drew the ornament close and squinted. "How did the artist carve everything in such tiny detail?"

"That is one of the secrets passed down from father to son."

"But how—" Will squinted, attempting to focus in on the extra figures in the background. "Are those the three brothers?"

"Standing behind the three kings, yes."

"It looks like the tallest one is holding—"

"—the wooden star they gave to baby Jesus," Nick finished.

"You wouldn't happen to have a magnifying glass handy, would you?" asked Will.

Nick chuckled, placed the manger scene back on the tree, and retrieved another ornament from a higher branch. This scene depicted a sleigh soaring over rooftops through a moonlit sky.

"My forefathers were the ones who first discovered the Magic of Christmas—magic that allowed them to hear children's wishes and make those wishes come true. Magic that could even make reindeer fly."

"Wish I had been there to see that," said Will.

Nick smiled. "I wished the very same as a lad."

The next scene Nick chose illustrated an old-fashioned craftsman's woodshop in all its minute detail.

"Santa's workshop?" guessed William.

"The very first. Humble in size and means, but created by folk whose fine hearts more than made up for what they lacked in property and goods."

Nick searched the tree for the next ornament and spotted it just out of reach. "It was my Great-Great-Grandfather Zachariah who built The Great Toymakers' Hall, a much larger and more elaborate workshop." He stretched his arm as far as it would go and did a little hop to retrieve it. "And he chose Carrington, out of all the places in the world, to be its secret home."

William studied the petite setting of a lone mountain lodge nestled between two snow-covered peaks. "Is this what it looks like now?" Will asked, placing it back on the tree with the others.

"Not quite, that would be . . . this one," he said, plucking the next ornament and handing it to Will. "My Great-Grandfather Kristoff kept the Toymakers' Hall that his father built, but added more buildings to the surrounding estate, which my father named *Kringle Towne* when he was a boy, after his favorite Santa name, and we've called it that ever since." He pointed to the scene. "That's what Kringle Towne looks like from the top of Christmas Mountain."

"Wait a second. Are you saying Santa's Workshop is here? In the Swiss Alps? Isn't it supposed to be at the North Pole?"

"Oh . . . well, that was a useful myth. We didn't start it, but Grandfather Kristoff knew a good thing when he heard it. That one little misconception insured that our location remained a secret for over three hundred years now."

"So you are saying that your great-great-grandfather was Santa Claus?"

"He was known by many names in many different cultures. But you must understand Will, Santa Claus has never been just one person. It is a family legacy passed down from father to son." Nicholas smiled. "Yes, my great-great-grandfather was Santa Claus, as was my great-grandfather, my grandfather, and even my father, briefly . . . before he died."

"Your father died too?"

"In a winter storm the night I was born."

William felt a tug at his heart. No wonder it seemed like Nicholas understood. He'd lost his father as well. "I'm sorry that happened to you, Nicholas."

"Always be grateful that you had opportunity to know your father, Will. Some of us never get the chance."

William nodded. Only then did the whole of what Nick had been saying begin to sink in.

After a moment, Nicholas pulled another ornament from the tree and continued.

"A clock?" said Will, taking the ornament from Nicholas.

"Not just any clock. It's a metachronome. A magical time device which made it possible for my grandfather Kristoff to deliver toys to children clear 'round the world all on Christmas Eve."

"I always wondered about that." Will had more questions about the metachronome, but something else caught his eye—a wooden carving of an elaborate mechanical key.

One thing was certain, keys were special things, and often led to special places. Will thought of the wonderfully ornate key to the attic back home and how it had led him and his family to Carrington.

"Nicholas?" Will pointed. "What about this one?"

"Ah, the Clockwork Key!"

"Can you tell me about it? What does it open?"

"That, good Will, is a story for another time. But, you might find this one interesting," said Nick, handing William an ornament from the back of the tree. "My grandfather cared for my elder brother and myself after our parents died."

William pointed to two boys standing with a man who resembled Santa, in what looked like a toy factory. "Is that—?"

"Me, yes, and my older brother, Simon. It was up to Simon to take the reins when the time came, but well . . . it didn't work out that way."

69

"What happened?" asked Will, now fully invested in the story.

Nick let out a long, weary breath. "There are no ornaments for what came next. I'm afraid the last chapter of my story is not as glorious as the rest." The old man began to shuffle back to his place by the fire. "But you need to hear it, Will. This story belongs to you as much as to me. And it will aid you in your search for answers."

William didn't understand. He had a thousand questions crowding his thoughts, but he didn't want to interrupt again.

"After my Grandfather died," continued Nicholas, "the responsibility of becoming the next Santa Claus fell to my brother, being the firstborn son of my father, but Simon wanted nothing to do with Christmas. In fact, he hated it."

"How could anyone hate Christmas?"

"I don't know, but he did. And he had no intention of following in our father's footsteps."

"What did he do?"

Nicholas sank into his well-worn, familiar-as-home leather chair and stared at the dwindling fire for a moment. As he spoke, his gaze remained fixed on the dying flames.

"When Simon came of age, he just . . . left. It was up to me then, to fill his shoes—to become the next Santa Claus. And I wanted it. I wanted it more than I've ever wanted anything. But I was a young boy at the time, too young. I hadn't found my footing yet. And Simon leaving hurt me more than I was willing to admit."

"I can't believe he would just abandon you like that," said William, "abandon everything your family had built."

Nick straightened in his chair to fortify his courage. "He did. But not before crushing my hopes of ever taking his place. He said I wasn't strong enough, brave enough to do what had to be done. He said that I would never amount to anything."

Nick stopped, glanced down at his tattered leather shoes, and mumbled, "I suppose he was right."

Shifting his gaze to the Christmas tree all aglow in the dimly lit lobby, he continued his tale. "Even though Grandfather said he suspected all along I might be the one, even though he believed in me, I never mustered the courage or the faith in myself to make it happen. Oh, I tried. God knows I tried, but I never found the magic, so I couldn't deliver the gifts on Christmas Eve."

Nicholas made a fist involuntarily. "I let everyone down; my father, my grandfather and all those who carried the family legacy before them, all the way back to the first toy made for the first child."

"By the three brothers?"

"Yes."

"They were your ancestors—the ones that made the four-pointed star for the baby Jesus!" said Will, connecting the dots. "So you really could have been Santa Claus!"

"Yes," repeated Nick, but this *yes* was different from the last—a deep and private sorrow had crept into his voice.

"A very significant individual," mumbled William.

"What's that?"

"Something Father said in his letter—the letter that brought us here. He said he planned to introduce us to *a very significant individual.* I've been trying to figure out who that might be, but it's you, isn't it?"

"Yes," said Nick, and this *yes* he barely spoke.

"He knew," said Will. "Father knew who you were!"

Nick gave a single nod.

Will peered at Nicholas for a long moment, trying to fathom the idea. "Santa Claus."

Nick gave a sad smile. "Is it so hard to imagine?"

The boy scrutinized the man before him—bushy black and white speckled beard, rose-red cheeks, a twinkle in his eye that had dimmed a little in the last minute or so, but it was all there. Will finally shook his head. "No. It's not hard to believe. Not at all."

"I did my best," added Nicholas, "but it wasn't good enough."

"You said you never found the Christmas magic. Didn't your grandfather tell you how? You said he believed in you."

Nicholas nodded. "The day Grandfather died, he called me to his bedside. He told me of his concerns about Simon, and showed me The Book of Christmas."

Will's eyes widened. "The Book of Christmas?"

CHAPTER ELEVEN
SEVEN LETTERS

Nicholas leaned forward, a look of earnest intensity in his eyes as he spoke: "The Book of Christmas is a sacred family tome passed down from one generation to the next. It holds all the family secrets and wisdom gleaned through the years," said Nicholas. "Grandfather showed me this book and entrusted me with the secret of his magic."

As he reached for the iron poker to stir the fire, Will thought he saw Nicholas' hands shaking, but he quickly steadied them.

"If Simon refused to take the reins," Nick continued, "I was to journey into the mountains above Carrington, find the marker stone that designated the entrance to the hidden cave as he had shown me, and bring back the magic. But . . . I failed. So for thousands of children, Christmas never came that year, nor the year after that, nor any year since. The letters continued to pour in from children all over the world, but none were ever answered."

"Didn't you try again the year after?"

"I didn't get the chance. When Simon received word of Grandfather's death, he returned just long enough to close down Kringle Towne, putting half of Carrington out of work in the process. Many of us were left to survive on the streets that winter."

"Is that how you ended up here at the hotel?"

"The owners of The Carrington Grand, Gertrude and Harold Mills, were old friends of the family. They offered me a room, but I couldn't pay, and I was too proud to take charity. I was young and foolish. I didn't understand that a gift benefits the giver as much as it does the receiver, and in receiving graciously, you offer a gift of equal value in return."

Nicholas stopped just then, his expression stern. "I want you to promise me something, Will," he said, his tone suddenly grave.

"What," said William, not at all sure he wanted to hear what Nicholas was about to say.

"As you grow to be a man, don't ever let pride stand in the way of asking for help, or receiving it when it is offered. It does a disservice to those who love you and dishonors the spirit of giving." Nicholas took in a deep breath, fighting back a wave of cresting emotion, and then looked directly into Will's eyes with a fierce resolve. "Promise."

"All right," said William, not really understanding why it was so important. "I promise."

"Because, my boy, the consequences of such an act are often indefinable in the moment," said Nick. "You could change the course of your entire life without realizing it. That is how I ended up in the lobby. I refused to take a room I couldn't pay for, and they refused to let me live on the streets. They even asked the post office to send my mail here, and that's a lot of letters and postcards to handle, even for a hotel of this size, especially around the holidays."

Nicholas glanced over at the front desk, smiling at the memory before continuing. "Every single piece of mail addressed to St. Nick, Father Christmas, or any form of Santa Claus, in any language started pouring into The Carrington Grand. Sometimes hundreds a week."

"Does the mail still come here?" William remembered writing a letter to Santa a few years back. He'd wondered if it ever reached its destination.

"No, the letters dwindled as each subsequent Christmas passed without Santa Claus . . . as mothers and fathers started filling in for him, buying gifts, wrapping them in the wee hours of the night, and secretly placing them under the tree before their children woke on Christmas morning."

"So it's all true," Will mumbled to himself.

Nicholas cleared his throat, battling the grief constricting his voice. "I believe the post office began writing 'return to sender' on them, but a few got through—seven altogether—the ones addressed to *Mr. Claus, Care of The Carrington Grand Hotel*. I don't know how these seven children knew I was here, it's a bit of a mystery to me, but our Postmaster in town, Mr. Brinkley, considered them personal mail and sent them on through. I actually saved them. Got 'em all right here." He patted his breast pocket. "Keep 'em with me wherever I go."

"Those letters must be pretty old by now," said William. "The kids must all be grown."

"Yes, but I still dream of answering them someday . . . to apologize for never sending a reply, and to tell them how much their kind thoughts meant to me."

"Weren't they just like all the rest? I want a dolly with yellow hair, I want a rocking horse with a red saddle?"

"No, these last seven letters were special. Their requests were not like other boys and girls. They weren't asking for toys or gifts. They were not concerned for themselves."

William stared at the place where Nick said he kept the letters—the breast pocket of his old weathered coat. If the letters were really there, that would be proof enough that his story was true.

"Would you like to see one of them?" Nick whispered.

Will hesitated, not knowing if he wanted proof. He was starting to believe, and he decided he liked believing in Nicholas. He didn't want to ruin that. But his curiosity got the better of him, as it always did. "Can I?"

Nicholas thought for a moment and then said slowly, "It would be an honor to share them with you." He took out all seven letters and carefully selected one for William to read. "Here. This one's written in English. It is from a young girl named Anne. She lived in Boston."

William read aloud:

> *Dear Santa,*
>
> *May I please have a moment of your time? I hope this letter finds you safe and well. I know that you are busy and you've many things to do, but if you could please hear my request,*

I would be so grateful. You haven't been to our house in a year, maybe even two, and I was wondering if you might have overlooked us. Please know it is not for me that I ask. My little sister is very ill, and it would mean the world to her, and to me, if you could bring her something special. I'd really like to see her smile again.

Affectionately yours,

Anne Marie Harris

"You see?" said Nick, "Why I couldn't throw them away?"

It might have been a trick of the firelight, but Will thought he saw the glint of tears in Nick's eyes. His heart heavy, he began to comprehend the entirety of Nick's sad tale.

Until that moment, he wasn't sure what part of Nick's story was real, and what part was just an old man's wild imagination. But he had to admit, from the very start he felt there was something wholly genuine and sincere about Nicholas. Now he understood. It was because his story was all true.

"William!" Nora called. "Come now. We're retiring for the evening."

"Yes ma'am," called William. He looked at Nick, peering into eyes soft with memory and regret. "Thank you for trusting me with your secrets," whispered William.

"You are worthy of them," said Nicholas. "Thank you for listening with your heart. It is good to have a new friend."

"Nicholas? I need to tell you something. It's about Mother. She's planning to—"

"William!" Nora called again, this time from the stairs.

"Coming," William called back.

"Go," said Nick. "You mustn't keep your mother waiting."

"But I have to tell you—"

"Run along now. We'll talk tomorrow."

Will rose from his chair. "Goodnight, Nicholas."

Nick waved a quick goodnight as he turned toward the fire, retrieved an old leather-bound novel from the mantle, and settled in for his favorite evening pastime.

CHAPTER TWELVE
AN ANGEL'S LULLABY

Nora and Becca waited for William to catch up. As they began to climb the stairs, Becca rubbed a few sticky crumbs from her chin and licked her fingers.

"You missed the best bread pudding," said Becca. "And the creamiest vanilla cream too! I told them to save some for you. Maybe you can have it for breakfast in the morning."

William smiled. "Thanks, Bec."

"Out of the question," Nora interceded, "dessert is not for breakfast."

"That's okay," said Will. "I don't really want it anyway."

"I thought it was your favorite," said Becca.

"Are you feeling all right, darling?" Nora put a hand to William's forehead as if to check for a fever.

"I just have a lot to think about."

"You were with that old man in the lobby for a while," said Becca. "What did he say?"

"His name is Nicholas, and he was just telling me a story."

"A story?" said Nora. "About what, may I ask?"

"About Christmas."

"Oh, well I suppose that's acceptable. But you shouldn't be pestering the poor man. He hasn't had a moment's peace since we arrived. I'm sure he is rapidly growing weary of your questions."

"How do you know I'm asking questions?" said Will.

"When are you not asking questions? Both of you." Nora laughed, putting one arm around her son and the other around her daughter. "I declare, you have got to be the most curious children on either side of the Atlantic Ocean." She squeezed them tight as they arrived at their suite. "But I wouldn't have it any other way."

Nora turned the key and opened the door. "Now off to bed, you two! I've planned a full day in town tomorrow, so I want you both rested and ready to rise for an early breakfast. No staying up to whisper through the door after the lamps are doused."

William grinned. "Us?"

"Yes," Nora tapped Will on the nose, "you. Now run and get ready for bed, both of you, and I will come tuck you in."

A few minutes later Nora glided into their rooms to kiss them each goodnight.

She found William already snug in his bed, but she could tell in a single glance that he was wrestling with something. A new thought or idea had taken hold and wouldn't let go, making sleep all but impossible—a trait he'd inherited from his father.

Nora narrowed her gaze on her son. She'd kept close watch on her children's grief since their father died, but she could tell this was something else.

"Would you like to share whatever it is that has you so preoccupied?" Nora asked, tucking William's covers in at the sides.

"Not yet," said William. "It's still baking."

"All right then," said Nora. "You will let me know when it comes out of the oven?"

William nodded.

Nora doused the bedside lamp. "Try to get some sleep." She kissed his forehead. "Sweet dreams, my boy."

In her daughter's room, she found Becca dressed for bed, standing at the window, gazing up at the stars.

Turning down the covers, Nora said softly, "Becca, love, come. Time for sleep."

"What do you remember about Papa?" asked Becca, her eyes still fixed on the sky.

"What sweetheart?"

"Willy says if we don't talk about Papa, he'll disappear and we'll lose him forever. I don't want to forget him."

"Oh my sweet girl, we'll never forget him." Nora crossed the room to her daughter. "But your brother is right. It is good for us to share our memories with each other. Our hearts heal a little more with each sweet remembrance." Nora smiled at the twinkling heavens framed by the window like a sparkling portrait. "Did you know you get your love of the stars from your father? He used to stand out in the grass field across from our first home and stargaze for hours."

"He did?"

Nora nodded. "Even in the dead of winter. I remember browsing a bookshop one afternoon just before you were born. I showed him a book of constellations I thought I might get him for his birthday, but I was surprised to learn he wasn't the slightest bit interested."

Becca brushed a stray strand of hair from her eyes, "Why not?"

"He told me he didn't want to know about the stars, he wanted to dream about them. He said 'I don't want a book to tell me their names. I want the stars to tell me themselves'."

"He must know all their names now," said Becca, pointing at a constellation.

"And has no doubt made friends with each and every one of them," added Nora with a tiny half-suppressed giggle. "Heaven must be very pleased to have him there."

"So . . . Papa's in Heaven?" Becca asked, her gaze unwavering.

"Of course he is, honey."

"Maybe he's not."

"Oh dear, what ever would make you say such a thing?"

"Maybe he's here . . . in Carrington, looking after us."

"I see." Nora touched her daughter's cheek. "I believe he can be in Heaven, *and* also be here with us."

"At the same time?"

Nora wrapped her youngest in a warm embrace from behind and joined in her stargazing. "That's what's so special about Heaven. You can be everywhere at once. There's no time or space to keep us apart. You can still love and be loved, but you don't feel any loss, or lack, or pain."

"So there are no broken hearts in Heaven?"

"Not a single one."

"I like that." Becca yawned.

Nora glided over to the bed and patted the covers. "Hop in."

Becca did as she was told. After snuggling down into the fluffy warmth, she said with a soft sadness, "Heaven sounds like a nice place to live."

"I believe it is. And I believe your papa is happy there."

"Mama," said Becca, her eyes suddenly filling with tears, "are you going to go live with Papa in heaven?"

"Not for a very long time, my love."

"When you do, can I go with you?"

"We will all be together again someday, sweetheart. But for now, we must hold him in our hearts and know he is here with us."

"I miss him so much my heart hurts."

"Mine too." Nora's eyes closed for a moment to steel herself. "It will get better, darling. I promise."

Nora reached over and opened a silver music box sitting on Becca's bedside table, where it had always sat at home. It tinkled and plucked out a pleasing little melody that had been in their family for so many generations Nora no longer remembered where it came from. She began to sing the words that accompanied the lullaby, remembering all the times in her youth, when she was upset or afraid, and her mother sang it to her:

Close your eyes and think of a place,
So peaceful, soft and safe.
And I'll be there by your side,
To say love will abide,
To help you to find your faith.

Where the world you've known,
Is not so frightening and cold,
Because all that you love surrounds you.
Where no harm will come,
No wrong will be done,
Where your dreams have finally found you.

And here, you'll be free,
To live, to love, to be . . .
Where all that's good can be known.
And those you have lost,
Gone at such a cost,
Will be there to guide you home.

Close your eyes and sleep dear one.
Dream until the night is done.

Nora continued to hum the melody until Becca fell asleep. She pressed her lips together to quell a sudden quiver and kissed her daughter's forehead.

"I love you, Mama," whispered Becca, sleepily.

"I love you too. More than you will ever know. Goodnight. Sleep tight. See you with the morning light."

Nora retreated to her bedchamber, crossed to the window and once again gazed up at the star-lit sky.

"Garrett, my love," she whispered. "Help me through this. Guide my soul so that I may know what is right for our children. Please help our hearts to heal. In a few days it will be Christmas, but I . . . don't know what Christmas means without you."

Nora placed a hand on the cold glass, trembling with all she had not allowed herself to feel. "Everyone expects me to be strong. And I know you'd want me to be brave."

She looked up, eyes gleaming with unshed tears. "But the truth is . . . I'm afraid. Afraid I won't be able to find my way without you." Her voice wavered. "You were my strength, my heart, my home. How can I . . ." Her voice failed her.

Squeezing her eyes shut, breath quick and shallow, she let her forehead rest against the cool glass.

Hand to heart, she took one deep breath, then another, struggling to calm her threadbare emotions.

When she opened her eyes again, her gaze fell upon the midnight blue satin drawstring pouch she'd placed on the desk next to the window when they first arrived—the pouch that protected the urn containing her beloved's ashes. Reaching out, she clutched it to her breast and finally . . . let go.

Out poured all the love and pain that she'd kept locked inside for far too long, shattering the protective walls she'd carefully constructed around her heart.

As sobs and gasps finally slowed to long deep breaths, Nora began to hear the haunting music box melody again, this time so faint and far away that she thought at first she'd imagined it.

An instant passed. Time slowed.

Breath held. Thoughts stilled.

Somehow, impossibly, she began to hear her husband's voice, echoing from somewhere far away, answering her prayer in the same tender melody and words that had just coaxed their daughter to sleep . . .

Close your eyes, my love, and think of a place, so peaceful, soft and safe. And I'll be there by your side, to remind you love will abide, to help you find your faith . . .

The light in the room wavered, pulling her gaze back to the desk. Next to the blue satin pouch, the flame of a porcelain oil lamp quivered for a moment as if struggling against some unseen force.

Nora gasped. "Garrett?"

An inexplicable movement of air caught a stray strand of her hair. She whirled around. The swish of her dress filled the silence as the music box melody ended. "Garrett?"

Her skin tingled with a luminous warmth as an effervescent calm washed over her, and she *knew*.

A moment.

Just a moment.

Then gone.

But for that single moment . . . he was here.

Garrett was here in this very room, reaching out to her, across the gossamer divide that separates Heaven and Earth.

She didn't know how. She only knew that it was so.

The lamp-flame grew brighter and steadied itself, drawing her attention to the faded brown file folder on the desk, holding the two-dozen or so letters Garrett had penned to Mr. Staub.

Nora gathered her strength, and, releasing her breath through pursed lips, sank into the velvet-cushioned desk chair.

Hands shaking, eyes stinging, she opened the file and began to read.

CHAPTER THIRTEEN
A CLANDESTINE MEETING

By first light, Mr. Staub was already of an unpleasant disposition. In the last fifteen minutes, he had: found a crack in one of the casement windows in the main dining room that wasn't there yesterday; learned that the list of tasks he'd given the night staff had been utterly ignored; and, just this instant, received an urgent request for his presence at a meeting in town, carried by an incompetent courier who delivered the message at the very moment the meeting was set to begin.

Mr. Staub read the note again to verify its contents, then tipped the courier begrudgingly, and hurried to retrieve his coat from the cloakroom. He called Ben and André over with a few quick snaps.

"André, prepare the horse and carriage at once."

"Already done, sir. Mrs. Eda Lowenstein requested a conveyance at daybreak, but had a last minute change of schedule and canceled moments ago. We can leave whenever you are ready, sir."

"Good. We are going into town. I've just received word that I am to meet Mr. Worthington posthaste."

"The bank manager?"

"Yes, quickly now, bring the carriage around."

"Yes, sir." André dashed off.

"Ben, you and Fiona are to look after the hotel in my absence. I shan't be long."

"But the bank is not open at this hour, sir."

"I am well aware. It would seem Mr. Worthington wishes to keep this meeting off the books. Why, I do not know."

"Might this summons have something to do with our new owners?" asked Ben.

"We shall see." Mr. Staub spun on his heels to head out.

"Sir, wait!"

Staub huffed in aggravation. "What is it, Ben?

"Your hat, sir!" Ben sprinted to the cloakroom to retrieve his supervisor's bowler hat and cane.

"Ah yes," mumbled Staub as he accepted his essential accoutrements. "Much obliged."

When they arrived at Carrington's only bank, a small stonemasonry building that stood on the corner at the far end of Main Street, André helped Mr. Staub out of the carriage.

"Sir, may I pick up a few spices for Fiona at the general store while I wait for you to conclude your business?"

"If you must," said Mr. Staub.

"She provided me a list," said André, with an apologetic grin. He pulled a small piece of paper from his pocket. "I dare say if I return empty-handed, she will have words for me, and none too pleasant."

"Very well, but make certain to return before the end of my meeting. I have no wish to wait in the cold."

"Yes, sir."

As André crossed the street, Mr. Staub turned toward the bank's prodigious double doors and took in a quick breath to steel himself. He hadn't been summoned since the sale of The Grand, and wasn't at all sure this summons was a good portent.

As he entered, a middle-aged man in a black suit held out his hand. "Mr. Staub, good of you to come. May I take your coat and hat?"

"A summons at such an hour raises suspicions in the more discerning mind," said Staub, shaking the man's hand and offering only his hat. "And your unceremonious note was decidedly vague. What's this all about, Worthington? Why am I here at this ungodly hour?"

"It is at the bequest of another that I have called you here."

"Whom, may I ask?"

"Please, follow me to my office and I shall explain."

Mr. Staub trailed the bank manager into a dimly lit, windowless office at the back of the building.

"This gentleman," Worthington said, gesturing to a tall man stepping out of the shadows, "is here to purchase The Carrington Grand Hotel. He has made a generous offer."

Staub peered at the man, scrutinizing his harsh features and dead expression. "The Grand is no longer for sale," said Staub. "You have been misinformed. Mr. Garrett Hillerman bought the hotel last year."

"Yes, but Hillerman is deceased now, is he not? And his death presents an opportunity that did not previously exist."

"Opportunity?" asked Staub.

"I am informed that his widow is now in possession of the hotel. Her loss will no doubt render her susceptible to external influences, making this an opportune time to acquire the property."

Staub took an instant disliking to this man. "I'm sorry. I didn't catch your name."

"I did not offer it. You may refer to me as Klaus."

"Mr. Friedrich Aschwin Staub," offered Staub in return, extending a hand, but the man did not shake it.

Mr. Worthington pulled a document from his desk and presented it to Staub. "Klaus is willing to purchase The Grand for nearly twice what the Hillermans paid for it. A very generous offer."

"As I have said, the hotel is not for sale."

The black-cloaked man took the document, rolled it into a tight scroll, tied it with a tiny piece of black ribbon, and offered it to Staub. "I am certain that Mr. Hillerman's widow would be pleased to be relieved of her husband's burden, especially at such a profit. If you would kindly deliver my offer—"

"I'm afraid," interrupted Staub, "that you are wasting your time . . . and mine."

Mr. Staub did not know why, but at that very moment, he had the unprecedented, and quite ungentlemanlike inclination to knock this man to the floor. Of course, he considered himself much too refined to do anything so crass. Instead, he looked the man squarely in the eye and said, "Mrs. Hillerman has given no indication that she has any intention of selling The Carrington Grand, and I have no intention of delivering your message."

It wasn't that he was averse to the idea of carrying a message for Mrs. Hillerman, it was more that he felt suddenly and unexpectedly protective over her. Something about this encounter just didn't sit right with him. Staub's well-honed intuitive sense about people had put him on the defensive with this man, and although that came as a bit of a surprise, he knew he didn't want this stranger to have anything to do with Mrs. Hillerman or The Grand.

The man leaned in and lowered his tone. "If you support this acquisition, I can offer you a substantial monetary reward for your cooperation."

"A bribe, sir? If you think me of so low a caliber as to be persuaded by such an inducement, you are sadly mistaken. And your presumptions regarding Mrs. Hillerman are—"

The man snarled. "You know as well as I that a woman cannot manage an establishment as substantial as The Grand. The weaker sex is born lacking the business sense required to make such critical calculations and decisions."

"I assure you," said Staub with equal intensity, "Mrs. Garrett Hillerman is a very intelligent and capable woman."

"In the home, perhaps, but she and her like should not be permitted to meddle in the affairs of enterprise and industry. How would this world fare if we allowed feminine histrionics to enter the professional arena?"

"I dare say, quite a bit better than if the likes of you ran it."

"Now, gentlemen," said Mr. Worthington, intervening to avoid an incident, "I'm sure we can come to an equitable arrangement if we simply agree to—"

"I believe, Mr. Worthington," interrupted Staub, "that our business is concluded. Now, if you will excuse me, I must return to my staff. It is, after all, the holiday season."

As Mr. Staub turned to go, the dead-eyed gentleman caught his arm, his skeletal fingers digging into Staub's flesh.

"Mark my words, Mr. Staub. I *will* own The Carrington Grand, and when I do, I will see it reduced to rubble as it should have been years ago."

"If Mrs. Hillerman should ever choose to sell The Grand, I shall certainly be advising her *not* to do business with you, *or* your representatives," said Staub, unrattled.

"By the time I am through with this town, she won't have a choice and neither will you. You would both do well to consider my offer."

"This conversation is done," said Staub, breaking free from the man's grasp. "Do not contact me on this matter again." He headed for the exit, hoping André would be waiting just outside so he could make a hasty departure.

The bank manager stopped him at the front doors, holding Staub's bowler. "I'd advise caution, Mr. Staub," he said with hushed urgency. "Klaus has just purchased this bank!"

"That is no concern of mine."

"He plans to collect on all debts. Immediately."

"The Carrington Grand is not indebted to this bank, Mr. Worthington."

The bank manager returned his hat. "No, but *you* are."

"Good day, sir," said Staub, placing his hat atop his head.

Mr. Staub stepped out of the bank and into the brisk air. Relieved to find his coachman standing by with the carriage, he took in a deep breath to shake the tension of the unpleasant encounter and slipped on his white gloves.

"André, let us be off!"

"Are you all right, sir?" asked the coachman.

"I will be as soon as you get these horses to a gallop!"

Trev, who waited behind the bakery each morning before it opened to receive the day-old goods the baker's wife handed out, spotted Mr. Staub leaving the bank in a huff and then recognized the tall man who exited through the same doors only moments later. As the man turned the corner on foot, Trev thanked Mrs. Brimby for the bread and took off to follow the cloaked stranger.

CHAPTER FOURTEEN
A FINE SPRING DAY

Three days remained before Christmas, and all of Carrington had an air of excited anticipation. Nora and the children headed in to town, with André at the reins, intent on spending the day Christmas shopping, as long as weather permitted.

Every delightfully ornamented storefront displayed the best handmade crafts, delicacies, wares, and gifts the hamlet had to offer. As they wove their way down Main Street, snow, crunchy and crisp underfoot, blanketed the town with glistening white accents. Everyone who passed by smiled and greeted the Hillermans with holiday cheer.

One couple stopped and tipped their hats. "Top of the morning to you, Mrs. Hillerman," said the polite gentleman.

"And to you," said Nora, "Mr.—?"

"Drescher," finished the gentleman. "I am Hanz and this is my wife, Hilda. We're guests at The Carrington Grand."

"Oh, yes, of course. Pleased to meet you both," returned Nora. "These are my two children, Rebecca Rose and William Thomas."

"How do you do, Master William? Miss Rebecca?"

"Fine, thank you," the children said together.

"Are you enjoying your stay at The Grand?" asked Nora.

"Oh, yes, very much. We have decided to spend our winter holidays here from this day forward."

"What a splendid idea. I do hope we will be seeing you at The Carrington Grand Christmas party tomorrow night."

"Of course! We wouldn't dream of missing it," said Hanz, putting his arm around his wife. "It is why we came to Carrington, after all."

"The party?"

"Yes," said Hilda. "The formal announcement arrived by courier at our home months ago requesting our presence in Carrington for the holiday, and, of course, our attendance at the hotel for the Christmas ball. The letter also affirmed that all arrangements had been taken care of, including the cost of our entire week's stay at The Grand."

Nora stared at them in surprise. "Truly?"

"In fact," said Hanz chiming in, "other guests have said as much and are equally confounded. Whomever our host is, he is exceptionally generous."

"It would seem so," said Nora.

"It's all so mysterious, and I do love a mystery!" Hilda added in a conspiratorial tone. "Do you know, Mrs. Hillerman, who he might be?"

"I haven't a clue, I'm afraid. I suppose we shall all discover our benefactor's identity tomorrow night at the celebration."

"We look forward to seeing you there," said Hanz, tipping his hat. "Good day to you, Mrs. Hillerman. We're off to do more Christmas shopping!"

"Tomorrow then," called Nora as they walked on. Nora glanced around. "Rebecca, where is your brother?"

"Over there," Becca pointed, "talking to the man at the flower cart. Shall I fetch him?"

"I think not. He seems quite engaged. As long as he hasn't wandered off."

"Look, Mama," said Becca, drawing her attention to a beautiful window display in a nearby hat shop. "You would look so pretty in that."

Nora turned to see what her daughter had found.

"I like it here," said Becca, as Nora gazed through the shop window. "The people seem nice."

"They do," said Nora, her thoughts far away. "I like it here too, sweetheart." The hat that caught her interest—not the one her daughter had pointed out, but the one just behind it—was made of cream liberty satin, plaited and edged with Chantilly lace and loops of rose-colored ribbon sweeping the left side of the brim. A white velvet rose encircled by a wreath of tiny silk buds garnished the back as a finishing touch. It wasn't precisely the hat that enchanted her, but the memory it brought . . .

Miss Nora Lynne Becker and Mr. Garrett William Hillerman had recently become betrothed. Arm in arm, they walked proudly down the avenue, in the city where they first met and eventually made their home, Charleston, South Carolina. It was on this bright afternoon that Garrett pointed to a particularly fine hat in a handsome storefront window, and said . . .

"Oh my sweet, you would look so lovely in that hat! But truth be told, you would look lovely in any hat or no hat at all. You are the most beautiful woman in the world, Miss Becker."

"The whole world?" said Nora, with a good-natured grin, ever playing practical and pragmatic to Garrett's lofty goals and dreams, though she believed in him unwaveringly.

"Yes! The whole world!" he said, grinning like a man in love.

"I dare say, Mr. Hillerman, you are inclined to no small amount of exaggeration."

"That may be true," said Garrett, "but I embellish none where you are concerned, my dear. And I want to buy you this fine hat because I want you to have beautiful things! You deserve to be surrounded by things as beautiful as you."

"I'm sure this lovely hat is far too expensive."

"Perhaps, but I won't always be a man of such modest means. Someday I will own a chain of fine hotels. I've already decided on a name.

"Oh? And what might that name be?" teased Nora.

"I'm going to call it Hilltop Hotels."

"Clever, Mr. Hillerman."

"I promise you this, my sweet. We will be the richest couple in town, and when we are, I shall buy you a thousand stunning hats."

"And if I don't want a thousand stunning hats?"

"Then I shall get you whatever your heart desires!"

89

"May I tell you, Mr. Hillerman, what my heart truly desires?" she whispered, drawing close.

Garrett nodded almost imperceptibly, gazing into her eyes for the answer. "Just remember," he said, playing along, "you've already said yes to my marriage proposal."

"I want this." She put her hand in his. "For the rest of our days. It is all I want, my love. I don't need a new hat or a fancy dress or a big fancy house. Just you, and the children we will make together."

Garrett's smile beamed. "Don't you see, my darling girl, that only makes me love you all the more, which makes me want to buy you not only this beautiful hat, and a beautiful dress to match, but the big fancy house as well!"

Nora laughed. "Perhaps another time, my dear. For now, let's just enjoy our walk on this fine spring day."

Garrett took her hand into his and kissed it. "Agreed."

"Mama?" said Becca, pulling Nora out of her reverie. "Are you okay?"

"Oh yes, darling. I'm quite well," she uttered with a private smile.

They continued on their way, joined by William, who presented his mother a cluster of tiny flowers tied together with a thin yellow ribbon. "For you!"

"Why, thank you, William."

"The man said they're called Sweet Alyssum. He said it means 'worth beyond beauty.' But I just thought they were pretty . . . like you."

"Oh William, they're lovely." She poked a few of the delicate white blossoms into the arrangement on her hat. "How does it look?"

"Perfect!" said William.

Nora eyed a store across the street called The Lemon Drop Shoppe, brimming with holiday candies and toys, thinking it might just be the perfect place will need to fill her children's stockings on Christmas morning.

Glancing at the ornate clock tower at the end of Main Street, she turned to her children and said, "Your mother needs to take care of a few things in town. Do you think the two of you could manage to keep yourselves out of trouble if I let you run and play in the park for an hour?" She pointed to a snow-covered park across the way where children were busy making a snowman.

William and Becca nodded eagerly.

Nora knelt to tie Becca's knit scarf under her chin and button up her coat. "All right then. Stay warm. And have fun you two, but do not leave the park until I come for you."

"We won't," said Rebecca.

"William," Nora called after them, "look after your little sister!"

"I will!"

Just then André appeared by Nora's side.

"Thank you for keeping an eye on them for me, André," said Nora, in a hushed voice. "I wasn't quite sure how I would manage all that needs to be done today."

"It's no trouble, Mrs. Hillerman. Pleased to be of service."

"Well, I certainly appreciate your assistance. Between the town meeting and Christmas shopping after, I should think I'll be at least an hour or so."

"Take as long as you need, Mrs. Hillerman. Word has spread. Many of the applicants are already waiting for you down at the Town Hall. The Grand hasn't hired new staff in a very long time. There is plenty of interest. You should have no problem finding what you're looking for."

"Wonderful," said Nora. "And where might this Town Hall be located?"

"At the end of Main Street there, across from the bank." He pointed. "It's the tall building. The one with an unnecessary number of steps leading up to its entrance."

"Of course. Yes, I see it."

André sat on an ornate wood and ironwork bench facing the park in view of the children as Nora headed in the direction of the Town Hall.

CHAPTER FIFTEEN
THE ENCHANTED KINGDOM

As William and Becca crossed the street, Bec smiled and said, "That was nice what you did, getting Mama those flowers for her hat."

"I needed an excuse to talk to the man at the flower cart," Will confessed. "I thought he might know something about the stranger since he's out on the boardwalk all day."

"The stranger who watched us through the café window?"

"Exactly."

"Did the flower cart man know anything?"

"Not much. He said he has seen the man around, just in the last few days, but only from afar, so he couldn't tell me anything more. He did say that the man is not from around here, and that he knows everyone in Carrington. But he also said it's Christmas so he might be visiting family in town. I also asked the sign painter on the ladder in front of the barbershop. He said the same thing, so I have no more information than when I started."

"Well, I still think it was nice that you gave Mama the flower. It made her happy."

"I'd do anything if it meant she could be happy again," said Will.

"I know it won't fix anything," said Becca, "but I think I know what we should get Mama for Christmas."

"Really?" Will's eyebrows shot up. "What?"

"The prettiest hat you'll ever see. She stared at it in a shop window for the longest time. And she had that faraway look in her eyes . . . like she was picturing herself wearing it."

"How are we supposed to buy an expensive hat, Bec?"

"Well, I've been thinking," said Becca. "Maybe Mr. Staub can help us."

"Mr. Staub doesn't like children."

"No, but he likes Mama."

When Becca and William reached the park, they picked out the perfect spot to build their snowman and began construction. William snatched a tiny pinecone from the base of a tree.

"Hey, we can use this for his nose!"

"How do you know it's a *he*?" said Becca with hands on hips. "Maybe it's a *she*."

"It's called a snow*man,* not a snow*woman,*" sassed Will.

Becca scooped up two heaping handfuls of freshly fallen snow and covered Will in white fluff. "Hey, you can be our snow*boy,* Will!" she said, giggling.

William countered the gesture, dusting his sister's hair and eyelashes with tiny crystalline flakes.

Becca squealed as Will chased her around in circles until they both ended up tumbling and laughing in the snow.

As they got to their feet, a barrage of snow cannonballs came straight at them.

"Duck!" yelled William.

Too late. The snowballs pelted them, one after another, landing both William and Becca flat on their backs. Dazed, and a bit confused, they brushed themselves off and got to their feet.

Distant laughter reverberated through the park.

"You okay, Bec?"

"I think so," she said, holding her arm.

William turned and yelled, "Come out and play fair!"

Several of the town kids stepped out from behind a marble statue of a reindeer with a wreath around its neck. Several more emerged from behind adjacent trees.

"We're surrounded," whispered Becca.

Will did a quick count of heads. "Nine against two? How is that fair?"

"Such a bore," sassed Trev, stepping out from behind the others. "Playing fair? Not my style."

"You're the kids Mr. Staub kicked out of the hotel lobby the other day, right?" asked William.

"Could be," said Trev. "Depends on why you're askin'."

Becca pumped herself up. "Because it's *our* hotel."

Trev threw a nod to the gang. "See? Not a clue."

"What does that mean?" snapped Will.

"It means you don't get it," said Trev. "You're not from here. You don't belong here. And you don't know what's really going on here, so don't come into our town acting like you own the world."

"What are you talking about?" Will demanded. "What's really going on here?"

"Ask Nick," said Finn, the boy Will and Bec saw talking to Trev in the stables.

"You mean the old man living in the lobby?" William wondered how much the kids actually knew about Nick. "I know him. He's my friend."

"Everybody knows Nicholas," said a petite girl with a shock of bright red hair poking out from under a green woolen cap.

"He's a friend to *all* children," said a younger boy that must have been the red-haired girl's brother, for his hair was precisely the same color, and so was his cap.

"He's not like other grown-ups," said Finn.

They all began to chime in now.

"He talks to us."

"Plays games with us."

"He understands us."

"He tells us stories!"

"Lots of stories!"

William's eyebrows shot up. "Stories about Christmas?"

"No, about magic places," said a taller boy.

"Kings and dragons!"

"About hopes and dreams and stars that shine bright."

"And children the world over who see the same stars at night."

"Nick says dreams are real things," added Trev, getting caught up in the moment. "And that when you dream, you bring a story into being."

"And the same thing happens when a child makes a wish," said Finn. "It sets in motion what Nick calls 'a unique chain of events that makes it possible for that wish to someday come true'."

"Nick says wishes are just stories that haven't been told yet," said the taller boy.

"But what are his stories about?" asked Will. "Can you tell me one of them?"

"Trev can," said Finn. "She knows all Nick's stories."

"She?" asked a stunned Will, turning to Trev. Until that moment Will had assumed Trev was a boy. "I thought—"

"Well, you thought wrong," said Trev, tucking a wayward strand of honey-colored hair back into her cap.

"I know one of Nick's stories," said Red. "My favorite."

William peered down at the girl, for she was rather small compared to all the others. "What's it about?"

"It's about a magical city in an enchanted kingdom with a powerful king who's kind and good and sees things."

"Things that are to happen," added her brother. "Dreams that will come true."

Finn nodded. "And he knows all the thoughts and wishes of all the kids that live there."

"And the children of this magic city are never cold or hurt or hungry," said Trev.

"But there's a dark-hearted dragon named Simon, that tries to destroy the good king and his magic city," continued Red, her voice full of doom.

Will stiffened. "Did you say he called the dragon Simon?"

"Uh huh. And the dragon has no heart, no thought, no feeling. It cares only for its hordes of diamonds and jewels."

"But this dragon, the king cannot kill," said Finn, "for he carries the secret of the king's magic. And if the dragon dies, the magic dies with him."

"So Simon has the key to bring the magic back," Will muttered to himself.

"You're interrupting," said Red. "We're trying to tell you Nick's story."

"Enough!" bellowed Trev. "I'm bored. We're done."

"But the story isn't finished!" cried Red.

"And they all lived happily ever after," said Trev, "The end."

William glared at Trev.

"Come on, Willy." Becca tugged on William's coat. "We need to get back. Mama will be coming for us soon."

"Oooh," mocked Trev. "The babies need their mummy to find their way home."

Finn frowned at Trev, then looked at Will, who made no reply. Risking Trev's wrath, the boy said "I'm Finn, and you've probably figured out that's Trev. This is Colin," he said, pointing out the tall boy. "Luca. Roger. And over there are the twins Aldo and Ghita. Oh, and there's also little Jonah who's home sick, and Diona who's visiting her grandmother in Greece, but she'll be back next week, and you really should keep an eye out for her because she's the best of us when it comes to throwing snowballs. That's the whole gang."

Red crossed her arms and stomped down on Finn's foot.

"Ow! And the short ones here are Pawny and Mitsy, my little brother and sister."

Mitsy smiled and waved.

"I'm William Thomas, and this is Rebecca Rose." Finn extended his hand and William shook it in friendship.

"Hey," said Will, "next time you start a snowball fight, could you warn us first?"

"Consider yourself warned," said Trev as she hurled a snowball at William's head with the full force of her anger behind it. "Come on, rich boy. What'cha waitin' for? Let's go. Right here. We'll see who's king of Carrington!"

"Trev, I'm not going to fight you."

"Why? Afraid you'll lose?"

"We're going back to the hotel now," said Will.

"Chicken!" she said, making clucking sounds.

"Willy," said Becca, looking back at Trev.

"Just keep walking, Becca."

"Yeah chicken, go back to your room where Mummy can protect you, or better yet, why don't you go back to your own country! We don't want you here, rich boy!"

The children's jeering stung as William and Becca followed the slushy path out of the park.

"Why is that girl so mean to us?" said Becca. "We didn't do anything to her."

"Some people are just mad at things," said Will, "and if you get in the way, they're mad at you."

"Maybe they're right. Maybe we should go back to America."

"No Becca. There's something special about Carrington. It's not like any other place."

"How do *you* know, Willy? We've never been any other place."

"It's not easy to explain, but it's something I feel down deep. And because of it, I'm starting to look at Carrington differently."

"What do you mean?"

Will stopped and turned to his sister. "Just give it a chance, Bec. You'll see what I see—what Father saw—why he wanted us to come here. Carrington was important to him. Don't you think we owe it to him to find out why?"

Becca nodded reluctantly.

"And don't let those kids get to you. They're just trying to protect their territory."

"From us? Why?"

"They don't want the new owners of The Grand to come in and start changing things. They like their town the way it is."

"So do I," said Becca, feebly.

"Me too," Will agreed. "Hey, let's not tell Mother about today, okay?"

"Why not? It's not your fault those kids are so mean."

"I just don't want her to worry about us, that's all. She has enough on her mind."

Trev, who had been following them, ducked behind a tree to listen in on their conversation.

"Well, all right, but I'd rather tell her," said Becca. "She always finds out anyway."

William brushed snow off a park bench and they sat side by side to wait for their mother to return. Will looked down, fidgeting with his wet mittens.

"Go on, say it," said Becca.

"Say what?"

"You always do that thing with your hands when you have a secret you are dying to tell."

"I do?" The corners of Will's mouth turned down.

"So? Are you going to tell me what it is?"

William hesitated.

"Come on, Willy. You know you want to."

"Okay, but you can't tell a soul."

"I promise." Becca placed her hand over her heart.

"All right, what would you say if I told you I've met Santa Claus and he lives here in Carrington?"

"Oh, Willy, you're always making up stories."

"No really. I mean I met a man who says he was meant to be Santa Claus and I think he's telling the truth."

"How can you tell?"

"I don't know," said Will, "but I believe him."

"Who are you talking about?"

"Nicholas."

"That crazy old man in the lobby? Sure, Willy."

"He's not crazy."

"He lives in the lobby of our hotel. He makes up stories all the time. You heard the kids. They're just trying to trick you."

"They don't know! That story about a magic city, and the king who knows all the kids' wishes, and the dragon who threatens the kingdom, they think it's just a story, but it's not. It's real."

Becca laughed. "Dragons are real?"

"The dragon isn't really a dragon. It's Nick's brother, Simon. He's the one who threatened the enchanted kingdom, which is actually Carrington, and the magic city is really Kringle Towne."

"Willy, this is your silliest story yet!"

"I'm not making it up, Bec. When we get back to The Grand, Nicholas can tell you himself! Come on. Let's go."

"But Mama told us to stay in the park."

William felt a chill as the sun drifted behind a dark cloud. Wind stirred the treetops above his head. He squinted, peering down Main Street. Women suddenly clutched at their skirts. Hats toppled from heads and raced down the avenue. Street sellers closed up their stands.

"There's a storm coming," said Will. "We should find Mother and return to the hotel."

Becca pointed to a man in a heavy box coat, shoulder capes billowing in the wind as he made his way toward them.

"André!" called William.

The coachman waved a gloved hand in the air.

As William and Becca crossed the street to meet the coachman, Finn caught up to Trev.

"Find out anything good?"

"Enough to know we have to get rid of 'em and fast."

"What have you got against them, Trev? They're just kids like us."

"They're not like us. They have a rich father who gives them whatever they want. Everything comes easy for them. They think money can buy them anything. And their mum protects them from all the evils of the world."

"You can't blame them for having a wealthy father or a mother who cares, Trev. Just because you don't have—"

"Shut up, Finn."

"Trev, I know you've had it tough but—"

"I said shut up."

In the silence, Finn whispered, "I didn't mean to—"

"—You know," rasped Trev, her voice giving way, "you should mind your own business."

"It's starting to rain," said Finn. "I need to go home now."

"So go."

Finn didn't move. "Trev. Come home with me. Just until the storm passes. It looks like it might be a bad one."

Trev's jaw tightened as she watched the scene unfolding across the street. William and Rebecca ran to their mother, her arms full of string-wrapped packages. The family piled into the waiting sleigh.

"It's easy for them," said Trev with disdain. "They have *her*. I don't have anyone. Just Nick. He's my only family. And you have to protect your family, right?"

"Sure but—"

"Well, I have to do whatever it takes to protect Nick."

"From what?" asked Finn.

Trev nodded toward the sleigh. "From *them*."

CHAPTER SIXTEEN
THE DREAM YOU DARE TO LIVE

By the time the sleigh pulled up to the front entrance of The Carrington Grand, it had already begun to pour. André's grip on the reins tightened, but the horses, agitated by the violent winds, refused to settle.

"Hop out!" called the coachman, "Quickly!"

Nora and the children clambered free of the sleigh just in time.

Lightning flashed. A tree branch whipped through the air and sliced the space between the horses.

The team reared. The sleigh lurched.

Becca screamed as the whole rig nearly toppled.

With a fierce grip, André fought to keep the horses under control. "William," he called out. "Bring Nicholas! Hurry!"

Will dashed into the lobby. "Nicholas!" he cried. "Nick, André needs you! The horses—"

"I know!" Nick had already grabbed his coat and was on his way out. When they reached the court, they found the horses in a state of panic.

"Stand clear!" Nick yelled.

William pulled his mother and sister to a safe distance and they took shelter under The Grand's covered front steps.

Drenched, Nick stood in the stinging rain, his arms in the air as the horses reared. "Hey, hey! Greta! Gerda! It's me!"

"Nicholas!" cried William. "Be careful!"

Nick turned to the mare on the right. "Whoa, girl. You're all right. Whoa. Just a little mischievous wind."

The horses' manes whipped about in the savage gusts.

Sticks and stones, leaves, dirt, and snow all whirled into a violent twister underfoot. Greta whinnied and jerked away, but Nicholas had a fierce grip on her bridle. "Come here, girl." He reached up to stroke her nose. "Hey, hey, hey. There you are. Nothing to fear. Nothing to fear."

After more than a few reluctant snorts and foot stomps, Greta began to calm.

Using his thumb, Nick rubbed the space between her eyes, tracing the same little circle over and over. "There, there. You're safe now. That's it, Greta. Good girl."

Still agitated, Gerda jerked and pulled, trying to break from the harness and escape the storm.

"Greta, can you do something for me, girl? Can you tell your partner here to quiet down so we can get you both someplace safe and warm?"

With a few jerks of Greta's head, the other mare began to settle. And within the space of a minute, Nick had both them unhitched and preceded to walk them to their stalls.

André climbed out of the sleigh and joined the Hillermans under the shelter of the hotel's entryway.

Hand to his chest, heart still pounding, William turned to his mother and sister. "Did you see that?" Like watching pure magic, it was, seeing Nick work with the horses the way he did.

Nora nodded in slow motion. "Truth be told, I've never seen its like in all my years."

"Nick has a gift with all animals, ma'am," said André. "I'm just glad he's here to help with Greta and Gerda. They are, at times, temperamental old mares. Now, if you'll pardon me, I need to make sure they are fed and groomed."

"Oh, certainly," said Nora. "And thank you, André, for keeping us safe in the storm. You are a superb driver."

He bent at the waist in acknowledgement. "And may I recommend you spend a few moments warming by the hearth in the lobby before retiring to your rooms? It is extremely efficient at coaxing the chill from one's bones." And with that, the coachman turned toward the stables.

After warming by the fire, drying off in their hotel rooms, and changing for dinner, Will and Becca descended the stairs early to talk to Nicholas before meeting their mother in the dining hall.

"That was something," said William, "what you did with the horses out in the court."

"They were just frightened by the storm. All I did was let them know they were safe."

"Mother said she's never seen anything like it and she grew up around horses."

"I suppose I just know how to talk to them," said Nick. "But it's up to them to listen or not. They're good mares."

"I was scared they were going to hurt you," said Becca.

"Oh, Greta and Gerda would never hurt me. We're friends, you see. Like you and I will soon be. That is, if we can persuade Will here to give us a proper introduction."

"Nicholas," said Will, "this is Bec, my little sister."

Nick flashed William a disapproving look. "Oh dear, you can do better than that, good Will."

"Nicholas," said William, "this is Miss Rebecca Rose of Charleston, South Carolina." He turned to his sister. "Becca, this is Nicholas of The Carrington Grand Hotel lobby."

"Hello, Miss Rebecca Rose. I'm pleased to finally make your acquaintance."

"How do you do," said Becca, with a little curtsy. "Are you really Santa Claus?"

"Well now, that's a big question for a first hello."

Will piped up. "Tell her, Nicholas. She doesn't believe me."

"I see," said Nick, scratching his tangled beard. Then in a low voice he said, "Miss Rebecca, can you keep a secret?"

Becca nodded, wide-eyed.

"The truth is, I'm not really Santa Claus."

"Told you." Becca stuck her tongue out at Will.

"Oh, but I might have been," continued Nicholas, "had things been different. It was meant to be my destiny, I think, although I didn't know it at the time." Nick looked down at his ragged coat. "But, well, sometimes things have a way of not working out how you want them to."

"I know about that," Becca said in a soft voice, and William knew she was thinking about Father.

Nicholas took in a slow deep breath. "Sometimes at night I can still hear the children of the world call to me. And sometimes, in the silence, I know, like my grandfather knew, all of their best wishes and dreams. For a moment, I can even believe I have the magic to make those dreams come true. I even heard your wish last night, Miss Rebecca."

"My . . . wish?"

"Yes," said Nicholas. "About wanting the town's children to like you, and a quiet little prayer about going home for Christmas, and wishing your father could be there."

"You heard all that?" Becca flinched.

"I did."

"Only Santa could hear all our wishes and dreams," said William. "Now do you believe me?"

She gazed at Nicholas in awe. "So it's true then. You really *are* Santa Claus!"

"It doesn't matter now," said Nicholas with a sigh. "I had my chance and I lost it. I may still hear children's wishes and dreams at times, but the toys are not made, reindeer don't fly, and Christmas goes on without me."

"Oh Santa, there is no Christmas without you!" cried Becca. "Not the real Christmas!" She threw her arms around his neck.

He patted her back and then withdrew. "Thank you, Miss Rebecca. You're very sweet. But it's all gone now. There's no way to get it back."

It grew quiet around the crackling fire, and the three of them felt as if they were the only people in the world.

"But what if there is a way?" said Becca with a sparkle of excitement in her eyes. "What if it's possible to get the magic back?"

"The truth is, I don't know how," admitted Nicholas. "And even if I did, it may already be too late."

"Too late?" asked Will. "What do you mean?"

"Grandfather said the magic can only lay dormant for so long before it is lost forever."

"Then we had better get started!"

"No, William. It's just an old man's foolish fantasy. Better to let it go and accept my fate." He gave a little half-smile. "I don't have a bad life here. There are people who care about me, children who love my stories. I stay warm by the fire, and I even have the opportunity to fix a broken toy now and again. And making new friends, like the two of you, brightens my day immeasurably. All in all, I am quite content. Santa Claus exists only in our imaginations and that is where he will have to stay."

"You want kids to believe in you when you don't even believe in yourself!" said Will. "That's the trouble right there. What about dreams, Nicholas? You hear other people's dreams but you don't listen to your own!"

Nicholas sighed. "You don't understand."

"Your life is only as big as the dream you dare to live. That's what Father always said, right Bec?"

Becca nodded enthusiastically.

Nicholas sighed again and leaned back in his chair. "No more dreams for me, good Will. I'm just an old man. Nothing more."

William's face reddened as it often did when he was on a mission. "But you *are* more! Much more! You're Santa Claus!"

A few guests walking by looked at the trio by the fire.

"No one believes anymore," Nick said in a quiet voice. "Even you didn't believe in Santa Claus just a few days ago."

"Well, I'd never met him face to face before! And besides, it's never too late to change."

"Another something your father is fond of saying."

"Yes," said Will.

"Your father is a wise man."

"Was," corrected William.

"Our papa," said Becca, "he's gone."

"No," Nicholas said softly, "not gone. You might not be able to see him, but he *is* here. He's with you always. And if you look with your heart, you will know what I say is true."

"How could he be here and not here at the same time?" asked Becca, confused.

"Love transcends space and time. These aren't just words, Becca, they are Truth. If you could see what I see, you'd never again doubt the presence and power of love to reach beyond earthly boundaries."

Rounding his shoulders, Will crossed his arms. "Even if you're right," he said to Nick, "it doesn't make it any easier to be without him."

"That is also true. I know what it's like to lose someone you love," said Nicholas. "It's like there's a big hole—" he put his hand over his heart, "—right here."

"And it won't go away no matter what," said Becca.

"And it will be there forever and ever," added Will.

"Ho now, that's where you're wrong." Nicholas smiled inside at the presence he still felt in the room. "You have to keep remembering, keep your love for him safe, keep it in a special place, there inside your heart. And after a while, that empty hole will fill up with such fond memories—one right after another—that it will be overflowing with love. And then you'll find it won't hurt so much anymore."

William's brow creased in thought. "How do you know? Maybe it never stops hurting."

"I promise you, William Thomas, that is how it works. You just have to start remembering the love. And don't ever give up hope. The emptiness won't be there forever."

Becca's countenance brightened. "You just got to fill it up!"

"That's right!" said Nick. "There's nothing we can't do, as long as there is hope in our hearts!"

"If that's true, then you can be Santa Claus again!" said William with renewed enthusiasm.

Nicholas shook his head. "Except that."

"You said the children don't believe anymore. Well that's because they need someone to believe in. They need you!"

"Slow down there, good Will. It's not as easy as that. Being eager and willing helps, but it also takes time, energy, supplies, magic!"

"Magic is possible if you have the key," Will recited with dogged determination. "Seeing is not believing—"

"One must believe to see," finished Nicholas.

"I believe!" shouted Becca, a little louder than intended.

It stopped Fiona and Ben in their tracks as they hurried by, busy with their preparations for The Grand's Christmas party.

"My goodness!" said Fiona. "Aren't we full of life tonight? And what might we be believin' at this fine hour?"

"Magic!" whispered Becca, with only slightly squelched enthusiasm.

"Och aye," whispered Fiona. "I believe in magic too."

"As do I," Ben chimed in.

"'Twas Nicholas here who convinced me of it," said Fiona, "back when I first arrived in this fair town all heartbroken n'poor as a church mouse. Ye remember it, don't ye, Nick?"

"I do indeed. We were both a bit younger then."

"Aye, and ye spoke somethin' to me I'll nae forget. Ye said, *'Trust your heart, and you'll soon see, that all is not quite as it seems.'* Do ye recall?"

Nicholas nodded, and the three of them—Fiona, Ben and Nick—chorused the last line of the rhyme together . . .

" . . . *Life will be all it can be, if only we'd trust in the power of our dreams.*"

"I remember it well," said Nicholas, feeling something stir deep inside his soul. "I remember," he repeated, more to himself than to the others. "Perhaps you're right, William. Maybe all I truly need is to believe again."

Trev, who had come to tell Nick not to worry—that everything would be all right now—heard these last few words uttered by Nicholas, Ben, and Fiona, with William and Becca sharing their delight.

And seeing the joy in their eyes, the smiles on their faces, she felt her whole world starting to crumble.

"No," she whispered, taking a step back. "No!" She turned and ran out of the hotel, down the snow-covered hill, through the storm to the cobblestone streets of Carrington, and didn't stop running until she came to a wood and wrought iron door at 38 Mistletoe Lane.

She made a fist, hesitated, and then knocked.

"You best not be here to waste my time," came a thick gruff voice.

Trev whirled around to find the cloaked stranger trudging up the path behind her, his collar turned against the storm. "I have the information you requested," she said, shaking not from the cold, but because of what she was about to do.

CHAPTER SEVENTEEN
A CLOAK OF BLACK

Klaus snarled as he placed his top hat on a coat rack in the entry hall. "You are sure about this?"

Trev nodded. "I'm sure."

"You heard them say it?"

"I heard 'em. They're going to restore Christmas back to the way it was." Trev shifted from one foot to the other in the doorway, looking over her shoulder at the dimly lit street.

"Not possible. Not without my help," said Klaus. "They won't be able to retrieve the magic."

The man pulled off his cloak, hung it on the coat rack and then motioned for Trev to enter.

Trev didn't move. "They're going to try. Nicholas knows how. Your grandfather gave him the secret before he died."

"My little brother's not strong enough to brave the journey on his own," said Simon. "He never has been."

"He's not little anymore. He's stronger than you think. And the new kids have got Nick believing he can do it."

"Makes no difference," said Klaus. "They're just children. An inconsequential annoyance at best."

Trev shook her head. "You wouldn't be here if you believed that. And these aren't just any children. Their parents own The Carrington Grand."

The man's black eyes shifted side to side as he considered this new information.

"Listen," said Trev, "I've lived in this town my whole life. Something changed when they came. I don't know how, but it seems like there's hope again, hope that Carrington can be what it once was—"

"That will never happen."

"—hope that there's still magic here," Trev continued, "and there is. I can feel it."

"This ridiculous notion—that the world needs the magic of Christmas—has poisoned people for centuries. It does children no good to let them believe in magic. It breeds weak, undisciplined minds. Nothing is more dangerous than faith in what cannot be seen with one's own eyes."

"Maybe so," said Trev, "but if people start believing again, none of that will matter."

Klaus began to pace. "There is some truth in what you say. Belief is a powerful delusion that can have disastrous repercussions. And I know Nick. He would bring it all back if he could."

Hate flared in the man's eyes as if Trev had thrown fuel on a fire. He huffed and dropped a small wooden object into a leather satchel.

Trev couldn't see what it was he had been hiding, but he'd been clutching it so tightly it left an imprint on his palm.

Distracted for a moment, the man peered at his hand, stretched out his fingers, and then made a fist.

Expression hardening, he grabbed his hat and cloak from the hook. "I can ensure Nick will never be able to activate the magic." Klaus threw his cloak over his shoulders and bent the brim of his hat down to shadow his face.

"I don't care how you do it," said Trev. "Just stop them."

"Oh, I will." The man towered over her, his massive form made even more ominous by the thick dark cloak and tall black hat. He reached into his money pouch and pulled out a silver coin. "Here."

Trev took a step back.

The man stepped forward. "A job done well requires compensation. I am a businessman above all else. Take it."

It wasn't a request.

She took the coin and tucked it in her pocket. "I didn't do it for the money."

"Oh? Why then?"

"I got my reasons," said Trev, arms crossing her chest in a defensive posture.

"Let me guess. If Nick manages to resurrect the family business, he'll have better things to do than to mill about all day at The Carrington Grand with the likes of you, hmm?"

Trev's mouth tightened.

The man patted Trev on the head like a dog.

She recoiled. "Just stop it from happening and we'll both get what we want."

"If I didn't hate children so much," said the man, looking like the thought left a bad taste in his mouth, "I might consider you almost . . . tolerable."

"I assure you the feeling is *not* mutual."

Klaus gave a sinister laugh.

"Why do you hate children so much anyway?" asked Trev.

"I have my reasons," he echoed.

"Let me guess," mimicked Trev. "You got picked on by all the other kids when you were a little boy because you didn't want to take part in their childish games?"

"Go!" the man barked. "Keep your eyes and ears open and report back to me the instant they set out for the mountain."

"The mountain?"

"To retrieve the magic."

"I thought you didn't believe in magic," Trev said with a devious grin.

"I didn't say that. I said it was dangerous." He pushed her out the door and onto the icy streets. "Go!"

Trev took off running.

Klaus stepped out, closed the door, secured the bolt, and turned to head in the opposite direction—a black sweep of cape against a bank of white snow.

CHAPTER EIGHTEEN
THE ROSE BOX

It was truly, finally, wonderfully here . . . the night of The Carrington Grand Holiday Celebration Ball, just two days before Christmas. Inside the residential suite, Nora, William, and Rebecca dressed for the occasion.

Excited to be invited to her first Christmas ball, Becca twirled in her red velvet dress, trimmed with a white ruffled hem and tiny pink silk flowers accenting her waist.

William fidgeted in his finely pressed holiday suit and red bowtie.

Nora, still in her dressing robe, deliberated over which gown to wear to the ball, feeling awkward about shedding her mourning shades of black and navy blue at the urging of her children. "William," she said as she tried on another gown, "you'll be pleased to know I have some excellent news about your friend Mr. Nicholas."

"So do I," said Will. "I know who he is now."

William continued to explain, but in her nervousness about the coming festivities, Nora barely heard what her son had been going on about.

"Mama, it's true," said Becca, practicing her curtsey in the mirror. "Willy's telling the truth."

"The truth about what, darling?"

"About Nicholas, Mama. He really is Santa Claus."

"Santa Claus?" She held up a dress of aqua blue tulle over royal blue satin, then shook her head and threw it on the bed. "William really, you shouldn't bring your sister into your—"

"Mother, we believe him," said Will. "You would too if you heard his story."

Nora stopped and looked at her children with a sad smile. "William, Becca darling, Santa Claus is just an idea, a feeling. He represents the spirit of Christmas and the love that is in us all at this time of year." She pulled another dress from the wardrobe, held it up to herself in the mirror and then discarded it on the bed with the others.

"He's real and he needs our help!" said Will. There had to be a way to convince her.

"Yes William, Santa *is* real . . . in our hearts."

"No, he's actually real . . . in the lobby!"

"William, I know you've made a new friend and I'm proud of you for extending a charitable hand, but sweetheart, even Mr. Staub said Nicholas makes up stories to entertain the children. This is just another one of his stories. "

Becca moped. "Papa said Santa was real."

Nora sighed and reached for Becca's hand. Together they sat on the edge of the bed. "Becca honey, Papa just wanted you to enjoy the magic of Christmas while you were young. Santa Claus—the idea of Santa Claus—fills our hearts with wonder and hope. And what would Christmas be without wonder and hope?"

"Mother, don't you see? You're right. He *is* just an idea now. But it wasn't always like that. He was real once and he can be real again, but he needs us to believe in him!"

"Pleeease, Mama?" Becca pleaded. "Listen to Willy."

"What on earth has that man been saying that would have the two of you convinced so?"

"It's not just what he says, it's what he knows."

"He's magic," added Becca. "He can hear our dreams and wishes."

"And," said Will, "he understands things that no one else understands."

"He's not like anybody else, Mama. You have to believe us!"

"Just talk to him," said Will. "Decide for yourself."

"Well, I suppose I should have a talk with him," she said in a cautious, motherly way.

Will perked up. "After the party tonight?"

"Oh Will, I'm certain that would be far too late for the poor man. He will surely be sleeping."

"No he won't. Nicholas sleeps in the day so he can listen for the children's wishes and dreams at night. He'll be up. I know he will."

"William—"

"Please, Mama," Becca pleaded again.

Nora looked upon her children's earnest faces. "All right, my darlings, I'll endeavor to speak with Mr. Nicholas tonight, provided he is awake after the party."

"Then you'll believe too!" cheered Becca.

"We shall see. But nothing will happen if I don't first find something to wear tonight."

"What about this one?" asked Becca, her nose poked inside the wardrobe.

Nora's expression melted into a slight pout. "There are no more dresses, my sweet girl. Everything I brought on the journey is piled on the bed."

"No, there's one more, and it's beautiful!"

Nora reached in and gasped as she pulled out a stunning ball gown of cream and gold, as beautiful as any she'd ever seen. With a broché silk bodice, and golden crepe de chine ruffles cascading down the back, it was every bit the dress she dreamed of wearing to such a grand occasion.

Nora held it up, gazed at herself in the mirror, and recognized it at once. The memory rushed in to push all other thoughts aside. Nora had worn this dress once before—to the very first ball she and Garrett had attended as husband and wife.

He'd bought the dress especially for the occasion and presented it to her that night along with a silver brooch in the shape of a stylized rose, embellished with a single ruby at its center, which she still wore over her heart. In fact, that cherished rose was how Rebecca acquired her middle name.

For Nora, that night would always be one of the most romantic of her life, for it was not only their first ball as husband

and wife, it was also the anniversary of Garrett's breathtaking marriage proposal.

She smiled at the memory as she recalled Garrett's shining eyes when he presented his gifts to her that night, saying she had made him the happiest man in the world.

It had been the same for her. Their first year of marriage had been as near to heaven as ever she had come.

"I haven't seen this dress in over a decade," said Nora, her heart aflutter. She slipped it off the hanger, imagining herself young again, newly wed, and in love with the most wonderful man. She had considered herself the luckiest girl in all of Charleston.

"Wear it, Mama. It's perfect!"

Nora pressed it to her body. "It might still fit," she uttered. "But . . . how did it get here? Rebecca?"

"I just peeked in the wardrobe and there it was."

"William?"

"I never saw it before just now."

"Curious." She eyed the dress with wonder. "How ever could it have gotten here?"

"It's beautiful, Mama. Put it on! I want to see how you look!"

"I believe I will," said Nora on her way to the dressing area.

"Mother, what was the news you spoke of?" asked Will.

"Hmmm?"

"You said you had news concerning Nicholas?"

"Oh, I nearly forgot," she said through the dressing screen, "you'll be pleased to know I've found him a good home."

"What? Mother, no!"

"A boarding house at the end of town with a kind-hearted elderly landlady who prefers boarders of a similar age to her own. Of course, I had to promise a year's room and board in advance before she'd accept, but she finally agreed to take him in. I think he will be happy there. He'll have people his age to talk to and no little boys and girls bothering him at all hours of the night."

"But Nicholas doesn't need people his age. He needs to tell his stories. He needs to fix toys. He needs children around him, not a bunch of old people who don't care who he is!"

"What he needs, William, is a place to call home."

"He has that," said Will. "The Grand is his home."

"He needs a proper home."

"You just don't want him here because he makes your pretty hotel look bad! But if you put him in that boarding house, he might as well be dead!"

"William Thomas!" Nora popped her head out from behind the screen. "What a horrid thing to say!"

Will's voice cracked. "But it's true. I know it is. He'll die if you take The Grand away from him! And the magic of Christmas will die with him!"

"I understand you don't want to lose your new pal, but—"

"You *don't* understand!"

"Come now, William. Be happy for your friend. It's a nice place to live. He will have a room of his own and I'm told the landlady, Mrs. Muri, makes the best shepherd's pie in town."

Nora disappeared behind the dressing screen again, and William retreated into the adjoining room to set his mind to the task of finding a solution to this most recent development. He had to stop Mother from trying to move Nicholas out of the lobby.

"Mama," called Becca, from across the room, "there's a pretty matching handbag attached to the dress hanger." She untangled the cording from the curves of the hanger to examine the cream-colored velvet drawstring purse.

"Oh, wonderful," called Nora. "Can you lay it next to my wrap on the bed, sweetheart? Oh, and put my cream gloves inside?"

Becca stroked the soft velvet for a moment, then put her mother's gloves inside the purse and placed it with care on the bed.

"Would you like to pick out a necklace for me?"

Becca nodded and skipped over to the bureau. "This is a pretty box," Becca said, forgetting all about her search for the perfect necklace to go with her mother's dress. She ran a finger over the design on top. "It has a rose on it, just like my name!" She opened the box and read the words etched inside the lid:

Listen and the Past will Speak
of the Riches Love has Created

"It's another clue!" cheered Becca. She reached in and pulled out a palm-sized four-pointed star. "Where did this come from, Mama?"

"What, sweetheart?" asked Nora, emerging from behind the dressing screen, holding the back of her dress to keep it from falling open.

"The wooden star. It was in the rose box on your bureau." Becca squinted. "It looks like something made to hang on a Christmas tree. It's very pretty."

Nora held out her free hand to receive the ornament from her daughter and then sat on a short padded stool before a gas-lit vanity. "Oh, this is from your father's box," she said with a catch in her throat.

"The rose box was Papa's?"

As Becca finished fastening the buttons down the back of her mother's ball gown, Nora held the wooden star up to the light and studied its intricacies.

A superbly delicate little thing it was, evidently handcrafted with much love and care—so elaborately carved, it seemed the woodcarver meant it to resemble lace.

"What a beautiful little ornament," said Nora. She peered through the star. Its center was hollow, notched like a puzzle piece at the four points. "It would seem a part of it is missing."

Nora offered the star back to Becca and then turned her daughter around to tie the soft satin ribbon into a bow at the small of her back. When done, she stood and turned Becca to face the oval mirror on the vanity. "Well, aren't you pretty as a picture?"

"Mama!" said Becca, shifting her focus in the mirror to her mother. "You look beautiful!"

Nora smiled and did a little twirl. The dress's delicate gold beadwork sparkled with light.

"It's perfect!" Becca said, clapping.

"It is, isn't it?"

"All it needs now are the pearls Papa gave you for your birthday."

"You are right, my darling. They are in the top drawer."

"I'll find them!" said Becca, scurrying back to the bureau.

Crossing to the full-length mirror, Nora stopped and gazed at herself, seeing the girl she used to be—happy, full of hope, love, and wonder. Her world had changed so much in the last year that she no longer recognized it, or herself.

Running her fingers over the delicate glass beadwork hand-stitched into the bodice, she whispered, "Thank you, my love."

Mr. Hillerman appeared beside his wife and reached out to caress her cheek.

"I don't know how you managed it," she whispered, "but I know it was you." She smiled in a bittersweet realization. "You wanted to surprise me. Oh Garrett, I just wish you were here, looking at me with that silly grin of yours, unable to keep it in any longer. You'd burst out and say—"

"Are you surprised, darling?" Garrett spoke the words along with Nora, though she did not hear him.

Nora smiled to herself again. "Yes," she whispered, "it is a wonderful surprise."

"Mama? Are you all right?" asked Becca, holding out the pearls.

Nora snapped back to attention and accepted the necklace from her daughter. "Thank you, sweetheart. What would I do without you?" she said, clasping the ornate, triple string of pearls at the nape of her neck. She bowed to her daughter with exaggerated extravagance. "Come along, Miss Rebecca. Let us see if we can put a smile back on your brother's face."

"Can we give him this?" Becca held up the carved wooden star. "It might cheer him up."

"We certainly can. That is very thoughtful of you, Rebecca."

They strolled into the adjoining chambers and found Will brooding on a chaise in the sitting room.

Nora touched her lapel where her rose brooch usually rested. "Oh dear. I'll be right back."

"Willy, I found another clue!" said Becca in an excited whisper. "There are words on the lid inside Papa's rose box!"

"Words? I don't remember any words."

She ran to fetch the box. "It says, 'Listen and the past will speak of the riches love has created.' See?" She opened the box to show her brother the inscription.

"I didn't notice that when I found it in the attic. Good discovery, Bec! Maybe these words were put here as a hint for

Father . . . to encourage him to someday search out where he came from."

"And I have an early Christmas present for you, to cheer you up. Hold out your hand!" said Becca, hiding the ornament behind her back.

"What is it?"

"A Christmas tree ornament." She pulled the star out from behind her back.

Will's eyes rounded. "Bec, this was Father's. You shouldn't take things that don't belong to you."

"Now it belongs to *you*," said Becca, plopping the star into his palm.

The second it touched William's hand, it brightened for an instant.

"Did you see that?" said Becca, staring agape.

Will peered at the star, turning it over in his hands to see if it would catch the lamp-glow again. "Just a trick of the light."

"Maybe it's magic!"

"Or maybe it's just our imaginations," said Will, but as he gazed at the ornament, a tingle of familiarity quivered on his skin. He'd seen this star only once before, yet it felt familiar to him in a way nothing else ever had, as if it somehow always belonged to him and he'd just forgotten. It almost reminded him of—

He caught his breath. "Becca, what if this is—?" He stopped himself. "No. It can't be."

"Can't be what?"

"Nothing. Just a silly notion."

"Well?" asked Nora, entering and turning for her son in one continuous, graceful move. "Do I look presentable?"

William pocketed the ornament and shifted his attention to his mother. "You're going to be the prettiest of all the ladies at the ball," he said, and meant it.

"Why, thank you, William Thomas." Nora bent to straighten his bowtie. "Now come, you two! Let us attend this marvelous Christmas party that everyone has been chattering about."

She reached for their hands and they paraded out the door, the three of them, in their evening finest.

CHAPTER NINETEEN
THE LAST DANCE

In The Carrington Grand's sunken ballroom, decorated with silver candelabra emerging from lavish centerpieces and luminous gilded globes suspended above, a chamber orchestra played a Baroque Gavotte, adding to the magic in the room.

Couples swelled across the dance floor like a colorful tide. Nora stood with her children, taking in the sight from the top of the wide marble steps. She smiled a sad smile full of memory. The last time she'd danced was a year ago this very day with her husband at The Elldiwin's Annual Charleston Christmas Ball.

"Mama, may we play with the other children?" Becca asked, spotting a group of kids snacking on red and green speckled cookies next to a punch fountain bubbling over with the same colors.

Nora's gaze followed her daughter's to a group of children in their Sunday best and nodded. "Yes, yes, have fun you two," she said, and the children ran off to join the others.

"Good evening, Mrs. Hillerman!" Mr. Staub exclaimed, approaching from the lobby. "I am pleased you and the children have decided to attend our little soirée."

"Soirée, Mr. Staub? Come now. I would hardly call this *little*. There must be nearly a hundred people here tonight."

"Yes, well, given that we only have six families staying with us at the moment, in addition to yours, I thought it prudent to extend an invitation to the entire town. I do hope I haven't overstepped my authority in doing so."

Not at all, Mr. Staub. It's perfect. And you've done a marvelous job with the decorations," she said, surveying the spacious hall from their current vantage point. "The room is as grand as grand can be!"

"Thank you Mrs. Hillerman, but I'm afraid I can't take the credit. Ben and Fiona spearheaded the decorating, with, of course, the assistance of the new employees you hired from town. I did next to nothing. Didn't even have to manage the purchasing details or any of the arrangements!"

"Ben and Fiona managed those as well?"

"No, no the decorations, food, and beverages, desserts, swags and drapery, even the candelabra and centerpieces for the tables—virtually everything you see here—all arranged ahead of time and dropped at our proverbial doorstep three days ago—the same day the engraved invitations arrived. Well, all but the musicians, of course, who arrived this afternoon as befuddled as the rest of us as to who hired them. I must say, our benefactor certainly has spared no expense!"

"I am happy to see you in such high spirits, Mr. Staub."

"And I, you, Mrs. Hillerman." He presented his arm. "I'd be honored if you'd allow me to escort you in." Then, seeing the surprise on her face, he quickly added, "It is, after all, the most important facet of my job to see that all guests' needs are met."

"Oh. Certainly," said Nora, taking the manager's elbow with a delicate touch.

As he led her down the broad sweeping stairs, more than one set of eyes watched them descend.

"Have we found our mysterious host yet, Mr. Staub?" Nora asked, glancing at the faces of the guests. "I'd like to thank him."

Mr. Staub shook his head. "Odd as it may seem, he has not yet made an appearance."

"Perhaps he is here, Mr. Staub, and we simply lack the capacity to recognize him."

Mr. Staub offered Nora a quizzical expression. "It is obvious his guests are having a splendid time. Why would he not want to step forward and claim his praise?"

119

"With a true Christmas gift, the reward is always in the giving," Nora recited, remembering one of her husband's favorite sayings.

"Indeed," said Mr. Staub. He drew a chair from an open table to seat his guest. "Now, if you will permit me, I'll wander over to inspect the delectables Fiona has on display and return with a selection of her finest for all to share."

His words accompanied an amorous glint of the eye, but whether his obvious affection indicated an attachment to Fiona's treats, or to Fiona herself, Nora could not tell. Still, the thought brought a degree of bemused satisfaction.

While Mr. Staub perused the buffet table, Nora watched William and Becca play with the other children. What a delight it was to see them having fun again.

The youngest member of The Grand's kitchen staff approached with a full tray of luscious appetizers. "Would you like an hors d'oeuvre, Mrs. Hillerman?"

"Oh," Nora looked up. "It's . . . Camilla, isn't it?"

"Yes, ma'am."

"Well Camilla, they look delicious, truly they do, but Mr. Staub has promised to return with a sampling from the buffet table. And as difficult as it is to turn down your offer, I suppose it would only be polite and proper to wait for his return."

"Yes, ma'am." She curtsied.

"Oh, but I do appreciate how much care you have all put into this event. It's as grand as ever I've seen. Will you carry a message to the others for me? Tell them how genuinely impressed and pleased I am with the staff's accomplishments?"

Camilla curtsied again. "Yes ma'am. I will. Thank you ma'am." She hurried off.

Upon his return, Mr. Staub set two plates on the table, both heaping with gourmet delicacies and sweetmeats.

As they began to eat, both sat in silence a moment, listening to the chamber orchestra play, until Mr. Staub ventured a query.

Clearing his throat, he said, "Mrs. Hillerman, would you permit me to ask a question? It is regarding the hotel."

"Of course, Mr. Staub. What is it?"

"Might you ever . . . consider selling The Carrington Grand if the offer was favorable?"

"No," she said, without hesitation. "Never. Not for all the money in the world."

"Splendid. That is what I told him."

"Told who, Mr. Staub?"

"The man who came to call on Mr. Worthington yesterday afternoon. Mr. Klaus was his name. He made an offer on the hotel. I did not care for his manner of conduct. He was not the least bit respectful of you or Mr. Hillerman."

"How very odd."

"I made it clear that he was not to call again."

"Well, I am very sorry that you had to endure such a disagreeable encounter, but I'm grateful to you for handling the situation in my stead."

"I am, as always, at your service, ma'am."

She turned and gazed at the ballroom floor, watching the dancers in their sparkling gowns and tuxedo tails floating and spinning in a magnificent blur of light.

Mr. Staub cleared his throat. "It . . . seems a shame to attend such an extravagant ballroom party without so much as a single turn on the dance floor," said Mr. Staub. "If you would permit me to accompany you to the center of the room for the next dance, I will endeavor to be a worthy stand-in."

Nora nodded and curtsied respectfully, not wanting to be impolite, though it seemed strange, the prospect of dancing with a man who was not her husband.

They took their place on the dance floor and waited, a little awkwardly, for the music to start.

When the chamber orchestra played again, it was a waltz—but not just any waltz—it was a waltz Nora remembered well, for it held many a fond memory. She had danced it with her husband each year on their anniversary, for it was to this very waltz that they first danced, and it was during that dance that they first fell in love.

She'd been lovely then, but oh how much more lovely she was to him now, as he watched from on high. And though it was true—that when she recognized their waltz, her heart filled at once with love and sadness for what was and would never again be—still, she closed her eyes, surrendered

to the music, and let her feet move in time to the musicians' sweeping cadences.

Mr. Staub never saw Mr. Hillerman, nor felt his touch, but Garrett tapped the hotel manager's shoulder to cut in, and then quickly smiled to himself, for the transition between the two men was as smooth as the dance itself.

Next thing he knew, his beautiful wife was in his arms again, and they were dancing their waltz, sweeping across the ballroom floor, floating on air. Garrett's heart soared like never before. He had so longed to touch her, to hold her one last time, and the magic of Carrington made it possible. He wanted to tell her so many things—whisper in her ear that he had done it all for her.

In this moment, a moment unlike any other, they had found an evanescent bridge between their two worlds.

By her sudden gasp, Garrett knew that she knew it was he. She gazed into his eyes and saw not Mr. Staub, but the husband she'd lost and ached to see one last time, if only to whisper the words "I love you" and utter the grateful goodbye she'd never gotten the chance to say.

Her eyes filled with a soft mist but onward they went, their bodies remembering the steps, and each other, as if no time had passed, as if no distance had separated them. They both felt it—their love shimmering between them, growing ever stronger, lifting them up—a love so pure and powerful that not even Heaven could deny them.

As much as they longed to say to one another, when they gazed into each other's eyes, they knew . . . no words need pass between them. It was enough . . . to touch souls . . . to dance one last dance.

But like all good things, the song finally came to a close, and the magic dissolved with the last note. Garrett knew his wife could no longer see him, for she stiffened a bit and uttered an apology to Mr. Staub.

Nora quickly broke from his hold and stepped away. Her gaze swept the ballroom, searching for her husband's face, but the spell had been broken.

"Mrs. Hillerman, is there something wrong?" Mr. Staub asked, unaware that anything out of the ordinary had occurred.

"No," Nora said, flustered. "I just thought . . ." She broke off.

"Perhaps our dance has made you dizzy?"

"That must be it. Yes. It has . . . been a while."

"I'll have Camilla fetch you a glass of water," he said, snapping for the kitchen maid, who hovered over the food table, topping off the hors d'oeuvre tray.

"Don't trouble yourself, Mr. Staub. I'm fine. Truly I am. I only need a moment to catch my breath."

"Are you certain there's nothing I can do for you?"

"Yes, I'm feeling much better now, but I believe I shall retire early tonight."

"As you wish. I shall have Ben escort you upstairs."

Nora waved the suggestion away. "It is thoughtful of you to be so concerned, but I need no assistance. Let Ben continue to enjoy the festivities. Though if you'd be so kind as to gather up my children, I'd be exceedingly grateful."

"Of course."

"Merry Christmas to you, Mr. Staub."

"And to you, Mrs. Hillerman," he said, and hurried off.

Nora sat, hand on heart, attempting to catch her breath and regain her composure. She closed her eyes, trying to recall every step, every look, every turn of their dance together.

Garrett. If you can hear me, thank you my love. I know it was you, and I know it was real. I—

"Mrs. Hillerman?" came a soft voice from behind.

Nora looked up to find Fiona's concerned face staring down at her.

Upon seeing Nora's moist eyes, Fiona immediately pulled up a chair and sat beside her. "I guessed this might well be a bit rough on ye. First time n'all."

Before Nora could ask what she meant, Fiona added, "First big gatherin' since yer dear husband departed this world?"

"Yes," Nora answered. "How did you guess?"

"Oh, ye have memories floatin' in yer eyes like clouds threatenin' rain," Fiona said softly.

Nora dabbed under her eyes with the back of her hand, hoping she didn't look as out of sorts as she felt. "That last piece the orchestra played . . . it was playing the first time we danced, Garrett and I. It was . . . in that very moment that we fell in love. Exactly one year later he had the orchestra play it again and he proposed to me while we danced. I was wearing this dress." Nora looked down and touched the gold spun silk.

"You felt him here tonight with ye? No?"

"Yes." The word made barely a sound.

"That can happen at times," said Fiona. "When details n' events conspire to bring it all back."

Nora nodded. "It's just that . . . he would have loved it here. It breaks my heart that he didn't get to see it, that we never got the chance to experience this together."

"Och aye, life n' the timin' of it can be cruel that way. I lost my husband some time back, same as ye, with two wee *bairns* tuggin' at my skirts. Twins at that. 'Twas a heartbreak I did not think I could bear, but we had our memories, n' the house he built for us. For many years, both kept us warm on cold winter nights."

Fiona pulled a clean handkerchief from her apron and handed it to Nora. "In a sense, Mrs. Hillerman, The Grand is yer husband's gift to ye in much the same way. He may not've built it with his own two hands, but it wouldn't be standin' here today if not for his dedication and compassion. He left a part of his heart here for ye, same as my Patrick did for me."

Nora looked around and smiled through a blur of emotion. "I believe you're right, Fiona. I can feel him here."

"Death cannot put an end to love," said Fiona. "This we learn only through loss. 'Tis a powerful lesson to heal our tender hearts, n'heal they will. In time, the pain will abate, the memories will abide, and ye will make a new start of it. When I began my employ here, after my children had grown and my parents had gone to their heavenly home, The Carrington Grand offered me a second beginning. It brought purpose to my life. Perhaps it'll be the same for ye."

"I would welcome it," said Nora. "Thank you, Fiona."

"Anythin' ye need, m'dear, I'll be here." She reached for Nora's hand and squeezed it.

"It means more to me than you may realize," said Nora, with a catch in her throat. "And please know Fiona, the reverse is also true."

With a quick nod of respect and a warm smile for the beginnings of friendship, Fiona rose from her chair. "Is there anything I can fetch ye before I return to my kitchen?"

"Have you seen Mr. Staub? He promised to search out my children."

"An errand he is sure to delight in," said Fiona with a wink. "I'll put Ben to the task. That young man has an uncanny ability to scare up our wayward manager no matter the circumstance. 'Tis a frightful skill, to be certain, but mighty useful at times." And with that, she was off.

A private smile stretched across Nora's lips. She thought about all that had happened this night. A night of magic. A night of miracles. A night she would remember the rest of her days.

She rose from her place at the table and, in a glimmer of fleeting hope, glanced around the ballroom one last time for Garrett. She took in a deep breath and exhaled slowly, releasing the weight of her sadness and grief, now replaced with gratitude and love.

Her deepest wish had been granted. It was more than she'd ever thought possible. She'd had her moment, her chance to say goodbye, even if she hadn't quite uttered the words. It was truly the best Christmas gift she could have received.

As her eyes scanned the room, Nora spotted William and Becca making their way toward her. She waved them over.

"Are we going now, Mama?" Becca asked.

"Is it time?" asked William.

Instead of being disappointed to leave the party early, her children seemed positively thrilled at the prospect.

For a moment Nora could not fathom why, and then she remembered.

Nicholas.

She couldn't back out now. After all, she had promised.

"Did you two have fun playing with the other children?"

"We did," said William. "Can we talk to Nicholas now?"

"Of course," Nora replied to their eager faces. "A promise is a promise. And I suppose it is early enough for him to be awake."

"Oh, he'll be awake. He's waiting up for us."

"Well then," said Nora, arm swept out in front of her. "Lead the way, William."

CHAPTER TWENTY
THE HIDDEN DOOR

Nora and the children made their way out of the ballroom and into the lobby where they found Nicholas hard at work fixing the broken wheel of a toy train.

Perhaps it was the still-lingering magic of the dance, or maybe because Christmas was so near, but Nora found herself wanting to believe, in her heart of hearts, that what her children were saying about Nicholas was true.

Her mind, however, remained steadfast.

Nick greeted them with his usual cheer, putting the miniature locomotive aside to shake Nora's hand. "Very pleased to meet you, Mrs. Hillerman."

"And I, you, Mr.—?"

"Oh, please, I detest formality. Call me Nicholas."

"If you prefer." Nora bowed her head in agreement, feeling a bit uncomfortable being on a first name basis with a complete stranger.

"So you have come for the truth, then?" said Nicholas, offering her a seat across from him. "The children have told you who I am and you are doubtful. I don't blame you, of course. If I hadn't lived it, I wouldn't believe it either."

Nora settled into Nick's companion leather chair, relishing the soothing warmth from the fire.

"But you certainly have my children believing you are something rather extraordinary, and I would like to know why."

"I can respect that," said Nicholas. "But may I first ask you a question?"

"Certainly."

"Did you enjoy your waltz?"

"Waltz? Oh . . . with . . . Mr. Staub?" Nora stuttered. "It was pleasant enough, if not a bit awkward. Why do you ask?"

"It is not the waltz with Mr. Staub to which I refer."

Nora's heart skipped a beat. After a pause, she gathered her wits and turned to her children. "William? Rebecca? Would you fetch Mr. Nicholas some hot cocoa? And a bit of Fiona's Christmas cake, if there's any left."

Will and Becca trotted off, both looking a bit dejected.

Once the children were gone, Nora narrowed her eyes on the old man. "But," she said carefully, "Mr. Staub was the only gentleman who asked me to dance this night."

"True enough," said Nicholas, holding her gaze. "The other gentleman did not ask, for there was no need. He already knew what your answer would be. He knew that you believed in the love the two of you shared, believed enough to have one last dance together."

Nora's eyes misted. "But how?" she whispered. "How is it possible we . . . I . . . I don't understand."

"It's Carrington, ma'am. The resonance of Christmas magic still lingers here, like a faint echo of a beautiful song that once rang true through these mountains. It may be fading, but there was enough magic left to make it happen."

"Make . . . what . . . happen, exactly?"

"A brief connection between two souls whose love is stronger than time, stronger than the barrier between Heaven and Earth. It gave you a moment, a fleeting moment between heartbeats, but for that moment, you were together again."

Nora swept a solitary tear from her cheek. "It . . . it was enough," she stammered. "It was my only Christmas wish."

"I know." Nicholas spoke the words tenderly, in respectful reverence to her grief and her lost love.

"But how could you know such things?"

"The children have already answered that question."

127

"That you are Santa Claus?" Nora smiled wearily. "I'm sorry. That's just not possible. Santa Claus is a myth, a lovely story yes, but a story nonetheless. Everyone above the age of ten knows the truth of it."

"Just because everyone agrees on something, doesn't make it so."

"That may be, but in this case, I'm afraid common sense prevails."

"Yes, I suppose it does." Nicholas considered her words for a moment, and then an idea began to shine in his eyes. "Hmm, perhaps . . . you need to see for yourself."

"See what?"

"The truth."

"Perhaps I do," said Nora, slowly crossing her arms.

"Then I shall show you," said Nick, lowering his voice, "but you must understand, Mrs. Hillerman, this is a closely guarded secret as ancient as Christmas itself." He looked left, then right. "If you promise to keep my secret for the rest of your days and never tell a soul what you have seen, I will take you there."

"Where?"

Nicholas smiled. "Where I grew up."

Nora peered at the man before her, unsure of what to think. She had no cause to trust him, but for some unfathomable reason she felt she could. He might be senile or crazy, or both, she told herself, but his eyes conveyed a different story. And the children—the children believed in him, trusted him completely. *And* so did her husband. Garrett spoke of him often in his letters to Mr. Staub. His words of regard and respect, care and concern, even love, for this man, touched her deeply. He did not pity Nicholas his privation, he admired him, his integrity, his goodness, his purity of heart.

Nora intensified her gaze. "You . . . knew my husband."

"Yes," said Nicholas, returning her gaze with equal intensity.

"How? He never came to Carrington."

"No, sadly, he did not."

"And you have never left Carrington."

Nick frowned as if it stung a little to admit. "No."

"And yet you knew each other well?"

"We do."

"But you offer no clarity on the matter?"

Nick gave a little sigh. "A riddle easily solved by what I hope to show you, Mrs. Hillerman, if, that is, you will permit me."

Nora folded her hands in her lap. "My husband was a very good judge of character, Mr. Nicholas."

"Indeed."

"And I believe he trusted you, so I shall grant you this liberty, but do not misconstrue my consent for compliance. I've not altered my position on the matter and do not intend to do so."

"I understand," said Nick. "I will ask nothing more of you than to see with your own eyes and believe what you may."

She nodded. "Then we are in agreement."

"And you will tell no one what you have seen?"

She gave another slow nod. "And the children?"

"Yes, yes of course. And the children. They must come too! I already know they will keep my secret."

"And if we do this, there'll be no more talk about Santa Claus around the children. We'll consider the matter settled." Nora stood.

"Yes ma'am, completely settled," said Nicholas, grabbing his coat off the back of his fireside armchair.

"Now?" she said, a little surprised at the inkling of excitement sparking through her.

"The echo is fading, Mrs. Hillerman. I'm afraid there might not be much time left. Once the magic is gone, there will be no more proof of Christmas past, and Carrington will become just another mountain town."

"Where, exactly, are we going?"

"A place where few have ever been, except perhaps in their dreams. A place I have never shown anyone, until now."

"Is it far?"

"No, not far at all."

Nora glanced at the foyer and hesitated. "You are aware that some may consider it improper for a lady to leave a hotel unescorted at this hour."

"Of course. I humbly offer myself as escort," said Nicholas, bowing slightly, "and as for your remaining concerns, we won't be leaving the hotel. Not precisely. Well, not as far as its residents are concerned, in any case."

Nora's look of confusion quickly turned into a soft grin as William and Becca returned with hot cocoa.

"There wasn't any cake left, Nicholas," said Becca. "I'm sorry."

"Oh, that's fine with me, Miss Rebecca. I'm trying to watch my weight anyway." Nick rubbed his belly, winked and laughed. Will and Becca laughed with him. "But a nice hot cup of cocoa would not go amiss. Is that for me?"

Will handed Nicholas the steaming cup.

"Much appreciated."

Nora nodded toward the foyer. "Run and get our coats from the cloakroom, children. Mr. Nicholas is going to show us something no one has ever seen before."

"I didn't say that ma'am," Nick corrected. "It's just that I've never shown it to anyone . . . until now."

Nora and the children followed Nicholas deep into the bowels of The Carrington Grand Hotel. Holding a candle out to illuminate their way, Nicholas led them into a long, dark tunnel that spiraled down a seemingly endless flight of stone steps to the basement below.

Candlelight cast dim splashes of light into the dusty air, giving the deep cavernous basement an ominous haze. They had no way of knowing that the eerie feeling they felt—a feeling augmented many times over by the dark, scary expanse—was compounded by the fact that there were too many footsteps echoing in the shadows.

At the far end of the basement stood an ancient wooden door, hinged in rough black iron, but conspicuously lacking in any other hardware. No knob, no latch, not even a keyhole.

"This is the way," said Nicholas. "But I must warn you, this door doesn't work like other doors. It is protected and activated by magic."

"Magic?" said Nora, doubt evident in her tone.

Nicholas set down his nearly-finished cup of cocoa and began searching the area, humphing and gumphing in the dim light until he found a small iron hook projecting an inch or two out of the wall beside the door. From it hung a tarnished silver-linked chain with a solid silver, palm-sized ball at the end.

William pointed. "What does that do?"

"It summons the magic, but only for the right person." He turned to Nora. "Ready?"

They all nodded in anticipation.

Nicholas reached up and tugged on the silver chain. Eyes closed, silently praying that there would be enough of Grandfather's magic left to get the mechanism to function, he waited, listening for any audible indication of movement.

Nothing happened.

He opened his eyes and let out his breath. His heart clenched in his chest. "I'm sorry. It's too late. The magic must all be gone."

"Try it again, Nicholas," said William. "It's not gone. Not yet. I can feel it. Try again."

He tried again, but it was no use. Then looking at William, he said, "Perhaps you should try it, Will."

"Me? How could I open the door? I don't have magic."

"How do you know?"

"I think I'd have noticed."

"Remember what I said by the fire when I first told you my story? That it is as much your story as it is mine?"

Will nodded.

Nick gestured to the pull-chain and stepped aside. "Go on. Reach up and give it a good tug. You never know what you are capable of until you try."

William did as he was told. Still nothing. "See?"

"Try it again but this time, close your eyes and picture the door opening as you pull. Wish it . . . no, *will* it to open."

William hesitated, but with Nick's encouragement, he finally wrapped his fingers around the weighted silver ball once more. He closed his eyes, focused his mind, and pictured the door opening. Then, with all his hope and strength, he held his breath and . . . pulled.

CHAPTER TWENTY-ONE
THE CLOCKWORK KEY

The door whooshed opened, creating a quick cloud of dust. Becca squealed. "You did it, Willy! You did it!"

They all peered into the darkness beyond the door but could see, quite literally, nothing.

"The adventure awaits," said Nicholas, but neither Nora, nor Becca, nor even William made the slightest move.

"It's not as scary as it looks," said Nick, stepping through the door. The light from his curious candle, which somehow never went out, lit up the rounded, wainscoted walls of a passageway, accented with a painted holly leaf pattern that ran its length. "See?"

As Nicholas led the way, Will tugged on the tail of his old coat to get his attention.

"Nicholas," whispered Will, "where are we going?"

"My grandfather's workshop," Nick whispered back.

"Your grandfather's workshop is under the hotel?"

"No, but this is the quickest way to get there, not to mention, the most fun!" he said with a wink.

Nick stepped onto a platform and held up the light to reveal a set of antiquated tracks disappearing around the bend of a subterranean tunnel, not unlike the ones they were just

132

starting to build beneath New York City, William thought, with a rush of excitement.

Nick pulled an old wooden lever next to one of the tracks. "Hope it's still serviceable," he muttered under his breath.

A moment later, an elaborately painted, open-air rail car with a sleigh-like carriage rolled into place and stopped.

"Still works," Nick said with a sigh of relief. He opened a little side door that creaked in protest, revealing two plush, roomy bench seats, each facing the other. He dusted the surface with his handkerchief and said, "All set."

Nora hesitated.

"We call them rail-sleighs," said Nick. "They were used on a regular basis to transport supplies and workers up the hill. Daily deliveries to the hotel, which no one questioned, seemed the best way to keep Kringle Towne shrouded in secrecy. And the rail-sleighs made the transporting of goods more efficient."

Nora and the children stepped up onto the loading platform.

"Is it . . . safe?" asked Nora, barring her eager children from boarding the sleigh. "It seems awfully old."

"This system was built by the best craftsmen and engineers in the world, Mrs. Hillerman. I assure you, no harm shall come to you or your children. We are just taking a short ride up the hill." Nicholas dusted the seat with his handkerchief and offered Nora a hand. "In truth, it is safer, faster, and warmer than hitching up the horses and taking the hotel's sleigh through the snow."

Nora took Nick's hand, stepped up, and then nodded her consent to William and Becca, who climbed in, bubbling at the prospect of a hidden passageway to a secret workshop.

William considered the thought that they might just be the first children ever to see Santa's real workshop.

Once they had all boarded, Nicholas pulled another lever; this one inside the carriage, and the fancy rail-sleigh began to roll along the tracks on its own unseen power.

Just before they rounded the nearest bend, William glanced back to watch another empty rail-sleigh take its place at the platform in automatic response to the system's activation.

Clickety-clack-clack. Clickety-clack-clack. Picking up speed, the conveyance carried them upward and onward, away from the basement of The Carrington Grand Hotel.

After a few minutes, and more than a few twists and turns in the track, the rail-sleigh slowed to a stop at a richly embellished landing station—its style and flair matching that of the rail-sleigh's design, resplendent with bright colors, gold accents, and delicate metal scrollwork. If not for the thick layer of dust on every surface, it might have looked like something out of a dream.

Nicholas sighed as he took it all in. "I'd forgotten how beautiful it was," he said to himself, and then turned to his passengers and said, "Welcome to Kringle Towne!"

Nora quieted the children's exuberant response as they stepped from the rail-sleigh and made their way to a set of massive arched double doors rising up like sentinels before them. With its gilded flourishes, marble tracery, and jeweled rivets, it could have been the entrance to a royal palace.

"Why is it so big?" asked Becca, staring up at a door that seemed to be made for giants.

"Grandfather Kristoff thought that if perchance an intruder were to make it this far, he would think twice about entering if the entrance was twice the necessary height. After all, one would have to wonder if giants lived here, would they not?" Nicholas winked at Becca. "Grandfather appreciated clever security."

Nora pointed to the beautiful hand-painted script written in an arc over the door. "What is the meaning of the words at the top?"

For he whom heaven knows to be true,
here no sorrow will come to you.

"For he whom Heaven knows to be true, here no sorrow will come to you. It's a warning for those who don't belong and a blessing for those who do," said Nicholas.

"So how do we open it?" asked William, anxious to move on with the adventure.

"Ahh," said Nick, "first we need to find the key. It is well concealed. That much I remember. Hmmm. William, I wonder if I could trouble you to hold this for me?"

Nicholas handed him the candle—a candle that, Will noted, had not melted or burned down in the slightest.

While Nicholas searched for the key, William amused himself by trying to blow out the candle, which apparently possessed a will of its own, for it grew brighter with every attempt.

"Willy, what are you doing?" whispered Becca. "We need that light to see by."

"Just testing a theory."

"This is it!" Nick exclaimed, pulling open a hidden trap door in the wooden floor.

William held the candle close to peer inside. The secret compartment held a single glistening key, unlike any key in the world. Not only was it bigger than a key could ever hope to be—he guessed its length at just over a foot long—but the construction of this key resembled that of a machine. Metal gears, cogs, and wheels flanked both sides of the iron shank, and an elaborate star pattern filled the oval handle at the top, which was inlaid with silver, copper, and gold.

"The Clockwork Key," muttered William.

"Ah, you recognize it!" exclaimed Nick.

"It looks just like the ornament on the tree, only bigger."

"Remember how I told you it was a story for another time? Well, now is that time! This key and the lock it fits were created by my great-grandfather's most devoted and loyal craftsman, Artemis Eckermeyer, who spent the better part of a year on its construction. Upon its completion, he claimed that no man or beast or spirit, no matter how clever or cunning, could enter uninvited, for one must not only possess the key itself but also affect the precise measures in which it must be employed."

Becca peered over Will's shoulder. "It looks magical!"

"It is!" said Nick. "Stand back, children. This will all happen very quickly."

William and Becca took a few steps back with their mother and waited for what would come next.

With both hands, Nick carefully lifted the heavy key from its hiding place, and as he did, the trap door in the floor began to close on its own.

It was at this precise moment that it did a very strange thing. Once closed, it proceeded to flip on two axis points in the floor, and transformed itself into a set of six steps, extending one by one up to meet the door a good five feet in the air.

Nick carefully climbed the mechanical staircase, feeling a rush of conflicting emotions crowding his thoughts. This place had kept all his hopes and dreams safely locked away—so safely that he didn't have to think about what happened fifty years ago—so locked away that he didn't have to feel the pain of his brother's betrayal.

And now he was about to open it back up again and let out all those murky memories. He wasn't at all sure he wanted to revisit the past, but this family had become very important to him, and he needed them to believe his story, whatever the cost.

Nick stopped at the highest step and stood before the largest keyhole any of them had ever seen. He lifted the key and pressed the star handle between his two palms setting the gears in motion. When he inserted the colossal key into the lock, it began a series of rhythmic clicks and ticks, sounding a bit like percussive music.

Nick began the exact sequence required to activate the unique interaction between lock and key as the family gazed up from below. "I just hope I remember the correct progression after all these years," he mumbled.

He turned it once to the left, once to the right and then back to the left, continuing all the way around until it rested in its original position.

With each turn, he stopped and waited for the gears to rotate and click in before advancing to the next position. As the lock's final tumbler settled into place, the gears inside began working and churning again, until a loud triple-click brought the whole sequence to a halt, plunging them back into silence. Nick exhaled his relief.

The metal stairs retreated back into the platform, returning Nick safely to the floor, and the twenty-foot tall double doors parted automatically to let them in.

The hall, dark but for the faint glow of Nick's candle, smelled of musty dampness and dried pine needles. Recesses of deep blackness loomed all around them.

Becca grabbed Will's hand.

"Don't be afraid, Bec," whispered Will. "Nicholas won't let anything bad happen to us."

As the candle mysteriously grew brighter, details began to emerge. They seemed to be in some kind of industrial factory. Cobwebs laced every right angle. Bags and piles of letters, presumably to Santa, lined long wooden tables. Greying sheets encased a collection of oddly shaped equipment scattered throughout the space, some of them over twenty feet tall. An enormous clock, with its inner workings exposed, dominated the west wall. Four ornate hands graced its face.

"I've never seen a clock with four hands," Nora said, peering up at the monumental timepiece.

Nicholas pointed. "Hours, minutes, seconds, and days."

"Days?"

"See the outer ring? Twenty-five numbers in reverse order? The fourth hand counts down to Christmas and tells us at a glance how many days we have left before delivery."

"That's why it's pointing at the number two!" exclaimed Becca, working it out for herself. "It's two days before Christmas!"

"Exactly! That hand stays frozen in place all year and only starts moving on December first."

"Very practical," said Nora, not quite sure what to think.

"Oh, it possesses a few other useful attributes as well," said Nick with a secret smile, knowing her skepticism would soon meet within incontestable proof.

Nick pulled the sheets off a few dusty heaps to expose fantastically shaped, elaborately decorated machinery.

William noted obvious signs of neglect—gears and levers stiff with rust and age, paint faded and chipped—but in its day it must have looked splendid, with many of them painted as colorfully as candy.

Thoroughly enchanted, Becca ran to uncover the rest of the machines, squealing and clapping with each new discovery.

Nora apologized for her daughter's enthusiasm, but Nicholas stopped her, saying, "Enthusiasm is a gift adults all too often squander in favor of maturity."

William didn't share his sister's glee. In the shadowy light, the place looked very sad and lonely, not at all like the cheery, bustling workshop it was obviously meant to be. But he longed to know the secrets this workshop held, and the wondrous stories it could tell. "Is this really where your grandfather made all the toys when he was Santa?"

Nick nodded, moving to a huge circuit breaker on the wall above a row of convex amber-glass meters. He threw the switch, raised his arms wide and said in a grand tone, "*This* we called The Great Toymakers' Hall!"

His voice echoed in the vastness of the room, but the effect was apparently not as grand as he'd expected, for he frowned at the lighting fixtures flickering on, one struggling bulb at a time.

The children, however, were beyond impressed, despite Nick's apparent disappointment.

"Not quite the dazzling effect I had hoped for," Nick mumbled. "It was rather extraordinary in its day."

Nora could not hide her surprise as she took in the sheer size of the room. "What a magnificent hall." She uttered, almost in a whisper, feeling a bit like she'd just stepped into a church. "Is that electric light?"

"Ahh, well, yes and no. The fixtures are electrical, of course, but they are, shall we say, augmented by a more mysterious energy source."

"And . . . how long did you say this workshop has been dormant?"

"Fifty years, Mrs. Hillerman. My grandfather was the first to bring the innovation of electric light to Kringle Towne. This was the achievement of a lifetime for him. He had his best engineers working on it for nearly a decade before it was finally able to be implemented in 1840."

"Wait," said Will, "are you saying they invented the light bulb decades before Thomas Edison?"

"Edison wasn't the first to dabble in electric light, Will. The first incandescent light was developed in 1802, followed by a more practical version, the arc lamp, in 1806. My grandfather's engineers studied all the prominent inventors in the field at the time, and came up with their own version that proved very efficient."

Gazing up at the buttress supported ceiling, the extensive carved wood scenes on the walls, the high Baroque style windows of thick, leaded glass, even the craftsmanship of the delicate stone inlay in the floor they stood upon, Nora had to admit, it all took her breath away. "I don't know what I expected. Certainly not this."

"It is a sight to behold," Nicholas said, remembering the starry-eyed boy he used to be, always in awe of his grandfather's larger than life manner and the mechanical palace wherein he made his magic.

Nora squinted. "The hall seems to go on forever!"

"Nearly," Nick said, taking the candle from Will. "With Grandfather's magic in the air, there always seemed to be enough room to accommodate the increase in toy production each year. We never ran out of space."

"You have quite a rich family history here," said Nora, recalling how Garrett often admired those who had what he called 'heirloom stories.'

"My grandfather did all his best work right here in this hall. As a child, I used to sit and watch him for hours."

Nora saw Nicholas' smile fade as a wave of something akin to regret seemed to take him over. "How long has it been?" She asked in a soft voice.

"Hmm?"

"Since you were last here?"

"I was thirteen-years-old when the factory was shut down." Nicholas moved over to a combination workbench, conveyer-belt system, and reached out absentmindedly to finger a knob on the control panel. "I don't even know if any of it is still operational, Mrs. Hillerman. I fear it's been dormant far too long."

"Only one way to find out," said Nora. "Give it a try."

Nicholas hesitated and then nodded, moving to the wall. After saying a little prayer, he heaved a second massive breaker switch into its ON position.

No movement. No sound. No churning of gears. Not even the slightest bit of valve flutter or piston chatter—only the faintest little momentary whir, as if it had made its final effort and deemed itself simply too old and too tired to fulfill its function.

Nicholas sighed in resignation. "Machines, like people, need to be in motion to stay in good working order." He rubbed an arthritic elbow. "Remaining idle for protracted periods of time cements the gears and stiffens the joints."

Becca tugged on Nick's arm to get his attention.

"Yes, Miss Rebecca?"

"May we play with the toys?" She pointed to a corner piled high with an assortment of toy drums and tiny trumpets, kaleidoscopes and puppets on ropes, hobbyhorses, seesaws, and tin trains, colorful puzzles and fun games, popguns, books about talking foxes and jack-in-the-boxes, yellow-haired dollies and even a dollhouse or two, and knickknacks aplenty, all magically new—and unlike the factory's machinery gears, the toys had managed to stay dust-free over the years.

"Certainly," said Nick. "That's what they're for after all!" Then glancing at Nora, he added, "That is to say, if your mother approves."

The children turned to Nora, who nodded, but as they hurried off, she called after them, "Behave yourselves, you two! Stay where I can see you. And keep away from the machinery!"

Nora turned to Nicholas. "It is kind of you to let them explore. They are very curious about all this."

"Curiosity is one of my favorite traits among the children. We adults know too much, or at least we think we do, and eventually we stop asking questions. What a shame that is, don't you think?"

"I'm inclined to agree," said Nora, "but there are times when my children can get a little overzealous. I believe they got that from their father."

Nicholas glanced around at the dormant machinery and sighed. "Like Garrett, your children are convinced we can bring it all back. I don't want to disappoint them, but I'm afraid there's not much chance of getting things to be the way they were."

"If you are who they say you are, there should be more than just a chance. The children believe you're magic."

"Yes, I know. They believe in me. Sometimes I can even believe in myself with their faith so strong. But all you see here, Mrs. Hillerman, despite its glorious past, now only represents what I might have been. My chance to be Santa expired long ago."

Seeing Nora's eyebrows raise, Nick added, "Oh yes, there was a brief moment where it could have come true. Grandfather entrusted me with the secret of his magic." Nicholas looked away. "But I failed him. I let everybody down." He glanced over at William and Becca who were now diving into the vast collection of toys left over from the final Christmas. "I guess I'm going to let them down, too."

"Listen," said Nora in a hushed voice so that her son and daughter could not overhear. "I'm not quite sure what to think about all of this, but you have my children convinced you are Santa Claus and they've had enough disappointment this year, so—"

"You think my story is false? A tall tale to entice the children? Mrs. Hillerman, I would never do or say anything to hurt them. I would not lie to them. What I have told them, and you, is the honest truth."

"I've tried to keep an open mind," said Nora, "but I fear when all is said and done, this will be just a toy factory like any other, and you will be just a man, like any other—a man who has lost his way. And I promise you I will do everything I can to help you find it again."

"Help me? How?"

"Well, as you know, Christmas is a time for charity." She produced a note card from her handbag and offered it to him. "I have found you a new home, Nicholas. The address is written on the card."

Nicholas glanced at the card. "Hanover House?"

"Yes. It's quite nice."

Nick chuckled to himself. "Mr. Hanover worked for my grandfather. Nice man. He always managed to produce a butterscotch from his pocket just as I happened by."

"Of course I shall pay your room and board for as long as it takes you to get back on your feet," continued Nora. "It will be our gift to you."

"The greatest gift you can give me at this moment, Mrs. Hillerman, is to believe that what I have told you is the truth and that I, too, want what's best for your children, indeed for all the children of the world."

"I'm sorry, but your story is simply too fantastic."

"Your husband believed in me. It's why he brought you and the children to Carrington. It's why he saved The Grand."

"He believed in the magic of Christmas, yes, but that's not the same thing as believing in Santa Claus," said Nora. Her definitive tone left no margin for dispute.

Nicholas sighed. "Garrett knew the truth in his heart. He didn't need proof. But I can see that you do," Nick said, motioning for her to follow.

He led her over to a set of glass doors with swirl-frosted etchings. "This was my grandfather's office—the headquarters of Kringle Towne." He stopped with his hand on the knob and said, "No one outside of the family has ever seen what I am about to show you."

CHAPTER TWENTY-TWO
MUSIC OF THE MACHINES

Nora followed Nicholas into a richly decorated wood paneled office, warmly lit with stained glass lamps leaded in a recurring snowflake pattern. Over a pinecone sprinkled mantle hung a gleaming eyed portrait of Mr. and Mrs. Claus posing arm in arm amid dozens of brightly wrapped Christmas presents in front of a shimmering tree.

Nick motioned to a tall, slender rosewood bookstand, carved with the same holly leaf pattern seen throughout the Hall, inlaid with luminous gold and silver highlights. On this pedestal rested a sizeable burgundy leather-bound register.

The wooden stand appeared to be made especially for this book. It even included a small protruding shelf to hold a candlestick at a perfect distance from the book for reading and writing.

As Nicholas set the candle in its place, Nora noted that the bookstand, and the book it held, had not been protected by dustcovers, and yet, like the toys, didn't seem to have a speck of dust on it.

Nora stepped closer, her curiosity brimming.

"Your maiden name before you were married," Nick said suddenly. "Becker, right? Nora Lynne Becker?" Nick touched the book and as he did, Nora thought she saw a faint sapphire glow emanating from its parchment-like pages.

The children, who were playing out in the workshop, must have seen it too, for they came running into the office to join their mother and Nicholas, oohing and ahhing at the luminous book.

"This register is where Grandfather kept all his secrets. He also recorded here all the children's dreams, wishes, letters, and requests."

"Is this The Book of Christmas?" asked Will, bubbling with excitement.

"It is, indeed."

"So it wasn't buried with your grandfather after all."

"Nope. It's been right here all along. Wait until you see what comes next. You're going to like this part."

Nick picked up the book, letting it rest on its spine, then spoke Nora's full name aloud and quickly withdrew his hands to let the book fall open where it may.

Nick pointed. "In this column here, he listed the toys the children would receive on Christmas day." Nick squinted in the candlelight. "Let's see. Ah. Becker. Here you are. Nora Lynne, Charleston, South Carolina." He placed a finger on the line. "Here's a Christmas you may recall. You were six years old, and you sent a letter asking for a rocking horse painted—"

"Red and white. I remember. It was on the porch Christmas morning," Nora murmured. "It was all I wished for that year. I loved that horse."

"See this mark here?" Nick slid his finger across the page to stop on another tiny inked symbol. "A four-pointed star. That means it was special somehow. A good deed or an unselfish act attached to the gift after it was received. You must have—"

"I gave it to my little sister that same day. She loved it even more than I did, even though she was too weak to ride it. She was so sick that year." Nora looked at Nicholas. "I've never told anyone that."

"He knew. Grandfather knew every time one of his gifts met with an unselfish heart or a courageous soul. He recorded every one of them in this book."

"Excuse me," said Nora, now intrigued. "What is this line here?" She pointed to a red line that ran from her name to the edge of the page, ending at a tiny, intricate, ornamental mark.

"Ahh," said Nick. "My favorite part." He tapped the symbol twice, and suddenly the page looked very different. An elaborate diagram of connecting dots and lines scrolled across the page as the register entries dissolved.

"It's a Heart Line," said Nick in a tender voice. "It connects your heart to another's."

Nora traced the line with a finger and gasped as she reached its destination. The name read *Garrett William Hillerman.*

"My husband," Nora whispered, touching the name.

"Grandfather had a way of sensing certain, well, destinies, I guess you could call them. Probable futures. He sometimes knew when two people were meant to be together."

"He knew we were going to be together when we were children?"

"All a part of the Christmas magic," said Nicholas.

Nora peered at the book in wonder. She wasn't sure how, but she was starting to believe. She found herself recalling how it felt to wake up on Christmas morning at the break of dawn, the sweet scent of fresh-baked cinnamon cakes in the air and presents under the tree, wrapped in brown paper and yarn.

If she closed her eyes, she could still see her bejeweled hometown adorned for the holidays, the warm smiles on the faces of those passing by. She could even feel the grace-filled reverence of Christmas Eve when she and her sisters joined their mother and father for the candlelight ceremony at their neighborhood church.

Growing up in Charleston, Christmases were pretty near perfect. The only two wishes that never came true were her wish for snow each year, and a little baby brother, which would have made the family portrait complete.

She looked down at the book again and noticed a small note next to her husband's name. So minuscule was the handwriting that Nora had to lean close and squint to make it out, but before she'd gotten a good look at what it said, the beautiful diagram suddenly and inexplicably vanished and the register reappeared.

Taken aback, Nora pulled away.

"It's like that sometimes," said Nicholas. "The book is very protective of its secrets. I apologize if it startled you."

"Nicholas. This book. This place. I think I understand now. I believe I've misjudged you. I am sorry."

"These are memories, Mrs. Hillerman, nothing more."

"But . . . the magic exists."

"What's left of it."

"It was all real." Nora placed a hand on the book. "When I was little, I knew it was true. I knew it with all my heart and soul! But I allowed myself to forget."

"Everyone forgets." Nick fell into a disheartened silence.

Nora, now too excited for silence, wanted to know more. "Nicholas," she said, noticing a date written next to her name, "what is this date, here?" She pointed. "December twenty-third, eighteen hundred and seventy-nine? I was about Will's age then."

"That's the day you stopped believing in Santa Claus," Nick said with a catch in his throat. "My grandfather called it 'losing a heart,' and it saddened him a little more each time it happened."

"Oh dear," said Nora, remembering that fateful Christmas Eve when she saw her mother wrapping a present that, on Christmas morning, she claimed came from Santa Claus.

At once, an elegant feather pen seemed to spontaneously appear next to the register the moment she thought about writing in the book. Taking the pen into her right hand, she bent to inscribe new words next to her name.

The children saw their mother writing and stood on tiptoes to glimpse her inscription. "What are you doing, Mama?" asked Becca.

She finished by crossing off the older date and then stood back to admire her work.

"What's this?" asked Nicholas.

"December twenty-third, eighteen hundred and ninety-nine," William read aloud. "That's today's date."

"Correction. *That,*" said Nora, "is the day I started believing in Santa Claus again."

The book instantly self-corrected, replacing the old date with the new one in perfectly aligned, elegant lettering as delicate as lace, and beside it, a tiny heart appeared.

Nick's shining eyes twinkled as the kids cheered.

"No wonder all the entries look so perfect!" said Nora.

Carefully closing the book, Nicholas touched the elaborate bejeweled key insignia on the front cover—a perfect miniature replica of the clockwork key that permitted their passage through the entrance into The Great Toymakers' Hall.

The instant Nicholas touched the key, the book began to glow with the same faint sapphire light they had seen earlier.

In that very moment, the factory brightened, the colors intensified, and the machines whirred to life.

The children ran out to watch the toy factory come alive in a complicated series of rhythmic clacks and pops. Old engine gears, pulleys, cogs and wheels all grumbled and groaned into motion, humming and whirring, squeaking for oil. Conveyer belts started conveying, pistons began pumping in swishes and spurts, compressors thumping, valves clanking, all in an elaborate rhythmic symphony.

In short order, whistles blew, radiators creaked and hissed, and a complicated counterweight system started hoisting wooden pallets high into the air carrying toys to a railed loft above.

"What's happening?" asked Nora as she and Nick followed the children out into the factory to watch the old building burst into action.

"Christmas magic!" Nick exclaimed, his eyes as sparkly as the twinkling lights. "If there's still enough to run the toy factory, then it may not be too late after all!"

Indicator lamps flashed on and off in complex sequences. Needles danced inside numerous dials and gauges. Great puffs of steam billowed out of hinge-capped pipes.

"The last time I saw such a spectacular exhibition of industry," shouted Nora over the factory din, "was in the Machinery Building at the Chicago World's Fair in eighteen ninety-three!"

"Now that is something I would have loved to see!" Nick shouted back.

"It was even louder than this!"

Nora laughed as Will and Becca danced to the music of the machines. She hadn't seen her children this excited about anything in a very long time. It filled her heart with such joy to see them so happy. In fact, she was obliged to admit that she, herself, hadn't felt this good in just as long. She decided then that whatever this adventure turned out to be, it was all worth it, just to have this moment.

"It *is* quite noisy, isn't it," called Nicholas. "I never noticed as a child! Pardon me a moment." Nick moved to a central control panel, made a few adjustments, and dialed back the speed of the machines. The factory went from clamorous to almost calm.

William and Becca ran to join their mother and Nick.

"So what do we do now, Nicholas?" asked William.

"Now? What do you mean?"

"Now that you know everything still works!"

Nora placed a hand on Nick's shoulder. "Now that you know the magic isn't gone."

"Yet," mumbled Nicholas.

Becca chimed in. "Now that you know you can be Santa Claus again because that's who you are and will always be, forever and ever."

Nicholas placed a gentle hand on Becca's cheek. "You are right, child. I am who I am. No sense denying it any longer."

"So what do we do now?" repeated Will.

"Now," said Nick, heading back to his grandfather's office, "I suppose we need to find the cave where Grandfather's sleigh, and the source of all its magic, lies dormant, waiting. It's the only way we will be able to deliver all the gifts 'round the world on Christmas Eve. That is the real magic of Santa Claus."

"And where is this cave?" asked Nora.

"Christmas Mountain." Nick pointed out the tallest window at a moonlit peak.

"And the reindeer?" asked Becca. "Are they there too?"

Nick nodded. "In hibernation . . . a kind of magical slumber," he said to Becca's crinkled nose. "Waiting to be woken from their long sleep!"

"So reindeer really do fly?" asked Becca.

"They do! The stories are all true!" said Nick, entering the office as the family followed.

"Except for the chimney rumor," he added. "There are more magical ways to drop presents off that don't involve soot and fire hazards!"

Becca giggled.

Nicholas crossed to a wardrobe, its split-door facade painted with a wintery mountain scene.

Before opening the cabinet, he paused, ran his fingers through his beard, and took in a deep breath. In the long exhale, he muttered, "I can do this," and then pulled open the doors.

There, right where he'd left them so many years ago, were his Grandfather's woolen cap and mittens, his boots, and what he called his Christmas coat. "I hope it's still here," Nick mumbled, reaching into one of the coat's many secret pockets to produce an elaborately carved four-pointed star, hollowed out at its center.

"What's that?" asked Nora, her eyes fixed on the familiar shape.

"It's another magic key of sorts," answered Nicholas. "One-third of it anyway. This key is how my grandfather gained entrance to the cave on the mountain."

"Nicholas, may I see it for a moment?" asked Becca.

"Its magic is activated when the three parts are united," continued Nicholas, as he handed it to Becca. "I have the first part, but I'm afraid I don't know where the other two reside."

Becca tugged on her brother's arm and pulled him into a huddle. "Willy," she whispered. "You see it, don't you?"

"I see it," said Will. He pulled the matching ornament from his pocket and gave it close inspection. Slightly smaller than Nick's, to be certain, but the variety of wood and the style of carving were nearly identical. The tingles returned.

"Nicholas? I have something you need to see," said Will, enthusiasm brewing. "Is this one of the missing pieces?" He handed his star to Nicholas.

"William Thomas!" Nick exclaimed. "This is the second puzzle piece—it connects my third of the key to the center piece. Where ever did you find this?"

"It was in Father's things."

Nick looked at Nora.

"I honestly haven't a clue how it got there," said Nora. "It seems he intended to share it with us when we opened our Christmas presents this year. It was with the tickets that brought us here."

"And this too." William handed Nicholas the old tintype photograph from his pocket.

Nick gazed at the photograph in pensive silence.

William frowned. "Are you all right Nicholas?"

"Oh, much better than all right, my boy!" he burst out, offering the photograph back to William. "It seems I too have been looking for clues, Will, and your photograph there, well, that might just be the most important clue of all!"

Nick's gaze momentarily shifted past Nora and the children to the empty space beyond. Nodding in acknowledgment, his smile soon had a light of its own, and it brightened the spirits of all who stood near.

William stared at the photograph, befuddled.

"Nicholas?" said Nora, hopeful of an explanation.

Nick held up the two star ornaments. "These four-pointed stars are an important part of my family's history," said Nick. He turned to William. "You know, don't you, Will? What these are?"

"The first toy from the first Christmas," said William, "carved by the three brothers."

"Indeed!"

"And they have magic, right?" added Becca.

"Ah, it is good that you have both been paying attention!" said Nick. Then, turning to Nora, he added, "This star puzzle, carved in three parts to resemble the star of Bethlehem, became the first toy ever given to the Christ child. 'Twas made for him on the evening of his birth, fashioned out of the same wood as the manger, and imbued with all the magic of that night."

"But how did *you* come to possess it?" asked Nora.

"Ah, how it came back to my family after giving it to Mary, Joseph, and Jesus is a bit of a mystery. You see, thirty-four years after the birth of Christ, the star, as the story goes, was miraculously returned to its makers, who were, all three, still alive and well and making their way as traveling craftsmen in the Holy Land.

"It was said to have passed through many hands, traveling many roads across many kingdoms before it found its way home. And when the star was restored to them, they knew in their hearts that they were meant to be the keepers of its magic. This star has been kept safe by my family for nearly two thousand years."

"What an extraordinary tale," said Nora.

"When my great-grandfather found a way to reach all the children of the world on Christmas Eve, he used the power of this star to create that magic, and also to protect it in the secret cave on Christmas Mountain."

"Is all this true?" asked Nora.

"Here, let me show you," Nick said, grinning. "I haven't seen this since I was a child." He fitted the two stars together and, with a flick of his wrist, rotated them into alignment.

The pieces clicked into place, nesting perfectly, and then fused together in a flash of brilliant light to make one intricately interwoven four-pointed star. But the last piece was plainly missing, for the heart of the ornament was still hollow and dark.

"Unfortunately," said Nicholas glumly, "there's still one more part to the puzzle, and I fear they must all be together for the key to work."

"Then let's go get it!" said Will. "Do you know where it is?"

"I don't know *where* it is," said Nick, "but I think I know *who* might have it."

"Who?" asked Nora, now swept up in the adventure.

Nick's jaw tightened. "Simon."

"The man who closed down Kringle Towne and put everyone on the streets?" asked Will. "*That* Simon?"

"Yes, and if I'm right, there is little chance we can ever recover his piece of the star."

"Maybe the key will work without it!" said Becca.

"I don't think so, Miss Rebecca," said Nick.

Will's hands went up. "Has anyone ever tried?"

"I suppose not."

"So try! We can't give up now!"

Nora touched his arm. "I agree with the children, Nicholas. You owe it to yourself to try."

Nick smiled. "That's the first time you called me by my name without putting Mr. in front of it." As Nora nodded, he said, "Then . . . I'm not a stranger to you any longer?"

"No. From this day forward, I will consider you a friend."

Becca jumped up and down. "Papa always said you never know what you can accomplish until you try!"

"How right you are, child!"

"What are you going to do, Nicholas?" asked Will.

Nick looked down at the star in his hand. "I guess I'm going to go climb a mountain."

CHAPTER TWENTY-THREE
A MOMENT OF TRUTH

"Now," said Nick, "if you're going to continue working while I'm gone, you'll need to reference this." He pointed to a handwritten manual adhered to the wall in Grandfather's office. "All you need to know is right here. Each piece of equipment has its own function."

He shuffled over to a strange oversized typewriter-like machine with tubes that extended out the back and disappeared into the ceiling. "And they're all connected to this contraption here, called a *Duplagraph*, where the names and toys are inputted from the Dear Santa letters, which then sends—"

Nora placed a hand on Nick's shoulder. "We'll figure it out."

"Go get the sleigh and the reindeer," said Becca.

William nodded his assurance. "We'll keep working, Nicholas. Don't you worry. We'll be ready for you when you return. Go save Christmas."

Nick gave Will a little half-smile. "I'll do my best." He pulled his grandfather's large, fur-lined, burgundy velvet Christmas coat from its place in the wardrobe and slipped it on.

"Perfect fit!" said William.

"It would seem so," mumbled Nick, stepping into his grandfather's boots. "We shall see if I can truly fill his shoes."

He wrapped the hand-woven fuzzy wool muffler around his neck and tucked the two ends under his lapel.

Will laughed. "You're starting to look like Santa already!"

They all joined in, but the laughter soon withered in the seriousness of what Nick was about to do.

"Godspeed, Nicholas," said Nora, the worry evident in her voice.

Nick raised a hand. "No time for sentimental goodbyes! I hereby dub thee Santa's special team. Now get to work!"

"Don't forget these," said Nora, handing Nick his wool cap and mittens.

As Nick took them, he squeezed Nora's hands and whispered, "Thank you, Mrs. Hillerman . . . for everything, but most of all, for believing."

"I believe . . . it's time you call me Nora."

Nick smiled.

"Take care," she said, and then, sensing Nick needed a moment to himself, she led her children out into the factory.

Nicholas lingered in the office a long moment, remembering all the hours he'd spent there watching his grandfather manage the workshop.

His eyes fell on his old patchwork coat hanging on a brass hook next to the painted wardrobe. From it, he retrieved the seven Dear Santa letters he had carried all these years.

Looking through the factory windows at William, Becca, and Nora sorting the toys churned out by the magical machinery of his boyhood, he felt a great surge of love come over him, and then sighed to himself, hoping beyond hope to survive the mountain and return. He had family now. He had a reason to stay alive. He hadn't felt that in a very long time.

Placing the string-bound bundle of Dear Santa letters in the breast pocket of his grandfather's coat, Nick patted them for safekeeping as he had always done, but for a moment his hand rested there. "The time is now," he muttered to himself, a tingle of rightness coursing through him. "He needs to know. He needs to know before I . . . "

Nick stopped the thought, sighed again, and pulled out the letters. After untangling the string, he sifted through the envelopes until he came to the one he was looking for. He retied the six remaining letters and placed them back where they had been kept safe for 50 years, next to his heart.

Then, from a different pocket, he retrieved another letter—one he'd kept separate from the others, a letter he'd never told anyone about, not even William.

Nicholas pressed the two letters between his palms, knowing what he had to do. He'd held on to them all these years, and they'd become very dear to him. In fact, he read them whenever he began to lose hope.

To Nick, these letters represented the innate goodness in all of mankind and the true spirit of Christmas. He didn't want to give them up, yet it filled him with joy to finally have someone to share them with, someone who'd cherish them as much as he did.

Garrett Hillerman appeared at his side. *Yes. It's time.*

Nick called William over so they could speak privately.

"Nicholas, I'm worried that we won't get our work done in time for you to deliver all the gifts before Christmas Eve."

"Oh don't fret about that good Will. There's always enough time. It's all part of the Christmas magic. Time will move as slow or as fast as we need it to. Just keep an eye on the big clock out there on the wall in the main hall."

William looked over his shoulder.

"Pay particular attention to the second outer ring. The one made of copper. It shows the passage of time within Kringle Towne, rotating to the next click precisely once every second. You will see the space between those clicks slowly lengthen as the night goes on, like a metronome increasing its silence between beats to slow time in music."

"Is it happening right now?"

"Yes, it is granting us the time we need to have this moment together, you and I." Nick paused, his expression suddenly very serious.

"What is it, Nicholas?"

"William, if there was one thing you could have for Christmas above all else, what would it be?"

"My father," said William, without hesitation. "I would want to see my father."

"Well, I can't bring your father back, but perhaps I can offer you the next best thing." He held out the first of the two envelopes. "This was the final 'Dear Santa' letter," said Nicholas. "It's for you."

"For me? Why?"

"It's from your father."

"My father?" William felt a familiar lump in his throat.

"It's a letter he wrote to me when he was your age."

"My father wrote one of the last seven letters?"

"Yes, but this letter didn't come with the others. It came years later. I had been living at the Grand for so long, it had become my home. At the time, I hadn't the slightest notion how he knew, but it came addressed to Mr. Nicholas Claus, care of The Carrington Grand Hotel, just like the others, but with my full name." Nick paused, smiling at the memory. "When I read it, I knew it was special . . . I knew *he* was special. There was something in the words he chose—a kind of knowing—that told me it was more than just a child's promise soon forgotten. Read it. You'll understand."

William took the yellowed parchment envelope, opened it gingerly, so as not to damage the fragile paper, and read . . .

Dear Mr. Claus,

Please write and tell me if it's true. Somehow I feel you are very sad. I think you may be alone like I was, not so long ago.

I don't know how I know these things, but sometimes I can see when things will come to be. So I want you to know that although it may look hopeless to you now, it won't always be that way.

I know I'm only twelve, but please write back if you can, and tell me if there's anything I can do. I don't have much to give right now. I'm just an orphan taken in by kindly people who gave me a humble home and a name, but someday, when I'm grown, I know I'll do very well. So the time will come when I'll be able to help, and I promise you I will, in any way I can.

For now, just know that I am, and forever will be, your true friend.

Sincerely, Garrett William Hillerman
December 20th, 1876

Nick pointed to the letter. "He kept that promise."

"Thank you for this," whispered William, hugging Nicholas.

"You are welcome, my boy."

"I'm not sure why, but knowing father was one of the 'seven letters children' makes all the difference."

"I'd hoped it would."

Will offered Nick a sad smile. "It's the final clue."

"Not quite, good Will. There's one more." Nick produced the second envelope. "This letter, like the first, is from your father, but written many years later. It is a correspondence I received through Mr. Staub shortly after your father began to inquire about the hotel."

"You mean he wrote it after he was grown up?"

"Yes. Twelve years ago, to be precise. He wrote it the day you were born." Nick held out the envelope, open-palmed, and waited.

William hesitated and then took the letter.

"He loved you very much."

Opening the letter, William began to read, his eyes soon filling with tears. When he finished, he carefully folded the parchment and then sat very still.

Finally, he found his voice, softened by his father's words of love and pride for his only son. William peered up at Nicholas through a blur and managed a trembling, "Thank—" He swallowed, cleared his throat and started again. "Thank you for showing this to me. This has been the most wonderful Christmas I could have imagined. It would be perfect, if only he were here. Now, in a way, he is."

"More than you know," said Nick.

William offered the two letters back to Nicholas.

"No. Keep them. They belong to you now."

"But . . ."

"I finally know why I've kept these letters safe all these years. It wasn't for me. It was for you." He glanced at the big clock on the wall and watched as it clicked over to the next tick in slow motion. "Time to go."

Nicholas strode toward the side door that led not to the underground railway passage, but out to the blustery woods surrounding Kringle Towne, where the trail to Christmas Mountain lay waiting.

Nicholas stood before the door, feeling a familiar fear, the fear of a boy who was not strong enough, nor brave enough to do what had to be done. He took in a deep breath, grabbed a brass lantern off a nearby catch—its flame sparking to full brilliance the instant he touched it—and then pulled the release chain.

He waited as the heavy metal rolling door ratcheted open, revealing a white-laced, tree-lined view of the mountain. A flurry of snow whirled in. Nick remained frozen in place.

"Nicholas?" said Will in a quiet voice. "What is it?"

Nick stared out at the storm clouds, dark and ominous, moving in over the mountain, blotting out the light of the moon. "The last time I did this I . . . I failed."

"You were too young then. Things are different now."

"Yes, now I'm too old."

"You won't fail, Nicholas. I believe in you. We all do."

"There's . . . something else," said Nick, "even if I do make it up the mountain. Do you recall when I told you the magic can only lay dormant for so long before it is lost forever, and that I didn't think there was much time left?"

"I remember."

"The magic . . . it's dying . . . tonight. I feel it deep in my bones." He looked down at his boots. "The instant I step through these doors, time returns to normal for me, and there are only so many hours left. What if I get there and it's too late?"

"It won't be, Nicholas. I know it," said Will, his heart beating very fast now. "Let me go with you. I can help you!"

"You would brave the mountain with me?"

"You said this is my story too. Maybe this is why we came to Carrington. Maybe I'm supposed to go with you to bring back the magic!"

"I admire your courage Will, but it is just too dangerous. And besides, I need you here. There's much to be done if we are to be ready by Christmas Eve. I shall need all of you."

"If you don't get the magic needed to deliver the gifts, it won't make any difference if we're ready or not."

"I just . . . don't want to let you down, you or your family. I feel like that's all I have ever done. Let everybody down."

"But," said William, "this is what you've dreamed of your whole life, isn't it?"

Nicholas nodded.

"Well, this is the moment it all comes true. But you have to believe it too."

"Your life is only as big as the dream you dare to live?" said Nick, quoting Garrett Hillerman.

"Exactly!"

"Your father would be very proud of you, William Thomas."

"I'll ask him to watch over you when you're up there."

"I'd appreciate that." Nick gave a quick nod as if to say, 'I'm ready,' pulled on his wool cap and mittens, and then marched out to face the mountain.

As the door automatically closed behind him, William didn't move. He stared at the door for a moment, unblinking.

Nora approached from behind and put her arm around her son. "Is everything all right?"

"I don't know," said Will. "I'm worried about Nicholas. There's a storm coming and he's going up there all alone. There must be something we can do."

The line of Nora's mouth straightened. "I know you want to help, and I love you for that, but all we can do now is pray."

William closed his eyes, and bowed his head. "Father, if you can hear me, please watch over Nicholas on the mountain, and ask God to give him the strength he needs to face what may come. Thank you. Oh, and Father, I hope Heaven is beautiful and all your wishes come true there. I miss you. Amen."

"Mama! Willy!" cried Becca. "Someone's coming!"

Nora's eyes flashed to the entrance. "I thought no one else knew of this place."

"No one does," said Will, "Except—

"—Simon!" finished Nora with a gasp.

"Shut it down!" called Will. "All of it! Quick!"

Nora dashed to the wall and pulled, double-handed, with all her might, until both of the huge breaker switches slammed into their OFF position.

Beset by darkness, the workshop fell into silence, and they waited to see who would walk into The Great Toymakers' Hall.

CHAPTER TWENTY-FOUR
THE DARK-HEARTED DRAGON

William, Rebecca, and Nora hid behind the big steam engine that powered the extensive conveyor belt system. Will rubbed his nose. The machinery smelled of hot, stale grease and burnt dust.

As their eyes adjusted to the darkness, they noticed a dim glow coming from the office.

"Oh no, we forgot about Nick's candle," whispered Will.

"Too late now," whispered Nora.

As a small group entered the hall, Will squinted but could not make out their faces.

"Ouch!" one of them said. "You stepped on my foot."

"I did not," said another.

"Quiet, you two!" hissed a third.

Will recognized one of the intruder's voices. "Ben?" William called out. "Is that you?"

"Will?" said Ben, squinting. "Where are you?"

William exhaled his relief, and whispered, "It's okay," to his mother and sister. "It's Ben from the hotel."

They all three emerged from their hiding place.

"What are you doing here?" asked William.

"I could ask you the same question," said Ben. Then after an elbow to his ribs from Fiona, he added, "But I won't."

"Fiona?" called Nora, squinting. "Is that you?"

"Och aye, 'tis me."

"And André, the coachman, ma'am," mumbled André.

Mr. Staub stepped out from behind his team.

"Mr. Staub?" said Nora, surprised. "You too?"

William crossed to where they stood. "What are you all doing here?"

Ben cleared his throat. "We saw you descend the stairs to the hotel basement and wanted to see if you needed assistance."

"And," added Fiona, "we thought if ye talked Nick into becomin' what he was born to be, ye might well be needin' our help."

"Wait. You know?" asked William, surprised. "You know who Nicholas is?"

"What do'ye take us for, blind fools?" said Fiona. "We've known fer years."

"All but Mr. Staub, of course," said André.

"Aye, poor old Mr. Staub only just worked it out for himself this very night," Fiona said, attempting to stifle a laugh. "We had to show him the tunnel and the rail-sleigh before he was even willin' to consider the idea that we hadn't all gone mad as murmuring monkeys."

"And what do you think now, Mr. Staub?" asked Nora.

"Well, Mrs. Hillerman, I—"

"Turns out Mr. Staub has a soft heart inside that ironclad chest of his," said Fiona, interrupting her supervisor. "Seems he's had an affinity for all things Christmas since he was a wee lad. Gabbed on n' on 'bout it all the ride up."

Mr. Staub shrugged sheepishly.

Nora laughed.

Ben glanced around. "Where's Nick?"

"Gone to the mountain," said Will.

"To bring back the magic?" added Becca.

"So it's happening then?" said Fiona.

William, Becca, and Nora all nodded.

"Tell us," said Ben, "what can we do to help?"

"Aye, put us to work!" said Fiona.

Nora toggled the heavy breakers on once more, this time recruiting Mr. Staub for assistance.

The mighty machines of The Great Toymakers' Hall chugged back into action.

160

Everyone clapped and cheered at the sudden burst of activity except, of course, Mr. Staub, who got straight to work, as was his nature. But William caught the hotel manager grinning like one of Santa's elves whenever he thought no one was looking.

Jubilation. That was the general ambiance of the room as the magical machines began to create an infinite variety of toys and gifts. Until . . .

Thunder cracked.

Lightning flashed.

The factory labored to a halt and the Great Toymakers' Hall plunged into darkness again.

"Mama!" cried Becca.

"It's all right, sweetheart, I'm here." Nora found her daughter in the dark and wrapped her in a protective embrace.

William ran to retrieve Nick's candle, its unending flame still burning bright next to the Book of Christmas in the office.

Another flash of lightning outlined a tall, dark figure in a black cloak standing just inside the hall's grand entrance.

Becca screamed and hid behind her mother.

William came running, ready to protect his family and friends. Mr. Staub and André stepped in front of the women to stand beside Will.

"I am Simon Klaus," rasped the large man. "Kringle Towne and everything in it belongs to me. If you do not vacate the premises immediately, I will have you removed by force."

"I know who you are," said Will. "I know all about what you did fifty years ago."

The man drew down his hood. Gasps reverberated off the walls. Years of anger and hatred had twisted Simon's features into an ugliness befitting his dark heart. "Then you know," he said in a disturbingly calm voice, "I do not make idle threats."

William turned, handed the candle off to Fiona, and then marched right up to the man, folded his arms across his chest and planted his feet in protest. "You don't deserve to be here. You turned your back on Nicholas. You turned your back on Christmas, but we won't! You can't make us leave!"

Simon raised a hand to strike the boy.

Nora pulled her son out of his reach just in time. "What kind of man are you, striking an innocent child!"

"Innocent child? Parasites! Every last one of them!"

161

"How can you say that?"

"Leave now, madam! And take your little scum-rats with you before I—"

"Sir! We are not trespassing!" said Nora in as severe a tone as William and Becca had ever heard from her. "We are here as guests! Nicholas has—"

"Nicholas? Ha! That boy has no claim to Kringle Towne!"

"He has just as much right to this place as you do!" retorted Nora.

"More!" added William.

"Oh?" Simon looked at Will with a knife-edged gaze. "And how is that?"

William adjusted his posture—back straight, chin raised, fists on hips—and said, "Because he cares."

Simon's sinister laugh echoed through the hall. "You think that makes any difference to me, boy? Kringle Towne is still mine, and as long as it is, it will remain closed! Get out!"

"Come children," said Nora, taking their hands. "We'll have no more to do with this man and his malevolence."

"But what about Christmas?" grumbled Will.

"Hush now! We shall find another way to help Nicholas."

The children reluctantly agreed, and followed their mother as she paraded them toward the main entrance and out to the waiting rail-sleighs beyond.

Fiona and the others began to follow, but as William strutted by, Simon grabbed his arm and yanked him from the group. "You! Tell me where Nick is!"

"No," shouted Will. "I won't."

"Tell me, or I'll make you regret you ever—"

"Sir," said Nora, through gritted teeth, "take your hands off my son."

"Tell me where Nicholas is, and I'll let him go."

"William," said Nora slowly.

"No!"

"We are caught in the middle of something that is none of our affair."

"Let me go!" cried Will. "You're hurting me. I'm not telling you where he is!"

Nora marched toward Simon with all the fierceness of a mother bear protecting her young.

162

"Nicholas went to Christmas Mountain to bring back the magic!" Becca burst out. "That's all we know. Now let my brother go!"

"Becca, no!" shouted Will, but of course, it was too late.

Nora stopped and turned to her daughter. Becca ran into her arms.

William struggled against Simon's hold to no avail.

Mr. Staub stepped forward. "You got what you came for, Klaus. Let the boy be."

Simon shoved Will to the floor and headed for the same big metal door that Nick had exited earlier.

They watched as Simon Klaus trudged out the back and into the snow, disappearing in a blanket of white. All but Nora and Becca, that is, who rushed to help William up.

"Are you hurt? Let me see that." Nora inspected a scuff on Will's forehead.

"Mother, I'm fine."

"I'm sorry," cried Becca. "I couldn't let him hurt you!"

"I know, Bec. I'm not mad, just afraid . . . for Nick."

"I thank God you're all right," said Nora, breathless.

William glanced back at the open door offering a view of the stormy mountains. "I just want *Nick* to be all right."

"At least he got a head start," said Fiona, coming to check on William. "Maybe he'll be there and back before Simon can catch up to him."

Will frowned. "I hope so." Even as he said it he knew Simon was not far behind Nicholas. His only Christmas wish now was for everyone to be safe and back together again.

Nora stood, helped William to his feet and dusted herself off, realizing just then that she still wore her ball gown. "Come children. It will be dawn soon. We must return to the hotel."

"But we promised to be ready when Nick returned!" Will argued. "Simon's gone now. Can't we stay and work?"

"No, William, it's not safe. Mr. Klaus could return any time. We'll head back to The Grand to get cleaned up, have a bit of breakfast, a rest, and then figure out what to do next."

"But—"

A hand went up to silence his protest. "We shall wait for Mr. Nicholas to send word that all is well. I'm sure the others will agree."

"Your mother is right," said Mr. Staub. "My staff and I must return as well. We've left the hotel in the hands of the night staff, and need to relieve them before our guests rise." Then glancing over his shoulder, Staub called out to his footman. "Ben! Close the back gate! We're leaving."

By the time they arrived back at The Grand, the morning sun had just begun to peek over the mountain ridge, struggling to break through dark clouds. The storm over Carrington had all but moved on, leaving in its wake a fresh mantle of bright snow. The day of Christmas Eve had finally arrived.

Rested, washed and dressed for the coming day, William and Rebecca stood at the bay window in the parlor, gazing up at Christmas Mountain.

"Nick is going to be okay," said Becca. "I know he is."

"How do you know?" asked Will, worried for his friend.

"Because last night, when Nicholas left, I prayed for the storm to go away and look—" she pointed at the sun glistening on the snow—"it's gone."

"But now the storm is over the top of Christmas Mountain, right where Nick is headed." Will frowned. "And Simon."

Becca bit her bottom lip. "I didn't mean to get Nicholas in trouble."

"I know, Bec."

Nora entered with a determined gait, and summoned her children to sit at a nearby table.

"William, Rebecca," she said in a stern tone, "I want you to stay in the hotel today."

William's eyes widened. "What? Why?"

"I have some important business to take care of in town. I hope to return within the hour, but in the event that I am further detained, I've asked Fiona to look after you."

"But we have to go back to The Great Toymakers' Hall," argued William. "Tonight is Christmas Eve!"

"I am well aware of the date, William."

"We need to be ready when Nick comes back!"

"We can't let him down," added Becca.

"I know how important this is to both of you. It is to me as well, but Nick's brother is a dangerous man. Dangerous and unpredictable. There is no telling what he will do next. Your safety must come above all else. Do you understand?"

The two nodded, their expressions dreary. Neither felt hiding out in the hotel to keep safe seemed at all the right thing to do.

Nora waved a hand in the air to beckon The Grand's coachman. "Good morning, André," she said. "I . . . wanted to thank you for your part in keeping my family safe last night. You and Mr. Staub were very brave to stand with my son."

"It was William who showed great courage and resolve," said André. "You have a fine boy there, ma'am."

"I believe I do," she said with an inner smile. "André, I was wondering if you would be available to take me into town this morning? I have some urgent business to attend to, and there is little time to spare."

"Of course, Mrs. Hillerman. Always a pleasure," he said as if this day was like any other. "My sleigh is at your service. We can leave at once if you wish." He tipped his hat. "I'll have Ada retrieve your coat."

André dashed off, and Nora turned to her children. "I shall return as soon as I am able. Now run along to the café hall. Fiona is preparing a special breakfast for you—spiced griddlecakes with honey and lemon curd." She stood and kissed them both on the forehead. "Be good, children."

They nodded again, and she hurried off with André, heading in the direction of the carriage house.

"Come on," said Will, turning not toward the café hall, but The Grand's front doors. "There's something we need to do before Nicholas comes back."

"But Mama said—"

"She told us to be good and we will be. It's the right thing to do, Bec. I promise."

"What is? Where are we going?"

"You'll see."

"Can't we at least have breakfast first? Griddlecakes!"

"No time, Bec. Follow me. We need to get the others on board."

CHAPTER TWENTY-FIVE
THE MOUNTAIN STAR

Only Garrett Hillerman, being who and what he was, knew where William and Rebecca had gone and what they intended to do, but it was Nicholas he kept an eye on this day, to honor his son's fervent prayer.

The storm over the town might have broken, but the conditions on the mountain were far from kind.

As Nick struggled up the mountain path, he found himself wishing he'd had fewer helpings of Fiona's bread pudding and rich hot chocolate over the years, and at the same time, wishing he had both right now to warm his insides. Every bone ached. Every breath wheezed.

His limbs became leaden. Any minute now they'd seize up and refuse to take him any further. He'd gotten through the night, but only just, and his hopes of reaching the mountain peak before dusk were fast waning.

Boisterous winds fought Nick's every step. Snow twisted and howled like demon dogs, but he pushed on.

Walking beside his old friend, Garrett felt a great sense of love and pride cresting within his soul. He knew this was the hardest thing Nick had ever done, not only because of the harsh conditions, but because he had to face and conquer an enemy far greater than the mountain—that of his own fear and self-doubt.

It took a full day's light to hike the rest of what Grandfather Kristoff called 'The Tall Trail,' and now the threat of night closed in once again as Nick neared the top of Christmas Mountain. Worse, the storm had returned, and with it, a blistering cold. If darkness fell before he found the entrance to Grandfather's cave, there would be little chance he'd be alive come morning.

Exhaustion and despair took hold. *This would be a fitting end to my failure of a life,* Nick thought. *If I can't do this, then what point is there to any of it?*

Garrett heard the echo of this dispirited thought and reached out to Nick's mind, hoping to give him a spark of hope, but all Nicholas felt was a brief tingle that momentarily confused the senses.

Nick's whole body shook with fatigue, every step more difficult than the last. *Not much longer,* he thought. *I won't last much longer.* One more step and he felt his legs buckle.

Collapsing in the snow, he stopped fighting his fate and at long last accepted that his journey had come to an end. The brutal cold now permeated every inch of his Grandfather's thick coat as he lay on his back in the snow. Eyes closed, he uttered a silent prayer, not that his life be saved, but that it be taken swiftly.

"Grandfather," he rasped. "Grandfather, I'm sorry. I failed you . . . again."

A cruel silence enveloped him. No answer came . . . not an answer to his prayer, nor an answer from his grandfather.

The wind still thrashed, the icy cold still punished, but he could no longer feel them. The silence fell inside him now.

An unexpected sense of relief washed over him. This was it. He could finally rest. Just let go. Drift away. Sleep. No more pain. No more struggle. No more regrets. Just sleep, everlasting.

Garrett felt Nick slipping away. A few more seconds and he would be lost, along with everything he and Nick had worked so hard for. With the veil between life and death waning now,

Garrett appeared beside Nicholas and took his hand, though Nick felt nothing of his touch. Concentrating with fierce intent, Garrett sent Nicholas a message: *Don't give up. Don't give up. You're nearly there. Have faith, my friend. This is your destiny. Reach for it, Nicholas. Reach up!*

This time, Nicholas felt something—an inexplicable surge of energy and hope. Without really knowing how or why, he had new strength to move and a restored will to live.

Managing to get to his knees, he extended his right arm above his head to grope for a handhold. A stab of pain shot through his shoulder but he set his jaw and continued. His hand finally found a nearby rock, and with great effort, he pulled himself to an upright position. Winded by the ordeal, he leaned on that same rock and gulped air into his lungs.

Squinting up through icicle-lashes, he noticed it had stopped snowing.

Curious.

But as he peered into the distance, he saw that, no, the snow still fell . . . just not on him.

Even more curious.

Then he remembered. With a surge of excitement, he glanced behind him. Solid rock. In fact, the rock face curved around him and above him like the entrance to . . . a cave! Nick felt another wave of hope rise up.

His eyes quickly scanned the area. The granite alcove, while providing a modicum of shelter from the blustering storm, bore no indication of the hidden door that offered entry into Grandfather's secret cave. *But it has to be here,* thought Nick. *This has to be it.*

Dizzy in his search, Nick leaned once again upon the rock to steady himself—the very same rock he had used to pull himself to his feet only moments ago, yet this time he noticed something different about it. It wasn't rough like the other rocks of the mountain. It felt smooth to the touch, as if it had been cut and polished like . . . the marker-stone!

Forgetting his lightheadedness, he jumped up and whirled about to face the marker, remembering what his grandfather said the first and only time they'd climbed Christmas Mountain together . . .

"Memorize this stone, Nicholas. You will need to find it again someday. It shall grant you access to the magic when the time comes."

"But Grandfather," said little Nicholas, thinking the old man had forgotten that he was the younger son, "Simon is the one who will need the magic, not me."

"I have already shown Simon the way," said his grandfather. "He will have his moment. But you, Nicholas, you shall have yours as well. Someday, you will need to make your way here. This I know. It shall be a difficult journey, but you must summon your courage and strength when the time comes. Do you understand?"

Twelve-year-old Nicholas nodded, but he did not understand. It made no sense. Simon was going to be Santa Claus. Everyone knew that. It was Nick's only cause for sadness in a life of constant joy.

Now Nicholas understood.

With a mittened hand, he cleared the snow from the face of the stone. His heart leapt when he saw the inscription:

'Tis once again that time of year.
For thee, the magic shall appear,
If it be thy will, thy dream, thy fate,
The ancient star will open the gate.

Limbs protesting, fingers and toes frozen through, Nicholas knelt before the stone. "If it be my fate," he uttered, breathless, "let this part of the ancient star open the gate." He pulled the mitten from his right hand and reached into his coat pocket for the wooden star. Staring at the key with fierce concentration, he tried to recall what his grandfather did to activate its magic in order to open the cave door, but no matter how hard he concentrated, he could not remember.

Even if he could, he had no idea if the key would work with only two of the three pieces.

"Grandfather!" he called to the heavens, "Help me!"

He held the star over the marker-stone, hoping for some sign; a spark of light, a tiny glow, anything that might indicate how to set the magic in motion, but it was no use.

"Grandfather!" he called again. "Tell me what to do!"

Suddenly, the wind stopped, and an incomprehensible calm descended. Light from the near-setting sun burst forth from dark storm clouds and streamed through the pines, bathing the rock-hollow in a golden light.

With the low angle of the sun, a ray of light cast a shadow into a shallow impression carved in the stone, and an outline of a four-pointed star emerged on its surface.

Nick contained his excitement and again held the star key directly over the impression in the marker-stone.

This time something did happen. The stone began to emanate a faint sapphire glow just as the Book of Christmas had in The Great Toymakers' Hall.

"Thank you, Grandfather!" Nick called skyward.

He fit the star key into the marker-stone and stared at the cave, waiting for the stone gate to open.

"What's wrong?" he looked down at the star, with its center hollow and dark. The glow began to fade. "No!"

"Looking for this?"

The deep voice sent a shudder through him.

Nicholas looked up. The cloaked figure that stood between him and the cave entrance held in his right hand an imposing ebony staff, and in his left, the missing center piece of the four-pointed star. The heart of the key.

"Simon," Nick rasped.

"Surprised to see me, brother?"

"I knew you were in town the moment you arrived. Have you come to help me?"

His icy laugh chilled Nicholas far beyond the mountain's bitter cold.

"Ever the optimist, Nick. Ever the fool. You never change." He planted his dark staff in the snow and slipped the ancient carving back into the satchel at his waist. "I see now I made the trip for nothing. I couldn't be sure you wouldn't find a way to activate the magic without my piece of the star." The edges of his mouth curled into a malevolent grin. "I must admit it was worth the trip up the mountain just to see you fail, little brother. How pathetic that you ever thought you could be anything more than an utter disappointment."

"That is what you would have me be," said Nicholas, "and for far too many years I thought it was true, but no more."

"Oh? You have people who believe in you now and that makes all the difference?"

"Yes. It does. If you had anyone that believed in you, you'd know it was true."

"Then prove it." Simon pulled the satchel from his belt and held it out, dangling precariously from a single index finger. "Take it," he said with a piercing sincerity. "If you can take it from me, you can have it—fit the last piece into the star and open the cave. That's what you've always wanted, isn't it? Well, go ahead, brother. Take it if you can. Show me you are not the weakling I know you to be and I shall step aside."

Nick did not move.

"Come on, little brother. What are you waiting for? Time is running out."

Just then, something snapped in Nicholas. A guttural roar came from deep inside him. Age-old pain and quelled anger erupted in an explosion of rage. Charging toward his brother, he lunged, not for the satchel, but for Simon. They tumbled to the ground, battling their emotions and each other, neither possessing the strength for the struggle, but neither willing to give up the fight.

They rolled in the snow and fought with the last of their might, so matched in their sheer lack of skill and energy, it became clear that neither one would win.

In the scuffle, the satchel dropped. Nick caught sight of it, rolled and grabbed it before Simon could stop him.

With one last rush of strength, Nick stood in triumph, holding the bag in the air. Simon grabbed his staff from the ground and pulled himself to his feet, planting himself between Nick and the marker-stone.

Nicholas peered at his brother in disbelief. "You would go back on your word? You would stop me, even now, after I have met your challenge and prevailed?"

With both hands, Simon raised his staff across his body, barring his brother's way. "Don't go near the marker stone, Nick. I'm warning you."

Nicholas stepped back, feeling the weight of deep sorrow and utter exhaustion draining his last bit of strength.

"What will you do?" Nick rasped. "Hold me here at bay until we both freeze to death?"

Simon laughed. "Nothing as dramatic as that, dear brother. I need only detain you until nightfall. After tonight, Grandfather's magic will be gone forever. That's right, time's up." He glanced at the setting sun. "When the day is done and night has finally fallen, so will Christmas. The marker-stone will go dark, the magic will die, the cave will be sealed forever, and I shall finally be free."

Nicholas shook his head. "Free from what, Simon?"

"When Christmas is dead, no one will have to endure the curse of becoming Santa Claus ever again."

"Is that it? You see our family's destiny as a curse?"

"Isn't it? An entire family's fate sealed with the birth of one child, one gift, centuries ago, leading to what? Generations of simpleton toymakers toiling away in drudgery, not one of them able to choose their own path in life? Each son following blindly in the rut carved out by the father before him! Bah! Christmas is for irritating children and pathetic men with no aspirations of wealth and success! Not me! I was destined for greater things!"

"So you stole the heart of the star key to ensure the magic would not be restored and then left Carrington, but only after shutting down Grandfather's workshop so that I, and half the town, ended up on the streets? Why Simon? Why do you hate Christmas so much? Why can't you just let me try? You wouldn't have to do a thing. I'll do it all. You can go back to wherever you came from and live your life. The curse, for you, will be broken. Let me save the magic of Christmas before it's too late!"

"No!"

"Why?" pleaded Nicholas. "Why not?"

"Because she'll die all over again!" shrieked Simon, pressing his palms to his temples. "I've got to stop it from happening!"

CHAPTER TWENTY-SIX
THE CHRISTMAS GHOST

In The Great Toymakers' Hall, now shrouded in inky darkness, the painted machinery caught the tawny glow of an oil lamp as Will crept in through the massive front doors, left open from the previous visit. He looked around and then motioned for the others to follow, calling out, "All clear!"

Becca, Fiona, and Ben entered wide-eyed, all carrying oil lamps borrowed from The Grand's central supply cabinet.

"Is he here?" Becca whispered.

"Who?" asked William.

Becca shivered. "That mean old man."

"Simon? No Bec," whispered William. "He's not here."

"How do you know?"

"I just do."

"If no one's here, why are we whispering?"

Will grinned. "You don't want to wake the ghost, do you?"

"Ghost?" Becca gulped. "What Ghost?"

"You've never heard of the Christmas Ghost?" said Ben, chiming in. "It wakes once a year in December and haunts children who don't believe in Santa Claus. Do you believe?"

"Yes," said Becca, "but I don't like ghosts. They scare me."

"Don't worry, Bec. The Christmas Ghost wouldn't dare come around any of us."

"Why not?"

"Because we all still believe. Right?"

Nods and grins all around.

"Wait." Will's hand went up. "Did you hear that?"

"Hear what?" whispered Fiona.

"There it is again," said William, hearing a strange muted clicking noise. "Did you hear it that time?"

"I heard it," said Ben.

Fiona's head bobbed in acknowledgment.

"It's the Christmas Ghost!" cried Becca.

"Sounds like it's coming from over there." Will pointed to an awkward-looking apparatus sprouting all manner of tubes and copper piping.

"I thought you said all the equipment had been turned off," whispered Fiona.

"It *is* off," William snapped.

"Think it's the ghost?" asked Ben, with a conspiratorial grin.

Becca grabbed Fiona's hand. Fiona knelt to whisper "Och, nothin' to fear from ghosts, lassie. They're nae wha'cha think, n' they can do no harm. Only our thoughts make it so."

"I'll investigate," said Will. "Stay here."

Holding his lamp up to light the way, William headed in the direction of the sound.

"What do you see?" called Ben.

William shuffled around to the back of the machine and found Trev lurking in the shadows, her bootlaces caught in the teeth of a sticky gear, her face and hands splotched in engine grease. The clicking sound came every time she tugged to free her foot from its clutches.

William reached down and turned the wheel manually until it let her go, and then called out to the others, "It's the Christmas Ghost! And its name is Trev!"

William pulled her out into the open.

"Willy," said Becca, "that's not the Christmas ghost."

"Are you certain? Sure seems that way to me."

"Trev," said Fiona, offering her a handkerchief to wipe her hands and face. "What are ye doing here?"

"I'm . . . I'm worried about Nicholas."

"Me too," said Becca. "That awful man tried to hurt Willy."

174

"And now he's after Nicholas!" added Ben.

"You mean Klaus? I'm not afraid of that creepy old geezer," said Trev. "He doesn't scare me one bit."

"Trev, we saw you," said Will. "We saw you talking to him in the stables. You were making some sort of deal with him."

Trev straightened her newsy cap, tucking a few stray strands of hair inside. "And what if I was?"

"He wants to close it all down again," said William, his insides twisting, "close it down for good!"

"Fine by me."

Becca frowned. "How can you say that?"

Trev crossed her arms. "Because I don't care."

"I think you do care," said Will, "and that's the problem." He studied her face. "You don't want Nick to be Santa because then you'd have to share him with the whole world."

"You want to know what *I* think?" snapped Trev. "I think you should never have come here in the first place. You don't belong here. Nobody wants you here."

"*We* do," said Ben and Fiona.

Trev spat at Will's feet. "We were all just fine until you came, and we will be again once you leave."

"Trev, stop," said Fiona. "I know yer heart is good. You're better than this."

"It's time to wake up, Fiona. This is who I am."

"Taint so. 'Tis what fear has made ye into, but it's nae who ye truly are."

"Stop it! Stop trying to make me into somethin' better than I am. And while you're at it, stop acting like you're one of my long lost relatives."

"Yer too hard on yer own self, Trev, n' yer too hard on those around ye."

"Listen, I look out for myself. Hard is the only way to survive alone."

"You don't have to be alone," said William. "I'd be your friend if you'd let me."

"I don't need friends."

"Everybody needs friends."

Ben turned to Will. "I'll take her back to the hotel. Mr. Staub can look after her until we figure out what to do."

175

"—No, wait," said Trev. "Let me stay. Nicholas is, well, he's all I got. I need to be here when he gets back."

Ben scratched his cheek. "It's up to you, Will."

William weighed the moment. *This*, he thought, is what Father called a 'turning point incident' where you can either make someone into 'an enemy or a friend.'

Fiona moved to stand beside Trev. "Let her stay. She's as much a part of this as we are." Fiona retrieved a silver locket from her apron and placed it in Trev's palm.

"What's this?" Trev opened the locket and stared at the picture inside. "Is . . . is this . . . ?"

"Aye, 'tis yer mum. Merry Yule, me dear."

After an awkward silence, Trev whispered, "Thank you, Fiona."

Fiona gave her a hug. "No one should forget their mum."

Trev looked at William. "I need to stay. It's my fault he's in danger."

William nodded his consent.

"It was you!" cried Becca, finally working it out. Her face contorted at the betrayal. "You're the reason Simon's here! You told him what we are trying to do!"

"It's true," admitted Trev. "I did. And now . . . I just wanna make it right."

"But why? Why would you want to ruin Christmas?"

"Because if Nicholas becomes Santa Claus, he won't be just Nick anymore. He'll be somebody else. Someone I've never known. He'll have what he has always wanted, and then he won't need me. I couldn't bear that!"

"How do you think he'll feel when he finds out you betrayed him?" said Ben.

"The only thing that matters now," said Will, intervening, "is that Nicholas is okay."

"That's all I want," said Trev. "Tell me what to do."

"Haven't you done enough? None of this would be hap—"

"Ben, stop," said Will in a tone of authority that even Becca had never heard before. He softened his voice before continuing. "We're all scared. None of us want anything bad to happen to Nicholas. Placing blame will only make things worse." He turned to Trev. "I wish it weren't so, but there's nothing we can do now. Simon went up the mountain to stop Nick from bringing back the magic. And Nick said the magic is dying, so there will be no more chances after this. If he doesn't retrieve the magic tonight, it will be gone forever."

Trev gasped. "I . . . I didn't know. I swear."

"Nobody knew," said Will.

"I don't care about the magic anymore," cried Becca, "I just want Nicholas to come home!"

"'Tis for the two of 'em to work out now," said Fiona putting an arm around Becca. "Brother to brother."

Will's mouth fell open. "Oh no."

Becca stared up at her brother. "What's wrong, Willy?"

"Each piece fit inside the other," Will recited. "To honor the bond of brother to brother!"

"That's from Nick's Christmas story," said Trev, "about the star and how it got its magic."

"Nicholas thinks the magic is dying because it has been dormant too long, but . . ."

"But what?" said Trev.

"I think there's more to it than that. I didn't see it until now. The Christmas story has been trying to warn us all along. It says the star was made in three parts to 'honor the bond of brother to brother,' but that bond was broken a long time ago."

"Are you saying, even if they unite the three parts in time, the star key won't work unless—"

"—unless they mend the rift between 'em!" finished Fiona.

Will nodded. "They have to forgive each other. They have to become brothers again. I think it's the only way to save the magic!"

"If you're right," said Trev, "then it's over. Simon won't do it. He'll never forgive Nick. Hate is all he has left."

CHAPTER TWENTY-SEVEN
THE BROKEN BOND

The brother's stood face to face, in the eye of the storm.

"Who are you talking about, Simon? Stop *what* from happening again?" Nick's voice reverberated off the rock walls around them.

"You don't want to know," said Simon. "You never did. You just want to go on believing in your perfect little world."

"Maybe you're right. Maybe that's how it was. But I've changed. I want to know the truth now, Simon. Why do you hate Christmas so much?"

"If there was never such a thing as Christmas," yelled Simon, "our lives would be as they should be! You don't know what happened! You can't understand!"

"Then tell me. Help me understand."

"Christmas destroyed my life, so I destroyed Christmas!"

"How could Christmas destroy anything?"

"Oh, it can. It has."

"How?"

"How indeed," Simon sneered, stepping closer. Then, lowering his voice to a snarl, he said, "You never asked what happened to our mother, our father, not once in all the years you were growing up. Why is that?"

"Grandfather said they died shortly after I was born."

"No, they died *the night* you were born."

Nick shivered. "What?"

"Christmas Eve. Mother in childbirth, and Father in the storm trying to get to get help."

"Help?"

"With the birth. Something went terribly wrong. Father never told me what happened, but I could see the fear in his eyes before he left the cabin. I begged him not to go. I pleaded. I cried. But nothing I said made any difference."

"Where was Grandfather?"

"Our precious Grandfather was out delivering gifts to the children of the world." He spat out the words as if the bitterness of them had become intolerable. "You were restless. You couldn't wait. You had to be born on Christmas Eve. If Grandfather had been there instead of out delivering gifts, he could have taken the sleigh and gone for help. Mother and Father wouldn't have died, and I wouldn't have been left all alone. Alone with—"

"Me," said Nick with a sickening realization. "It's not just Christmas you hate . . . it's me. That's it, isn't it? When we were young you used to push me away. Whenever I asked you to help me make something or even just to play, you never wanted to have anything to do with me."

"You were free," said Simon with disdain. "Free from the moment you were born. You could choose. Choose what to do, whom to be. I was the eldest son. I had to be what they wanted me to be. I had to follow in Grandfather's footsteps."

"What's so wrong with that?" asked Nicholas.

"From the moment I was born my path was laid out for me. I always had to do this, do that, learn my craft. 'Someday you will be like me,' Father would say, 'so eat your vegetables and do your chores and mind your manners and work in the workshop and don't talk back.' I was going to be 'somebody important' someday."

"How could that be a bad thing?"

"They never stopped to ask me what *I* wanted. They never wanted to know me." Simon put his fist to his chest. "Me. They were so busy grooming me to be one of them, they never even noticed I had . . . a way with numbers, an eye for detail, a sharp mind. I was quick with words and clever with things. They never once said 'Simon, you could be a successful merchant, or a brilliant banker, or even a great inventor!' I knew my future had nothing to do with toys. I used to dream of someday showing them what I could do. They'd finally see something I accomplished and say to me, 'We never knew, Simon. You go on and be who you want to be and we will still love you.' But I never got the chance."

He paused, putting his emotions in check. "After Father died, it only became more important for me to learn the family business. I hated it. Every second of it. And there you were, playing with the toys, growing up happy, content. Everybody loved you. Everybody."

"Except *you*."

"I knew you would be able to choose your own destiny and that made me hate mine all the more. You were free, Nicholas."

"No, I wasn't."

"You could choose. You could be anything you wanted to be."

"No I couldn't!" yelled Nick. "Because the only thing I ever wanted to be was *you!*"

Simon stopped, halted by his brother's words. In the silence that followed, he stood staring at the dirty snow around his boots, as if trying to make sense of the patterns his footprints had made.

Finally, he returned his gaze to Nicholas. "Why would you want to be me?"

"You were the one who had the honor of carrying on the family tradition. You were the chosen one. You were special. Not me. I was just Nicholas Nobody. If you had only asked me, I would have switched places with you in an instant."

"Switched places?" He glanced at the marker, his heart turning as cold as the stone. "No, Nicholas. I can't let you bring the magic back." He aimed his staff once again, this time straight at Nick's throat. "Give me the satchel."

Nick felt a different kind of sadness seep into his bones as he tossed the star back to his brother. The kind of sadness one feels for the loss of a future that might have been.

Simon caught it with his free hand. "Now back away from the stone."

Nick took a step back. "I don't want to fight anymore."

"I said back away!"

Nick took another few steps back.

Simon placed himself between Nick and the marker stone.

"What are you so afraid of, Simon? You're not that little boy anymore. You can walk away from all of this."

"It's not that simple."

"Why not? I won't ask anything of you. Let me do this."

"No. It would all start up again."

"What would?"

Simon looked away.

"What would, Simon? What are you talking about?"

Simon's hands began to shake. He leaned heavily, falling against the marker stone, holding onto his staff as if it were a lifeline. He looked now like the elderly man he was; once tall and imposing, Nick saw who he'd become; a shell of a man, as hollow, dark and heartless as Nick's half of the star key.

"What would start up again, Simon?" Nicholas repeated, this time with more compassion.

"The pain, her screams, his tears, the cry of the howling wind, steam rising off scalding water, blood and broken glass, horrific images that haunted me every day of my life until I left Carrington."

"You . . . you were there," said Nicholas in a devastating realization. "You were there when she died."

"I was the only one there. Father left to get help, and I was alone. I was nine years old. I didn't know how to help her, how to stop the pain. I stayed at her side the whole time, but there was nothing I could do."

His voice was so weak now, Nick had to strain to hear it.

"I . . . I couldn't save her."

"I'm so sorry, Simon. I never knew."

"I can still hear her screams and her cries to God . . . to take her, but spare her child. And He did," Simon rasped through clenched teeth. "He granted her wish. He took *her*. And saved *you*."

Nicholas could see it all in his mind's eye now, as if it were happening right before him . . .

Wind raged outside the cabin. Little Simon knelt at his mother's side, silent tears streaming down his cheeks, as he watched her life slip away.

"Nicholas," she rasped with her last breath. "The child. His . . . name . . . is . . . Nicholas."

Nick's eyes welled. "She . . . she named me? I thought Grandfather named me."

Simon shook with the memory. "Her last words, her last thoughts were of you. Not the son by her side who loved her more than life itself. Her last act in this world was to save your life and forfeit her own."

"You never told me. Why didn't you tell me, Simon? How could I have known? I understand now what you've endured—the fear, the pain of losing her, a pain I alone was spared."

Simon rubbed his eyes red. "When we learned Father had perished in the storm that same night, Grandfather said I had to be brave, had to be strong, that it was up to me to carry on. I never got to cry for them. I was nine years old, Nicky! I wasn't allowed to be angry that they left me. I wasn't allowed to grieve, and you—"

"I never even got the chance to know them! Cried Nick. "At least you knew them. You knew what it was like to feel their love. I would have given anything to have known them as long as you did."

"And I would have given anything to have been spared the pain of losing them."

Nick closed his eyes against the sting of tears. "I wish I had known."

Simon dropped his staff, trembling not only from the cold, but from the unbearable pain seizing his heart. "I never told you because I . . . I needed to hate you . . . I needed to blame you."

"If it wasn't for me, they'd still be alive?" rasped Nicholas. "That's what you've been wishing all these years? That I'd never been born?"

Simon didn't answer, but Nick saw the truth of it in his brother's eyes.

"You could have been a brother to me, Simon. We could have been a family. But instead, you just left. Grandfather died and you saw your chance. You didn't say a word. You just took it all like a thief in the night. Even the star key. I . . . I lost everything that day. Everything!" Nicholas stopped to calm his spirit before continuing. "But I survived. I was thirteen years old when you left me to fend for myself on the streets, but I found a way to heal, and it made me strong. But you . . . you let it take you. You let it destroy your heart."

"Nicky, I—"

"And now you want to keep me from the only thing that ever meant anything to me, the one thing that can bring this old man's life any meaning." Nicholas gestured to the cave. "This is all I have left. You've taken everything else."

"Not everything," said Simon.

"You have been so cruel for so long, it has turned your heart black. It's been eating away at your soul all these years and now there's nothing left. I don't know how I ever looked up to you. I can't believe I ever wanted to be like you. In every way that counts, you are a wretched human being."

"I didn't steal the key, Nicky."

Nicholas blinked. "What?"

"You said I took the star key." Simon pulled the centerpiece of the star from his satchel. "I didn't steal it. Grandfather gave it to me. You need to know that."

"What does it matter now?"

"It matters to me. I am everything you say, but not that. I've never stolen anything in my life. Everything I have, I earned. I didn't steal the key. I took it with me because Grandfather said I must never let it out of my possession."

Nicholas peered at his brother, finally stitching all the pieces together. "Grandfather told me the same thing when he gave me *my* piece of the star. He knew. He knew this would happen."

"That's not all he knew," said Simon. "He told me that he gave you the second piece and that the day would come when we would meet the man who carried the third. He said until that day I must keep the heart of the key safe. So . . . I took it with me when I left."

"But don't you see, Simon, that means something. You saved it. You held on to it all these years. You could have destroyed it and destroyed the magic of Christmas right along with it, but you didn't. Some part of you must have held on to the smallest of hope that Christmas might someday be restored. Some part of you wants us to be a family again."

"You're wrong. I have no family."

"How can you say that?"

"Our family died long ago, and with it died that part of me that believed I could ever belong."

"But don't you want a second chance, Simon?"

"If life has taught me anything, it's taught me there's no such thing as a second chance. And even if there were, it's too late." He turned to go, and with his back to Nick he said, "If I can get off this cursed mountain without breaking my neck or freezing to death, I am going to return to Paris, resume my life, and forget this day ever happened."

"You won't forget, Simon, and neither will I."

"I shall try," he said simply, and started away.

"What do you do?" Nick called out. "In Paris."

Simon stopped but did not turn. "I own a successful chain of banks," he said over his shoulder. "I've done quite well for myself."

"Are you . . . happy there?"

"I've accomplished everything I've set out to do. I've become the man I always wanted to be. A man of affluence. A man of position. A man of power." He took another step.

"But . . . are you happy, Simon?"

"Sufficiently," was all he said.

"Then I am happy for you," said Nick.

"Doubtful."

"I guess it doesn't matter if you believe me, but it's true," said Nicholas. "I always wondered what happened to you. I always hoped you were all right . . . that you did well out in the world. I hoped you found whatever it was you were looking for. I tried to picture you happy, with a wife, children, a nice home—"

"No wife. No children. Never had the inclination to marry. But a nice home, that I have. Nothing but the best. I have everything I want."

"Then I suppose you really don't need a second chance."

Simon looked down at his piece of the star key cradled in his black-gloved hand. "No. I don't." He wrapped his fingers around the heart of the star and squeezed. "But you do." He slowly turned to face his brother. "I never told you this, but . . . you look like him."

"Who?"

"Our father."

"I do?"

"Now more than ever." Simon peered squint-eyed at his little brother. He finally knew what he had failed to understand in all the years that came before. "It was you. It was you all along, Nick. If I'd have had my eyes open I would have seen it."

"Seen what?" Nicholas looked down at his grandfather's coat, which had magically remained clean and pristine through the trials on the mountain. He pulled the sides together as much for modesty as for warmth.

"You were the one." Simon gestured to his brother's radiant face—his cheeks, red and chapped from the cold, his bushy beard dusted with snow. "Grandfather had it wrong. I'll bet you're great with children too. Am I right? Tell them stories? Fix their toys?"

Nicholas shrugged in shy acknowledgment.

"It was you all along. You were destined to follow in Grandfather's footsteps, not me."

"No. I tried. I failed."

"Not yet. There are still a few moments of light left." Simon pointed to the final sliver of sun about to vanish behind the ridge. "Huh." He looked down at the marker stone as a spark of inner realization lit his face with a wry smile.

Nick took a step forward. "What?"

"*This* is what Grandfather had in mind all along when he split up the pieces of the key. Clever old dog. He knew we would have to come together to make it work."

"Brother to brother," uttered Nicholas.

Simon opened his hand, revealing his piece of the star. "Take it." Seeing Nick's hesitation, he added, "It doesn't belong to me, Nicky. It never did. As Grandfather said, I was only meant to keep it safe. And I did that. My part is done. You were right. If I give you the key, I can walk away from all this. I can finally be free."

Nick looked at Simon, then at the heart of the star in his palm, and thought any second now he might wake to find this has all been some strange dream. He had wished, hoped for, and imagined this moment a thousand times over, and now, he couldn't help but wonder if it was actually happening.

Nicholas bowed his head to honor the immense significance of the gift and took his brother's piece of the ancient key.

Simon bowed back, uttered a raspy "farewell, brother," and turned once again to go.

"Simon, wait!" called Nick. "This was Grandfather's final gift to us—to bring us together, here on Christmas Mountain. We should . . . do this together. For Grandfather. For Father."

Simon stopped, hung his head, and let out his breath, creating a puff of white fog as he exhaled. "No," he said slowly, "not for them . . . but for our mother."

Nick nodded, his eyes shining. From his coat pocket, Nick produced his half of the star—which already contained the Hillermans' piece—and stared at it, for it had already begun to glow with a soft blue light.

He held the two parts side by side, took a deep breath and pressed Simon's centerpiece into the hollow heart of the star.

As it snapped into place, the three parts fused together, and the completed star burst into brilliance.

The last glimmer of radiance from the setting sun flared white-hot, blinding them with its final stab of light, and then went dark—and with it, the star.

"No!" cried Nick. "We're too late!"

"Maybe not. Look!" Simon pointed to the marker stone, glimmering with the last wisp of diminishing magic. "Hurry!" In that split-second, Simon acted on sheer instinct. He reached out, slapped his hand over his brother's and forced it down onto the surface of the stone.

Two hands working as one, they pressed the key into the star-shaped depression at the apex of the marker.

Light burst forth, streaming through the star's intricately carved design, casting lacy blue and white patterns on the rock overhang above.

Nick squinted as the light intensified. A rush of energy emanated from the star. It permeated every cell of his being, filling him with centuries of ancestral knowledge and wisdom; all their hope, their joy, their triumphs and failures, their clarity of purpose through hardship and adversity, their giving hearts, their unshakable faith, and their connection to the Christmas magic.

It all came alive within him. And the souls of all those who stood in this place before him, to activate that magic, joined with them now in a celebration of light.

There could only be one perfect word to describe what he'd just received . . . Love.

186

He gazed at his older brother and saw that he too had received the ancestral transference from the star. Nick watched as the miracle of this love filled Simon's dark heart, healing his wounds, and transforming the twisted features of his face into a face of compassion and understanding.

"I . . . never knew," gasped Simon. "All this time, I never understood." His eyes filled. "Nicky, your beard . . . it's turned pure white, and your hair as well!"

"Look!" Nicholas pointed to Simon's black staff lying stark against the snow where he had dropped it.

It too had begun to change. An opaque, milky smoothness started at the bottom and oozed across its length, transmuting every inch until the entire shaft was a luminous white. When the metamorphosis reached the top, it revealed a red ruby and a green emerald set side by side within a silver-and-gold-twined spiral, crowning the staff.

Simon bent on one knee, retrieved the staff and held it out to Nicholas. "I believe this is yours."

Nick shot him a questioning look.

"It belonged to our grandfather, and those who came before him. All who have carried the Christmas magic have carried this staff."

Nick received the staff with a noble nod to his brother, feeling like he had just become the crown prince of Carrington. With his heart full and bursting, he smiled, utterly speechless. None of his dreams had ever come close to the perfect beauty of this moment.

At that instant, the wind and snow began to flurry again, creating a whirlwind around them, picking up leaves, rocks, and dirt. The brothers clutched the marker stone for support.

"We need to find shelter!" Simon shouted over the roar, watching the trees whip in the fierce winds.

"Faith, Brother!" yelled Nicholas. "Have faith!"

Amid the din of the storm, Nick barely heard the sound of rock scraping on rock. He turned toward the cave to see the mammoth stone gateway starting to open. The same sapphire light that had emanated from the Book of Christmas and the marker stone, now escaped from the cave, bathing them in a radiant blue aura.

Simon, still staring at nature's fury, called out to his brother, "It's getting worse!"

"Turn around," said Nick, but his brother didn't hear him.

"How are we going to get down the mountain in this?" yelled Simon.

"The same way our grandfather did every Christmas Eve!" Nick put a hand on his brother's shoulder. "Turn around!"

As the stone doors opened, a gilded sleigh, surrounded by the silver and gold treasures of the cave, dazzled their eyes.

Nine sleeping reindeer began to stir, beckoned out of their long slumber by the awakened magic.

Draped on its own rosewood stand hung a majestic cream-colored, floor-length, hooded cloak, lined with fleece, trimmed in white fur, and adorned with the Claus family trademark design of holly leaf and berries embroidered along its edges. Nick smiled as a spark of memory quivered through him, for he'd forgotten the glorious cloak his grandfather donned every Christmas Eve before climbing into the sleigh.

Simon blinked. "I've never seen anything so beautiful!"

"Magnificent!" said Nicholas, transfixed.

As they walked toward the light, they began to see the transparent shimmering images of their mother and father, standing next to the sleigh, smiling at their two sons. Behind them stood Grandfather, and behind him, emerged every soul who had carried the magic of their family legacy, reaching back to the three brothers, where it all began. They had come to witness the next Claus taking the reins as they'd done for millennia.

And right there with them stood Garrett Hillerman, brimming with pride for the brothers as they entered the cave.

"Oh Simon, we did it!" said Nick. "The circle is finally complete again."

As the stone doors began to close behind them, Simon turned to his younger brother with a question.

"Go on," said Nicholas in his knowing way. "Ask."

"The key . . . it doesn't work without all three pieces. You must have already had the third piece of the star in place."

"Indeed."

"But how did you find it?"

"With a bit of heavenly assistance," said Nick, flashing a smile in Garrett's direction. "We have much to discuss, brother!"

CHAPTER TWENTY-EIGHT
THE FINAL GIFT

Trev scowled. "I swear, Will, I would never have told Simon anything if I had known he was going to hurt Nick."

"But he didn't, Treveena."

The deep voice came from directly behind them. They whirled around to find Nicholas and Simon standing in the entrance of The Great Toymakers' Hall. Nick held high a shining silver lantern from the Christmas cave, which cast a soft, warm glow on all their faces.

Ben snickered. "Treveena?"

"Shut it, *Benedict*," said Trev.

"Nicholas!" the group chorused, dazzled by his new Santa regalia, including cloak and staff. The air sparkled around him, and his smile shone bright as the sun.

Simon stood beside him, also dressed in holiday attire, though admittedly more subdued, with his burgundy tie and dark green waistcoat hanging loosely on his slim frame.

"Together," said Nick, "we were able to save the magic of Christmas!"

Trev ran to hug Nicholas. "I'm so glad you're all right."

Will joined them. "You did it, Nicholas! You really did it!"

"*We* did it. And it's all true, good Will. We found it all there waiting for us, just as Grandfather said it would be; the sleigh, the reindeer, the magic, everything!"

189

"I wish I could have been there to see that," said William.

Nick nodded again. "Someday you shall be."

Just then Nora stormed in. "William Thomas Hillerman! I suspected you two might be here. You should not have come without my permission!" Then, seeing Simon, she stiffened. "Sir, the children meant no disrespect. I will not allow you to harm them." She placed herself between Simon and her children.

"Mother," said William, "it's okay. Nicholas and Simon came here together."

Nora turned. "Nicholas? Is this true? Have you reconciled?"

"Indeed, ma'am, and we have brought the magic back from Christmas Mountain."

"That is . . . good news," she said cautiously, but it was then she saw the change in Simon's face, the compassion in his eyes.

He took hat in hand and said, "My deepest apologies for frightening you and the children, ma'am."

"Everything's all right now," said William. "Honest."

"Not quite, young man," said Nora, in a tone Will and Becca knew all too well. "What are you and your sister doing here after I made it abundantly clear that you were both to wait for me at the hotel?"

"Well," started William, "when you said you had to take care of some business in town, we decided we had some business of our own to take care of."

"Does your business have anything to do with the unruly bunch of bandits I ran into out on the rail-sleigh platform?"

William perked up. "Oh! They're here? That's great! I asked Finn to round them up."

"I know," said Nora, "They told me what the lot of you are up to. I asked them to wait outside until I had a chance to assess the situation. I can't imagine why you would bring them here knowing it wasn't safe, William."

"I invited the town kids because we're going to need their help if we want to get everything done by midnight!"

"William is right," said Nicholas. "We'll take any and all assistance that is offered!"

"Well, Nicholas," said Nora, "I'm fairly certain you will have all the help you need."

"Oh?" replied Nick, raising an eyebrow.

"I spoke with the townspeople. Many of them remember what your grandfather did for the town and their families, and they're eager to help. But that's not all I did when I was in town." Nora pulled a rolled piece of parchment from her bag and offered it to Nick.

"What's this?" asked Nick, handing the lantern to William. He took the scroll and tugged on the thin red ribbon that held the document in place.

"That is the deed to The Carrington Grand Hotel, and nearly half the town as well. I had no idea Garrett purchased so much property here, but it's all yours now. With the exception of that sweet Queen Anne house at the end of Holly Lane that just happens to be vacant. It's almost as though Garrett picked it out especially for us. He knows how much I love Queen Anne architecture."

"He does, indeed," Nick said with a twinkle in his eye. "Dear Nora, what you have done is very generous, but not necessary. I have everything I want right here."

"It was Garrett's idea," said Nora. "He wrote of it in his letters to Mr. Staub." She reached out to touch his shoulder. "This is Garrett's final Christmas gift to you. It's what he wanted, Nicholas."

Nick put his hand over his heart in gratitude. "Thank you, Nora."

Garrett's translucent being shimmered into view, grinning in agreement. Though Nick was the only soul in the room who could see him, all those present felt inexplicable warmth and joy lifting their spirits.

Nora smiled. "You're a rich man now, Nicholas."

"Even when I had nothing, I was a very rich man." He gathered William, Becca, and Trev around him. "It has always been about the children."

"Oh, the children!" Nora exclaimed. She hurried out to the railway platform and returned with a whole flock of town kids, led by Finn and followed by a smiling Mr. Staub.

Colin, Luca, Roger, little Jonah, who was all better now, Pawny and Mitsy, and the twins, Aldo and Ghita, along with several other new recruits, marched in, all carrying bulky white sacks of mail—the smaller the child, the smaller the sack.

191

Finn dumped the largest of the sacks out on a table in front of Nicholas.

"Mr. Staub?" said Nicholas, surprised to see the stoic hotel manager grinning at the little ones gathered around him. "Look at you. I thought you didn't like children."

"Well." Mr. Staub cleared his throat. "I thought it time for a change of heart."

Nick shook his hand with zeal. "Welcome to Kringle Towne!" He turned to face the children. "It was good of you all to come, but I don't understand." Nick peered down at the heap of mail sprawled on the workbench before him. He picked a random envelope from the pile and read the addressee aloud. "To Santa Claus at the North Pole?" He picked up another. "To Father Christmas? Kris Kringle? Saint Nick?" He continued to read all the Santa names from around the world, in their native tongue, for now that he was the one true Santa, he spoke every language there was to speak.

"We thought we'd pick up your mail," said William, with a wide grin. "The post office was very grateful."

Nicholas looked at the multitude of sacks on the floor with a sense of bewilderment. "All the letters, they never stopped coming?"

"Never," said Mr. Staub. "They've just been sending them back to the parents all these years."

William plucked a letter from the table. "So Nick, don't you think we ought to get started?"

"Excellent suggestion!" said Nick. "It is Christmas Eve, after all, and the hour of departure is approaching!"

Nicholas stood by to throw one of the two main power switches while Simon manned the other.

"Everybody ready?" called Nicholas.

A cheer rose up from the children as Nicholas and Simon heaved the breakers into their ON position.

Once again The Great Toymakers' Hall burst to life with lights sparkling, gears turning, whistles tooting, and steam billowing. The town kids all applauded.

As William and Becca opened Nick's mail, Nora retrieved the mysterious feather pen from its place on the bookstand and turned to a blank page in the register to record all the children's wishes and requests. But as they handed her the first letter, and she brought the quill to the parchment, the words magically appeared in shimmering script across the page.

"With that pen in your hand," said Nicholas, "you have but to think the words and they will appear!"

"Very efficient," said Nora, with a bright smile.

As for the rest, Mr. Staub began inputting information into the Duplagraph machine, Ben and André got straight to work organizing, categorizing, and tagging the toys that rolled down conveyor belts and shot from various shoots and tubes.

Finn and Trev began wrapping the new presents with the help of the town kids, amazed that the bows tied themselves as the fully revitalized Christmas magic provided all the finishing touches.

André took on the task of overseeing the rail-sleigh system since they expected more town folk to show up as the word spread throughout Carrington that the old toy factory was operational again.

And Simon fit right in as the shop foreman, making sure everything ran smoothly and stayed on schedule.

Nora put a hand on Nick's arm to get his attention.

"Things are coming along quite splendidly, I am pleased to report. With all the magic afoot, I believe we will be ready in time!"

"Excellent news!" said Nicholas.

"Nicholas, have you seen William Thomas?"

"Hmm," he said, thinking it over. "I may have spotted him heading toward Fiona's impromptu cafeteria. She set it up in one of the adjacent rooms." Nick pointed. "It has all manner of tasty treats."

"That must be where he is. My boy has a hidden talent for locating baked goods." Nora giggled. "Thank you, Nicholas."

"You are very welcome. I believe he has something he'd like to share with you."

CHAPTER TWENTY-NINE
A FATHER'S VISION

As Nora went to find William, Nick turned to climb a flight of metal steps leading up to a supply loft—a place he had gone many times as a child to watch the factory buzz along. He needed a moment to collect his thoughts and take it all in.

There he stood on the walk high above it all to survey the activity in the hall. After so many years dormant, it warmed his soul to watch the old workshop dance with a life of its own again, and best of all, to see it filled with people who loved and cared about Christmas as much as he did, all working together in harmony. What a joy it was to finally feel that he had, at last, come home.

Nora searched the extraneous rooms and found her son right where Nicholas said he would be—in the makeshift cafeteria Fiona had set up.

Sandwich wedges, rolled meats, fruits and melons, gingerbread and butterzopf, Christmas cookies and fresh baked apple strudel, not to mention Nick's favorite—hot chocolate with peppermint sticks—all spread across several decorated countertops.

Nora retrieved two cups of cocoa from the counter and joined her son at a nearby table.

"Hungry?" she said, but then saw he had no sweets or treats. She set the hot cocoa in front of him. "Your favorite."

"Thank you."

William's serious expression pressed on her heart. "Are you all right, sweetheart? What is that you're reading?"

"It's my Christmas present from Nicholas. It's a letter from—" Will's throat constricted.

"What is it, William?"

"It's . . . it's from Father."

"What?"

"It's a letter Father sent to Nicholas twelve years ago."

Nora shook her head. "I don't understand."

William offered the envelope as proof.

"This . . . this *is* your father's handwriting," she said. She touched the postmark. "He posted this the day after you were born?" Nora read the address on the envelope.

To Mr. Nicholas Claus
Also known as St. Nick,
In care of The Carrington Grand Hotel,
One Twenty-two Green Garland Lane,
Carrington, Switzerland.

She looked up, aghast. "Also known as St. Nick? He knew? Garrett knew who Nicholas was all along? But how?"

"Read it," said Will, offering her the letter. "Let Father tell you."

Nora hesitated, but only to catch her breath. She took the letter from her son and began to read aloud . . .

Dear Nicholas,

This day, the twenty-seventh of November, in the year of our Lord, Eighteen hundred and eighty-seven, I received my third gift from God. The first being my life, the second, my loving wife, and now, our son, born this autumn day, as pure and as beautiful as the breath of angels.

Now, you may ask, and it would be proper to do so, why I pen this letter to you, a veritable stranger, on this most momentous occasion, and I promise, by the end of this correspondence, you

195

will know what miracle motivates me to do so, but first permit me to introduce myself.

My Name is Garrett William Hillerman, and although I have never had the privilege of meeting you in person, we are far from strangers.

You see, sometimes I, like you, glimpse things the way they will someday be. And I saw one such vision as I held my son in my arms for the first time.

I saw you, Nicholas, in the lobby of The Carrington Grand Hotel and my son beside you as a young man. You sat together by a warm fire and spoke of important things. And between your two hearts there shone a golden light...a light that connected you, a light that reached back to the beginning of time.

I too was there, but only in spirit. And I felt great love and gratitude watching the two of you together, knowing that you had finally found each other...that you'd help each other to create the family I have always dreamed of, a family with a long, rich history of kindness and giving. I knew that you would be there to guide each other and keep each other safe. I knew you needed one another, without truly knowing why.

Before my vision cleared, I caught one more fleeting glimpse of the future as I held my newborn son.

I know for you there will someday be a grand reunion, and a joyful celebration will take place.

I myself won't be able to attend, but I shall send my son in my stead. And he will carry on for me, and be what I could not be. He will be your new hope, and restore Carrington to its former glory. He will be the new bearer of the Christmas story.

Please tell William, my son, I love him, and that I am proud of who he has become. And even though I cannot be there with him, I am a part of everything he's done, and everyone he loves.

And you, Nicholas, my dear friend, will understand what all this means when it is right for you to know.

In the interim, I shall keep my promise—the promise I made to you so many years ago as a boy—for I have become what I always knew I would be...a successful businessman, and I am,

*finally, in a position to help. So I make this promise to you again
. . . when the time comes, I will save The Carrington Grand,
and do my part to help restore the magic of Christmas.*

   You and William must do the rest.

   Sincerely,

   Garrett W. Hillerman

   Charleston, South Carolina

Nora folded the letter and returned it to its envelope, her breath shallow, her vision blurred by tears that washed away the deep sorrow she'd carried since Garrett's death.

William's mouth tightened. "He knew he was going to die. Why didn't he tell us?"

Nora smiled through her tears. She knew the answer. It was simply who Garrett was . . . who he had always been.

"Oh William, he didn't want us to live in fear. He wanted us to celebrate life to its fullest while he was here. Don't you see? If he had told us, it would have changed everything . . . the way we looked at him, the way we treated him. We would have wanted so much to protect him that we would not have allowed him to live the life he wanted to live in the time that he had left. It was his choice. He created his life on *his* terms. I admire him for that, now more than ever." She took William's hand into hers. "Do you understand, sweetheart?"

"I think so."

She looked deep into her son's eyes. "I believe you do."

"May I intrude?" said Nick, appearing in the doorway.

"Of course," said Nora. "Join us. Please."

Nick sat across from them at the table.

"Would you like a cup of cocoa?" Nora asked, rising from her chair.

"How could I ever say no that?"

"Can I have some too?" asked Becca, who had followed Nicholas in.

"Of course, sweet girl," said Nora, her arms opening to invite a hug. Becca scuttled into her embrace. They returned to the table with two additional cups of cocoa.

Nora touched Garrett's letter on the table. "It all makes sense now," she said to Nick. "Why he did what he did. All of it.

Why he brought us here. Why he purchased The Grand. Why he insisted that nothing be removed from the lobby." She looked at Nicholas, smiling at the thought. "Why you were listed as one of those things. But . . . why didn't you say something?"

Nick gave a little tilt of the head. "Why didn't I tell you that your husband believes in Santa Claus and, just in case you were wondering, I'm him?"

"Oh, I do see your point," said Nora.

"I knew you had to come to it on your own."

"You were right." She glanced at the envelope on the table. "And thank you for keeping his letter safe all these years. To hear it in his own words . . . means everything."

"It got me through some tough times, that letter."

Nora's face lit up. "Well, the tough times have ended."

"Indeed they have, Mrs. Hillerman. And it is because of you and your children, and of course, Garrett. You have all been a blessing beyond measure." Nick paused, his eyes full of hope. "Might I . . . ask a question?"

"On one condition," she said with an impish grin. "That you please call me Nora."

"Of course. Nora, forgive my boldness, but I am feeling quite daring since my mountain adventure."

"Go on, Nicholas, ask your question," said an impatient Will, who had already guessed what Nick intended to say.

"Nora, would you and the children consider staying on to help me run Kringle Towne? You can live at The Grand, or here, in a Kringle Cottage, or Carrington. I can offer you your pick of places, as I seem to have recently come into possession of quite a lot of property."

They all smiled at that.

Nick's expression grew serious. "It would please me greatly if you'd consider making Carrington your new home."

Nora thought for a moment. "To be honest, Nicholas, Carrington has felt like home since the moment we arrived. But it's not my decision alone." She turned to her children who'd been listening and had already made up their minds.

"Oh, can we stay, Mama?" said Becca. "Can we?"

"This is the way it's meant to be." Will pointed to the letter. "Father knew."

Nick brought his hands together. "So you'll stay then?"

"Yes," was all Nora managed to say, but it was enough.

"On one condition," said Will, surprising them all.

Nick's eyebrows arched. "What's that?"

William ran out into the workshop while Nick and the others anxiously waited to see what he was up to.

He returned to the café room with Trev in tow.

"On the condition that you let Trev live here too."

"Of course," said Nicholas, rising from his chair. "I wouldn't have it any other way!"

"Really Nick? You're not mad at me for telling Simon what you were doing?" Trev asked, searching Nick's face for forgiveness.

"If you hadn't told Simon, we would never have been able to retrieve the magic and Christmas would be gone forever. Trev, you have been as much a part of saving Christmas as any of us." Nick put one arm around Trev's shoulders and the other around William and Becca. "We're a family now. Nothing will ever change that."

Trev wiped her cheek with a dirty sleeve. "That's all I ever wished for."

"Me too," whispered Nick. "Merry Christmas, Trev."

CHAPTER THIRTY
INTO THE FOLDS OF TIME

They all followed Nicholas out into the workshop where the others were tending to the final gifts on the list.

"That's it," said Simon, pulling a lever. The machinery grinded to a halt. "All done . . . until next year, of course."

"And not a moment too soon," said Mr. Staub, looking at the Christmas Clock. "It's almost midnight!"

Simon smiled at Nicholas, and Nick smiled back, both knowing that the presents were always ready by midnight. 'After all,' said their grandfather every year, 'if the presents weren't ready, it wouldn't be midnight on Christmas Eve!'

"The reindeer have all been fed and watered, harnesses checked—all are ready to go, sir," said André, pleased with his new position. "They are excited to be back on the job. They told me so themselves."

Nicholas chuckled. "Oh, they do have a unique way of communicating, don't they?"

"Yes, sir," said the smiling coachman.

"Yer toy sack is loaded to its very brim," added Fiona. "It made 'nough room fer each n' every gift just as Simon said it would. I snuck a wee peak inside. A sight to behold, it was. Oh, n' if you're still takin' requests for Yule, St. Nicholas, I'll be askin' nothin' more than ta' have one just like it!"

Nicholas laughed. "And nothing would please me more than to grant you that wish, dear Fiona, but there's only one like it in the whole world."

Ben stepped forward with an armful of wrapped gifts. "Just add these to the top and you'll be all set, Nick."

"Thank you, Ben."

Nicholas looked toward the door that led out to the stables. A broad smile spread across his aged face.

Simon winked. "It's time, brother."

Nick turned to the group and called out, "Thank you one and all! Now if you will excuse me, I have a job to do!" He leaned in to whisper to Will. "Always wanted to say that."

"Nicholas?" Will whispered back. "Before you go, may I see the sleigh? I mean if it's allowed."

"Of course!" said Nick, glancing at Nora for permission.

Nora nodded her consent, the proud look in her eyes telling Nick all he needed to know.

"Fetch your coat, good Will, and follow me."

Nicholas and William left The Great Hall and entered a short stone passageway that led directly to the Kringle Towne stables.

Will had never seen such luxurious stables in all his life. He guessed not even a king and queen would have such lavish accommodations for their horses.

"Nothing but the best for our team!" said Nick, reading William's thoughts. He unhooked the heavy latch that held together two sides of a formidable wrought iron gate, then pushed the two halves open and stepped in. With a sweep of his arm, he gestured for William to enter.

Will caught his breath. Here was a legend come to life, a sight he thought to see only and ever in his dreams.

There they were, the nine reindeer, draped in the same posh finery as their surroundings, each fitted with a silver and gold harness, finely detailed in the now familiar holly leaf pattern, and a tasseled red velvet raiment on their backs suitable for royalty.

But it was the sleigh that caught Will's full attention.

The body of the colossal sleigh had a grandeur of style both simple and complex. Strong sweeping lines and spirals in its frame flowed into one another like liquid gold. The mountings and bearings, all etched silver, gleamed in the lamplight.

Will ran a finger along the engraved sideboard panels, painted in rich burgundy and deep Brunswick green, and relieved in white and gold. Its intricate swirl and vine motif echoed the flourishes at the entrance to The Great Toymakers' Hall.

"I've never seen anything so wonderful!" said Will.

"Hop in."

"May I?"

Nick nodded.

The plush interior of red and green velvet crushed in a delicate swirl pattern proved instantly warm and inviting, and a thick white woven coverlet, folded on the far end of the seat, promised to keep the cold at bay.

As Will sat himself down with a little bounce, the first thing he noticed was the display before him. Unlike any sleigh ever built, this sleigh had a front panel complete with gauges, dials, buttons and control levers.

Of course, the most intriguing and exciting aspect about it was that it possessed the adventure of flight, as no sleigh ever could unless imbued with magic. William hoped beyond hope that he might someday experience the full effect of its capabilities. What a marvel it would be to soar above the sleeping world.

Will pointed to a depression in the dash. "There's a space here. Is something missing?"

"Oh, only the most important component for the sleigh!"

Nick disappeared around a corner and returned with a palm-sized clock-like device. He reached over William and popped it into place on the front panel. It seated itself with a magnetic snap.

This timekeeper seemed oddly familiar to Will, and in an instant, he knew why.

"This looks just like the ornament on the tree! What did you call it? The meta . . . ?"

"Metachronome. You are correct, Will. That is precisely what this is."

Nick placed the last three gifts atop the bulging red and green velvet Santa bag weighing down the back compartment, which featured the same delicate swirl pattern as the upholstery in the sleigh. He cinched it up, retrieved the Christmas cloak from the back seat and whisked it over his shoulders, clasping it at the front with a cloakpin that resembled the star key in miniature.

As he slid in beside William, he said, "Remember when I spoke earlier of time moving slower in the Hall? *This*," he pointed to the Metachronome in the dash panel, "is the actual time-displacement mechanism that makes that possible."

"Time-displacement," repeated Will, noting the phrase for future reference.

"It's the only one of its kind," Continued Nicholas. "It controls time not only in The Great Toymakers' Hall, but in flight as well. It has the capacity to influence the pulse of time all over the world. Without this, we wouldn't be able to do our job."

"Wait. Are you saying this sleigh is . . . a time machine?"

Nick's eyebrows arched. "Where did you learn such a term?"

"It's a book by H. G. Wells. My Father gave it to me on my eleventh birthday."

"Wells, you say? Curious."

"But Nick," said William, attempting to fathom how any of this could be possible, "how did you build a time machine?"

"Ah, well, long ago, my grandfather granted a number of extraordinary requests from a young boy. Every Christmas the lad wrote asking for the strangest gifts: a length of copper tubing, a coil of wire, a pressure gauge, valves and switches, cogs and wheels, even minute clock parts and crystals. And each year the requests grew more unusual. Then one day they just stopped, and he heard no more from the boy.

"Years later, when the boy had become quite the clever young man, he sent my grandfather a letter thanking him for all the unusual wishes he had granted over the years. Included in this letter was a blueprint for an very unique timepiece. He called it a Metachronome.

"Grandfather knew in a single glance that it was something very special, so he found the best clocksmiths and inventors in the land to build it for him."

William peered at the mechanism in amazement.

"Well, we have tarried long enough! We've places to go, gifts to deliver!"

"Oh, of course." Will began to exit the sleigh.

Nick put a hand out to stop him. "I did say *we*, did I not? Would you like to accompany me on my rounds, Will?"

Speechless, William nodded, eyes full of excitement.

"All right then. Let us be off! Can you hop out and push the outer doors open for me?

Will climbed down and swung the king-sized barn doors left and right, to reveal a clear moonlit, snow-laden runway that stretched out from the stable doors. "The storm's gone!" Will said, gazing at the twinkling stars.

"Good!" called Nick. "Clear nights make smooth flights!"

By the time William got back to the sleigh, the precisely cut quartz crystal in the center of the metachronome had begun to resonate at the exact frequency required to alter time. The whole sleigh began to vibrate, rattling its brass and silver hinges.

"Is it meant to shake like this?" called William over the whirring tone steadily rising in pitch.

"Not to worry. It's just until we are airborne." Nick took up the reins and then offered them to William. "Would you like to do the honors?"

"Me, sir?"

"Just give it a good snap," Nick said, pantomiming the action with a wave motion of his arms and a quick flick of the wrists. "The team will do the rest."

"How will I know where to go?"

Nick chuckled. "The reindeer know. They're the best navigators on the planet."

Will gathered the reins, took a deep breath, and with Nick's nod of encouragement, snapped the leather as he'd been shown.

Nicholas yelled, "Away!" and they were off with a jolt.

The reindeer started at a full gallop as if they'd been waiting for the beginning of a race. Down the runway they charged, gaining speed until they reached the end of the line, which just happened to be—

"—a CLIFF!" yelled Will. "We're headed straight for a cliff! Nick! What do I do!"

"Have faith my boy. *Believe*."

"Believe what?"

He gave Will a knowing grin. "That reindeer can fly!"

And with that, they charged straight off the cliff.

But instead of flying . . . they . . . fell.

Will's stomach went topsy-turvy, and he heard himself screaming.

For a moment, amid the terror of plummeting to certain death, everything went still. The wind in his ears stopped thrumming, his heart stopped pounding against his chest, all fear dissolved, and his thoughts took on a crystalline clarity.

And in that singular moment, William thought, *this is it— the end of this grand adventure, and I will finally be with Father again.*

William found peace in that moment—a peace such as he'd never experienced. A radiant warmth of complete acceptance washed over him. *Whatever happens next,* he thought, *a beginning or an end . . . it is meant to be.*

Nicholas grabbed the reins from Will, forcing his thoughts back to the present moment. An instant later they were swooping . . . down and around . . . and back up to the top of the cliff . . . climbing higher still . . . soaring . . . soaring into the night, face to face with the brightest full moon William had ever seen.

Fists thrust in the air, Will let out an exuberant cry of exhilaration that could no longer be contained.

"Hold on!" shouted Nick, pointing to a brass handrail running along the inside of the door panel.

William clutched the handrail just in time to stop himself from flying out of the sleigh as they dipped down for a pass over the town.

Nick laughed. "I did the same thing on my first flight! After that, Grandfather decided to add a few safety features."

William looked down at the glistening scene below.

Warehouse-like structures hid behind quaint glass-front shops, cabins and cottages, all encircling a central star-shaped plaza with a familiar-looking fountain at its center, and all nestled in a hidden nook at the base of Christmas Mountain.

"That looks just like the fountain at the Grand!" called Will, over the rush of wind.

Nick nodded. "With the same inscription on its base too!"

"Kringle Towne is bigger than I thought!"

Nick's smile beamed. "I told Simon to light it up for you! It's a sight to behold!" He pulled the sleigh up over a slight ridge and pointed again. "Look! Carrington!"

A much larger town by comparison, the softer lights of Carrington, reflected by a blanket of white snow, glistened like polished gems. Seeing Carrington from above like this, William felt a deep affinity for the place. He'd only been here a short while, but he already knew he never wanted to leave. Carrington had become a part of him, a part of them all.

For William, it was like no dream he'd ever had, seeing all this from the vantage of sky. His heart soared as high as the moon, and he found himself laughing—laughing at the idea of flying reindeer, laughing at all that had transpired, laughing because he couldn't contain his joy or the immense gratitude he felt to be alive and soaring above the rooftops with his friend.

"This was my favorite part when I was a boy." Nicholas banked the sleigh around to make a low pass over The Great Toymakers' Hall, where all those they left behind waited out in the snow to catch a glimpse of Will and Nick in Santa's sleigh. They all cheered and waved, the children jumping and shouting, as they zoomed by.

William and Nicholas waved back and called out, "Merry Christmas and goodnight! See you with the morning light!"

Saying precisely the same words at the same instant, both smiled, knowing the meaning of their synchronicity. They were family now and would be forevermore.

"Are you ready, good Will?" called Nick, over the roar of wind in their ears. "Ready to see the whole world through Santa's eyes?"

"Ready, sir!"

Nicholas pulled a lever on the front panel, and off they dashed into the folds of time.

THE END

EPILOGUE

So it was that Santa returned to Christmas, and the magic of Christmas returned to the little town of Carrington once again, and in turn, to the world.

And though this happened long ago, it still lives in the memories of the townspeople, for mothers and fathers tell the tale every Christmas Eve at bedtime, tucking their children in for the night, whispering 'Merry Christmas and good night. See you with the morning light.'

Now I could end this story here, and tell you that yes, they all lived happily ever after, since that is the honest truth, but one part of my story remains untold, for what I saw in my vision the day my son was born has not yet come to pass, although it soon will. And, there are a few mysteries yet to be solved, so if you wish to see this puzzle completed, read on, dear ones.

After the gifts had been delivered on Christmas Eve and all the presents had been opened at The Carrington Grand on Christmas morning . . . after a superb holiday breakfast feast had been served up and devoured . . . after the children had all gone out to play with their new toys while the adults took afternoon tea in the parlor . . . after all this, there came a quiet moment in the early evening, when everyone had retreated to their rooms to dress for the Christmas day feast, where Nicholas and William returned to their soft leather chairs by the fire in the Grand's lobby to have a very important conversation.

"Nicholas?" said Will, leaning forward. "There's something I've been wondering."

Nick prodded embers back into flames in the fireplace, and then relaxed in his favorite chair. "I imagine there are a few *somethings*."

Will nodded with a shy smile.

"Not to worry. Pick one and we shall start there."

"Well, I understand where the star key came from, but how did my father end up with his part of it?"

"I too was baffled about that, until—" Nick stopped and held out his hand. "May I borrow your father's letter a moment? The one he wrote the day you were born?"

William kept it in his breast pocket, just as Nick had for decades. He offered up the letter, and Nick pointed to the last paragraph. "This line here, where your father said I would know what his words meant when it was time for me to know. Well, he was right. After I gained entrance to the cave and took full possession of the Christmas magic, I could see how everything connected—all of us a vast collection of stars joining together to make a perfect constellation. And you are at the center of it, good Will."

"Me?"

"It's time for you to know who you are."

"But I already know who I am," said William, confused by Nick's words.

"You know only the half that comprises your present. Your past has been shrouded by your father's adoption at an early age and your future, by his death."

"My father always told me that he was a self-made man, that he didn't need to find where he came from."

"Yes, but deep inside his soul, he longed to know of his lineage, and never stopped looking for it. His search led him here."

"To Carrington?"

Nick nodded. "And to me."

"Does that mean you know where my father came from?"

"I do," said Nick. "It is the same place I come from."

"My father was born here? In Carrington?"

"That tintype he left you. That's the proof."

William pulled the photograph from his pocket.

"See this inscription here?" Nick pointed to a name at the bottom. "H. P. Vanderveer. When I saw that name, I knew this photograph had come from Carrington. Henry Petrov Vanderveer was the only photographer in our little town. He spent his entire life here. When you said it belonged to your father, the pieces of this strange puzzle finally began to fall into place."

Will stared at the photograph.

"I was just a boy," said Nicholas, "but after I saw this, I began to remember. I knew your grandparents. They lived here, in Carrington, but it goes back much further than that."

"What do you mean?"

"You know how your father sometimes knew things before they happened?" said Nicholas. "And how he always seemed to know what you were thinking and feeling?"

"Yes. It's one of the things I miss most about him."

"There's a reason he was the way he was. It has to do with Christmas. Specifically, the magic of Christmas. Remember the story of the three brothers? Well, they each had their own families and in turn their own separate lineages. The oldest brother had a wife, a son, and three daughters, but tragically, the family perished in a fire. Their lineage was lost, but their part of the star was not."

"It survived the fire?"

Nick nodded. "No part of the star has ever met with harm."

"Because the pieces are protected by magic?"

"Yes, and that is how my family came to possess two of the three pieces. You see, my brother Simon and I are descendants of the second brother. And you, Will—you and Rebecca and your father—are descended from the third. It's all in the Book of Christmas. Once I knew what to look for, I found it all there."

"I still don't understand how my father had the star. He said when he was adopted he had nothing. No possessions. No name. No past. No future."

"That's not entirely true. Your father was just a babe when Simon shut down Kringle Towne and put everyone out on the street. Your grandparents, very young at the time, were left with nothing but a few possessions, some cherished memories, and an infant son to care for. They set sail for America, hoping for a new start, but sadly, they took ill on the crossing and never regained their strength. They perished within the year."

"That's terrible," said Will, feeling the weight of his father's story.

"Little Garrett spent eleven years in an orphanage before being adopted by Mr. Robert Hillerman and his wife, Beatrice, your grandparents. And because your father was so young when he lost his parents, he had no memory of them. But when they died, they left him with a handful of family heirlooms that the orphanage put away for safekeeping, and in turn, gave them to the Hillermans when they adopted your father. Beatrice stored them in her attic and thought no more of it until Garrett had his own son. She gave the rosewood box to your father the day you were born. Although it did not possess the beautiful rose design on top—that, your father carved the day your sister was born. And in this simple rosewood box, made by one of the three brothers while traveling in India, was the tintype of his family portrait and, of course, the star."

"But he didn't know what it was? That it was part of the key?"

"Exactly. That knowledge would come years later, when he started inquiring about the purchase of The Grand. After that, he began to put the pieces of his life and his family history together, although he did not reveal his findings to me, or to Mr. Staub. I believe he meant it to be a surprise for all of us."

"Well, I'm definitely surprised!" said Will.

"Once he understood the significance of the star he'd inherited, he began planning your family's journey to Carrington. It's why you are all here. To learn the truth. He thought he had more time. He didn't know you would be making the journey without him. But he *is* here, William. You feel him too, don't you?"

"I do," said Will, with a shiver. "So . . . if all this is true, that means we—you and me—we're related?"

"Indeed."

"So we're really family after all!"

Nicholas delighted in William's enthusiasm.

"I had a feeling," said Will. "I didn't know for sure, but I hoped. And then, in the sleigh, when you used the same words my father always said every Christmas Eve at bedtime—"

"—the same words *my* grandfather said to me each night," added Nick.

"Merry Christmas and good night. See you with the morning light," they recited together.

"That's when I began to believe it could really be true." William glanced toward the stairs. "Wait until Bec and Mother hear about this!"

"William," said Nicholas. He stood, and began to pace as if what he had to say was of great significance. "If you will permit me, I'd like to ask you a question. A very important question."

"Anything, Nicholas."

"As fate would have it, I never had the opportunity to have a family or a son of my own . . . someone to teach, and pass on the family legacy to. I'm going to need someone to carry on after I'm gone. Would you be that special someone for me, William Thomas?"

"I don't understand. How could I be—?"

"What if I told you that I believe this has been your destiny all along and that your father knew it too?"

"Are you saying Father believed I am meant to be—?"

"Santa Claus. Yes."

William sat very still trying to fathom all he had learned in the last few minutes. "I didn't even believe in Santa Claus when I first came here," he finally squeaked out.

"Since your family came to Carrington, the magic of Christmas has been steadily growing stronger. I thought it was the presence of your father's spirit, but I was wrong . . . it was you, Will."

Will felt a lump of pride swell in his throat.

Nick reached out to put a hand on William's shoulder. "What say you to my proposal, William? Will you be my successor?"

William leapt from his seat and blurted out, "Yes! Oh, yes. Most definitely!" Then, after putting his enthusiasm in check, he said, "I mean, I would be honored, sir."

The moment he agreed to Nick's proposal, William felt a rush of tingling warmth flood his entire being as the magic of his lineage permeated every cell of his body. And in that momentary bliss, he saw something magnificent.

His father shimmered into view right before his eyes as if he'd been standing there all along—smile radiant, arms outstretched.

"Father!" William cried. He ran into his father's embrace.

A deep sense of boundless love seized Will's heart and filled him with such joy that his very soul took flight.

The instant he returned, and he was again just a boy, his father's image misted in his embrace, becoming a million tiny points of light.

"The magic of Christmas is a part of you now," said Nicholas.

"My father . . . he was here. He was really here!"

Nick nodded. "For a moment you were able to reach out to each other across worlds. But, Will, he is always here—watching over you and your family. You know that now, don't you? This is the legacy you have been born into. And it's not just your father. All those who came before you will be here to guide you."

"And you, Nicholas? You'll be here too, right? You're not going away, are you?"

"I am Santa! Father Christmas! St. Nick! Where would I go?"

"And someday, I will be all those things too?"

"Indeed you shall. And more."

William gave Nick a grateful hug before they returned to their chairs by the fire.

Will exhaled, letting it all sink in. "Should . . ." He bit his bottom lip. "Should I tell Mother and Becca?"

Nicholas nodded. "You will know when the time is right."

William looked up just then and saw his mother and sister floating down the grand staircase in their new Christmas dresses.

Following behind them was another girl, about Will's age, whom he didn't recognize. This new girl was pretty, thought William, with her silky blond hair looking like liquid rose gold as it fell to her shoulders. She wore an emerald green dress that glimmered in the soft lamplight as she walked.

The two girls flopped onto a soft velvet sofa near Will and Nicholas, exhausted from their secret Christmas Eve activities in The Great Toymakers' Hall, and the morning's celebration, with so many presents under The Carrington Grand's Christmas tree that one could barely maneuver through the lobby.

"What a long night!" Nora exclaimed, settling beside the girls with a bit more grace and decorum. "We'll have to prepare much earlier next year."

My wife's words made Nicholas smile deep inside, for in that simple moment he finally, wonderfully, truly knew that he was not alone. Nick only ever had one Christmas wish—a wish he believed would never come true—to reunite with the family he had lost so long ago. But now, in this marvelous moment of moments, he realized his wish had come true, just not in the way he'd hoped, as wishes often do.

And because of this realization, I knew my wish had come true as well.

Nick had found his family—not the one he'd lost as a boy, but one that had been lost to time. And when I felt this moment heal his heart, mine too was healed.

Becca held out her hand to her mother, her fingers closed around a piece of jewelry. "You've forgotten something, Mama."

"I have?"

Becca opened her hand to reveal her mother's rose brooch. "You never go out without it."

"I wondered where that went! Thank you for finding it for me, sweetheart." She retrieved the brooch from her daughter and pinned it to her lapel. "Perfect!"

William's eyes grew wide. "I'll be right back!" he said, bouncing up from his chair, surprising everyone. He bounded up the marble stairs two at a time, sprinted down the hall and into his family's hotel suite.

In his bedroom, he found the rosewood box on the shelf where he'd left it, drew it down, and sat on the bed with it in his lap.

Carefully, he removed the remaining contents, and closed his eyes to say a little prayer, hoping he was right.

Then, opening his eyes, he held his breath and slowly turned the box upside down to look at the bottom panel. When he saw it—

the engraved inscription he somehow knew would be there—he let out his breath and smiled. It read:

A rose for my beautiful Rebecca Rose, carved by her proud papa this day, as she takes her first breath in this bright new world. May she always see the beauty and grace that resides within her, and may her light someday shine as brightly in the world as it now shines in my heart. G.W.A.

"Becca knew," muttered William. "She knew Father was here all along. She saw the magic in the garden when I couldn't see it. She never stopped believing." He considered for a moment and then said, "She needs to know the truth. She's as much a part of Father's legacy as I am."

William dashed back down the stairs to the lobby with the box cradled in his arms, but instead of approaching his sister on the couch with everyone else there, he stood by the Christmas tree and called her over in private.

"What are you doing over here, Willy?"

"Remember when you saw the roses in the garden and I couldn't see them?"

She nodded. "That made me sad. It was so beautiful. I wished you could have seen what I saw."

"Well, you were right, they were a clue. A clue I missed. But it's because they were meant for you, not me."

"What do you mean?"

"It was Father. He was trying to tell you something."

"He was?"

"I think he wanted you to have this," said Will, holding out the rosewood box.

"Papa's secret treasure box?"

"It's actually *your* box, Becca. He meant for you to have it."

"How do you know?"

"Turn it over."

Becca turned it over and read the inscription on the bottom. She ran a finger along the rough edges of the engraving. "Papa wrote this for me?"

"On the day you were born."

"Oh Willy, this is the best Christmas present I could hope for!"

"There's more, Bec. Father was born right here in Carrington. And he was related to Nicholas."

"Does that mean we are too?"

"That is exactly what it means!"

"So Papa finally found his family history?"

"It's why he brought us here," said Will. "He figured it all out. I've been searching for answers and they were all right here, waiting for us."

"So then . . . Carrington really is our home!"

Will nodded. "And always has been."

"Does Mama know?"

"Not everything. But she will . . . as soon as we tell her. Although, I think we should wait until after the Christmas feast."

Becca clapped. "It will be her best Christmas gift ever!"

"It will." He grinned. "Shall we join the others now?"

Becca placed her rose box under the tree and they headed back to the fireplace.

When William sunk into his favorite leather chair next to Nicholas, he looked around and said, "Has anyone seen Trev? I want to wish her a Merry Christmas."

The girls began to giggle.

"What's so funny?"

Nick took a look around with feigned concern. "Yes, where is that girl?" He called out to the room. "Has anyone seen Trev?"

"Very funny, Nick," said Trev. She kicked his boot.

Recognition dawned on William's face as he finally worked out who the new girl in the green dress was, sitting across from him.

Everyone laughed as Trev looked down and pretended to straighten her dress.

William, almost too stunned to speak, finally managed, "I um, I think you look pretty as a girl, Trev."

She reached across and socked his arm. "Gee, thanks."

Then leaning forward to whisper to Nick, who met her half way, she said, "I let Nora and Becca play dress up with me. It seemed important to them."

Nick gave her a quick wink. "That was very considerate of you."

Trev looked at Nick's new suit. "I'm not the only one playing dress up. You're looking quite dapper yourself there, Nick."

Nicholas leaned in. "Nice word, dapper. Very impressive."

"Like it?" Trev whispered. "Nora taught me. But seriously, you do look the part."

"You think so?" Nick looked down at his rich, dark chocolate suit and burgundy bow tie, feeling a bit self-conscious.

"Red velvet vest," said Trev, tapping his gold buttons. "Nice touch. Very *Santa Clausy.*"

"Well," said Nick. "I couldn't very well show up in my *comfys* now could I? I have a reputation to uphold."

214

Trev flashed a conspiratorial grin. "I'll bet you can't wait to get back into your perfectly-worn-in boots."

"Like old friends, they are," said Nick with a dreamy look.

Nora stood and took Nick's hands into hers to bring him to his feet, having something important to say to him.

The room quieted.

"Nicholas, you have given us so much. You have offered us a new home, restored our faith in Christmas, and in each other. You have brought us together at a time when we were lost in sorrow, and made us a family again. It is difficult to express the depths of our gratitude, but we are compelled to try."

"That is not necessary, Nora, for you and the children have given me much more than I have given you."

"Well, we have one last Christmas gift for you," said Nora.

Nick's eyes brightened with interest.

"You see, since the day we arrived, we have all been trying to solve the mystery of our anonymous benefactor who planned The Carrington Grand Christmas Ball and, indeed, brought us all here. Of course, now we know it was Garrett. And even though he couldn't be here with us, his surprise was so well orchestrated, his plan so complete, that it proceeded perfectly without him."

"Yes," said Nick, smiling.

"Garrett personally invited six couples to stay at The Grand and we now know why, thanks to Will," said Nora. "I hope it doesn't constitute a breach of confidence, but William told us about the 'Dear Santa letters' you have carried in your pocket all these years."

Nora signaled her children. They dashed out and returned with the invited hotel guests.

The six couples filtered in two by two, in their holiday finery.

"These six couples all have something in common," she said, looking at Nicholas. "You."

I'd hoped they would figure it out, for this was my final Christmas present to Nicholas, and the best part of the surprise. Now Nicholas, being who he had become, and in full possession of the magic from Christmas Mountain, knew instantly what Nora meant. He looked upon the faces of the hotel guests' and finally recognized them. He saw in their eyes the children they had been, and knew at once why I had brought them to Carrington. As children, we had all believed in him, and had never stopped believing, even after he stopped believing in himself. I wanted him to know that.

Nick turned as the couples approached to acknowledge him. He pulled the six remaining 'Dear Santa' letters from his breast pocket and, reading the name on each aloud, returned them to the children, now grown, who penned them so many years ago. "Hanz . . . Shiro . . . Isadora . . . Anne . . . Enric . . . Grant."

After all the congratulations had been shared, and the hotel guests had been honored and thanked for their contribution to saving Christmas, Trev plopped down next to Nicholas and said, "Fiona just brought in a plate of your favorite cookies. Would you like me to steal one for you?"

"I'd love a cookie. You know me too well. But Trev, you don't need to steal anything anymore. We own The Grand now, remember? You can help yourself to whatever you like."

Trev got up. "Where's the fun in that?" She flashed Nick a mischievous grin, one he knew all too well.

As Trev snuck over to the cookie plate, Nora sat beside Nick, and said in a small voice, "This is all so beautiful, Nicholas. I wish—"

"What do you wish?"

When Nora shook her head, Nick whispered, "You know, I happen to be in the business of granting wishes."

Nora gave him a little downturned smiled. "I was about to say, I wish Garrett were here to see this, but—"

Nick put a hand over hers. "He *is* here, dear one. He has been all along."

"I know that now."

"We are all, finally, together, just as he said we would be. A grand reunion."

"And I, my friend, am so very grateful for that." Nora's gaze fell away as her thoughts turned elsewhere. "Nicholas, there is a question I've been wanting to ask you."

"Might it have something to do with that blue satin pouch you brought with you from America?"

Nora nodded almost imperceptibly.

"You wish to spread Garrett's ashes in the gardens of The Carrington Grand?"

"Perhaps in the spring when the roses start to bloom?" Nora spoke in a voice as soft as her heart. "I believe that's what he would have wanted."

"Without a doubt," said Nick, "and of course, that is exactly what we shall do."

"Thank you, Nicholas. I finally feel it's time to move forward, time to embrace our new life here in Carrington."

"I am so pleased to hear it. And now that you are all a part of the Carrington clan, I have one last Christmas gift for you as well," said Nick. He handed her a gift box. "In honor of an ancient family tradition."

Nora smiled a shy smile and opened the box. Inside, were three hand-carved wooden ornaments every bit as intricate and exquisite as those already hanging on the tree.

"Oh, Nicholas. How ever did you find the time to make these?"

"I'm Santa!" he said with a chuckle. "This one is for Rebecca." He indicated a magical scene of the Grand's rose garden in full bloom, with her favorite angel statue at its center. Then he pointed to a flawlessly carved miniature family portrait of Will and Becca standing with Nora and Garrett on the front steps of The Carrington Grand Hotel. "That one is for William—something he has dreamed many times since arriving here. And this," he drew the last ornament from the box, "is for you."

Nora took the delicate sphere into her hands and peered at the scene it held within—she and Garrett in the Grand's festooned ballroom, dancing their last waltz together."

"Oh, Nicholas, it's perfect," she said, her voice tender with the cherished memory. "Thank you."

Nora hugged Nicholas, and when Trev returned with William and Becca, all three carrying plates of Christmas cookies, Nora hugged each of them as well.

And although Trev managed to squirm out of Nora's embrace, Nick saw a hint of contentment cross her face.

"Children, come see what Nicholas has made us!" Nora said, holding up the ornaments. "They are for the tree!"

"I have one for you too, Trev." Nick offered her the hand-carved scene. "It's you and me, sitting by the fireplace in our comfy chairs, and look," he pointed to the words etched at the top: 'Together Forever.'

"I love it," whispered Trev.

They all ran over to hang their ornaments on The Grand's towering Christmas tree, thus officially becoming a permanent part of Carrington's secret history.

And with these last few fragments of mystery finally solved, my time with you is almost done. I did not know it until this day concluded, but all is once again as it should be. My family is safe. I am finally at peace. My story is finished, my circle complete.

So with bittersweet sentiment, I shall say my goodbyes to you now, dear ones. Merry Christmas to each and every one of you. Know that

Christmas is always inside you. You will find it there, waiting to heal your hearts, whenever you need it to.

I am at peace now, knowing you will all be well, so I bid you a fond and heartfelt farewell.

It was at this moment that Simon made his entrance, sporting a dark blue suit, over which he wore a borrowed apron from the hotel kitchen.

"Simon?" said Nick, surprised to see his brother in an apron.

Fiona, Ben, André, and Mr. Staub, all wearing similar aprons, came to stand behind Simon.

"Dinner is served," said Fiona, stepping forward. "Featuring a delectable main course of braised duck with orange sauce and candied yams by Chef Klaus." Fiona's irrepressible smile charmed the room.

"And just wait until you see what we have prepared for dessert!" said Simon, "in honor of St. Nick!"

Nicholas stood and put a hand on his brother's shoulder, his smile every bit as genuine and as bright as Fiona's. "Simon, I didn't know you could cook!"

"There's a lot we don't know about each other, little brother, but in time, we will. I have decided to stay on in Carrington."

"I was hoping you would." Nicholas wrapped his brother in a tender embrace, pat him on the back, then turned to face the group and with arms stretched wide, said, "Merry Christmas everyone!"

"Here's to many more!" Simon called out.

"Let's eat!" William exclaimed. He reached over and tagged Trev. "Race you to the dining room!"

And race they did.

There once was, and perhaps still is,
a magical place called Carrington . . .

Merry Christmas From The Carrington Grand Hotel

Dear Reader,

Thank you for journeying with me to a hidden little town called Carrington.

The tale of how Carrington transformed from its humble beginnings as a short story penned in a single sitting, into the novel you now hold in your hands, spans more than 3 decades and has many twists and turns, epiphanies and pitfalls, and even some real-life miracles. It has been a true adventure for me, brimming with heroes and villains, ghosts and angels, and its share of life lessons.

Somewhere along the way, I fell in love with Nick and Nora, William and Becca, Trev and Simon, and The Carrington Grand itself. They have been with me for so long they feel like family. And somehow, whenever I've lost my faith in love or my belief in the magic of Christmas, Carrington has always brought me back to believing.

Over the last 30 years, The Saint of Carrington has taken many forms: a short story, a full-length theatrical musical, a screenplay, and now, a novel, which itself, has gone through numerous incarnations. And with your encouragement, it will continue to thrive (in new forms such as a special illustrated edition, an audiobook, and maybe even a sequel or two).

In my ventures as an author, I've learned that books have their own path to follow. We, as writers, plot the course and set the trajectory, but readers like you are the winds that fill their sails and propel them out into the world where hearts and minds await. So if you enjoyed the book and would like to help The Saint of Carrington heal more hearts and create more smiles for many holiday seasons to come, leaving an honest review on your favorite book-buying site is one of the best ways to help spread the word. Every review, no matter how small, makes a difference!

I hope *The Saint of Carrington* has touched your heart as it has touched mine and my family's. And if perchance you have lost your way, lost your faith, or lost loved ones dear to you, as I have, and are facing Christmas without them, it is my sincere wish that the message of hope herein, has in some small way helped to heal your heart, and maybe even offered you a bridge back to believing.

In truth, if I had my pick of anywhere in the world to stay at Christmas, it would be The Carrington Grand Hotel. Maybe someday, someone will build it on a snowy mountaintop and we can all meet there and share a cup of hot cocoa by the fire. Until then, this book can take us there any time we wish.

Thanks again for allowing me to share my stories with you, and for spending some of your wonderful holiday moments with me at The Carrington Grand.

Many blessings and heartfelt wishes,

Elayne Gineve James

PS If you're interested in "the story behind the story" and would like to read about the strange and wonderful real-life adventures of Carrington's evolution, (plus behind-the-scenes notes & extras), visit TheSaintofCarrington.com to download THE CREATION OF CARRINTON for free.

♡ *If you have a loved one, a family member, or friend who is struggling this season and you would like to give them a free copy of this book, write me via my contact page at ElayneJames.com and I will send you a link where they can download the eBook in its entirety for free. You, and anyone you send it to, can use this FREE FOREVER LINK year after year to give this book to any one who needs it.*

The Saint of Carrington
Contributors

Original Story & Novel
Elayne G. James

Editors
Jefferson Franklin UK

Adaptation
Musical to Manuscript
Cat Spydell

Book & Songs
Theatrical Musical
Elayne G. James

Score & Orchestrations
Theatrical Musical
James D. Peterson

SPECIAL THANKS TO
Carrington's Many Angels

Ken Henatay

Jim Rudolph

Elaine Rudolph

Cat Spydell

Greg Conway

Ishara Kassirer

Russell Taylor

James Peterson

Robert Stewart

Daniel Gordon

Dena Paponis

Dan Watt

Debbie Wastling

Larri Ryan

Pete Ledesma

Noel Hawkins

Gordon Firemark

Grant Rudolph

Corrina Lee

Bob Dworkin

and

(of course) St. Nick

❧ GRATITUDE ❧

I can honestly say *The Saint of Carrington* would have never been published without the help of some extraordinary people along the way. My deepest gratitude goes out to: composer James D. Peterson for partnering with me in the creation of the musical; my entertainment lawyer, Gordon Firemark, for saving Carrington when a real-life 'Simon' tried to take it away from me; my friend and CPA, Bob Dworkin, for keeping my head above water as I ignored the practical to focus on the fictional; Tony Fyler and his team at Jefferson Franklin Editing in the UK, who believed in Carrington's potential, and challenged me pushed beyond my self-imposed limitations as a writer, to transform the story into something…magical.

A very special thanks goes out to Russell Taylor for his in-depth story critique of the musical, which ultimately influenced the direction of the book, and for suggesting I make one small but crucial change to the title.

My heartfelt appreciation goes to my beta readers: Jim, Elaine, Ishara, Liz, Chris, Slater, Ken, Raena, Noel, Cindy, and Greg, who have given me the chance to make those final refinements and add the crucial finishing touches that are so essential to the life and flow of my books. And, of course, to my three wise sisters, Ishara, Raena, and Michelle, who have always been three of the brightest stars in my sky.

To my parents for their unconditional love, neverending encouagement, guidance and friendship, all of which inspired me to be brave in my creative pursuits as well as my personal growth, and to my wonderful extended family, for reading and celebrating everything I write, and always cheering me on.

And, of course, to Cat Spydell for being Carrington's dedicated midwife, for always making decisions in the book's best interest, and for taking that first step, so that I could eventually find the courage to write the book Carrington was destined to be.

But most of all, to my sweetheart, Ken Henatay, for all the love, support, and encouragement over the years. Through rough seas and smooth sailing, he's always by my side, helping me to keep the faith, never letting me forget who I am and why I am here.

Thank you one and all!

Elayne Gineve James

Scribbler of words on paper napkins in corner cafes. Musician. Artist. Explorer of dreams, myth, and imagination. Passionate pursuer of creative expression. Curious surveyor of unexplained phenomena and the mysteries of the universe. Dyslexic time-traveler. Elsewhere Girl.

Elayne Gineve James has a mischievous muse. There's hardly a moment when she's not jotting down story ideas on random sticky notes and scraps of paper. She typically works on 5 to 7 books at a time, all vying for brain space, even in her dreams.

A Northern California native, she began her writing career at age 11 when she read The Hobbit by J.R.R. Tolkien and knew she wanted to spend the rest of her life pursuing the fine art of "world building." That same year, she discovered her Pop's old guitar tucked away in a closet, and instantly fell under its spell. Her love affair with writing and music has remained constant throughout her life. Being a novelist and a songwriter provides a place of refuge, a sense of home, a purpose-driven life, and a creative outlet for her constant musings.

She now lives by the Pacific blue in Southern California with her sweetheart, focusing on her books, her family, and her continued studies of myth, imagination, and the inner-magic of personal transformation.